Jewel of the Nile

Cavanaugh Family Series

JC Wardon

A Mystic Waters Novel
JC Wardon

JC Wardon, Mystic Waters Books
TN. USA

JEWEL OF THE NILE
Copyright © 2014, JC Wardon
Trade Paperback ISBN: 978-1-944454-96-8

Editor, Gilly Wright
Cover Art Design by Calliope-Designs.com
Stock Art by Shutterstock.com

Original Digital Release, May, 2014
Original Trade Paperback Release, December, 2014
Trade Paperback Release: March 2016

JEWEL OF THE NILE

Will the lure of a past life forfeit her chances of a future in the present?

Dream-spinner? Time-traveler? Or Reincarnated?
Whichever family gift (or curse) has befallen her, Jewell Cavanaugh-White finds herself locked in a battle to remain in the present, so she must find the keys to her freedom by correcting a past wrong....

But how does she find out what needs fixing when she's thrust into the body of her ancient-self—a spoiled brat princess—who has gotten herself into serious trouble and is watched every moment of the day? And just what in the world is Jewell to do with the hunk of a man the princess is being forced to marry?

Prologue

His shoulders and chest were silk-covered muscle, his abs a rippling washboard that teased her palms and fingertips as her hand glided downward beneath the sheets. Gasping, she grasped the serpent's head while she trembled in both fear and desire.

She heard his sharp breath, his moan, and almost cried out in protest when he moved her hand away and smoothly rolled her onto her back. She could do nothing but whimper as his lips captured hers, and his large hands began a less tentative exploration of their own.

Tears slid from the corners of her eyes as his knee nudged her legs apart and his muscular thighs slid between her much softer ones. She wanted to tell him no. That she didn't want him. That she didn't want this. But she had no right to protest. Her fate was now sealed.

"Open to me."

She shook her head, refusing to look at him, though the hours they'd been doing this was weakening her resolve.

He said no more as he took her mouth again, still taking his time, still handling her with a gentleness she hadn't expected. His lips knew magic, witchcraft, trickery. His kisses were gentle one moment, teasing and tantalizing the next, and hard and demanding as his passion built, only to soften again when she reacted in what he believed was fear.

She tried to hate what he was doing to her. The aching tightness of her nipples, the butterfly-flutter of her belly, and the aching anticipation at her core, was a betrayal. His patience seemed endless, his temperament even, no matter how many times she denied him. The *gentleness of his actions while he was forcing her to comply to her father's edict almost persuaded her to cooperate. His ability to make her degradation and punishment seem more like a dance than a demand, an enticement rather than chastisement was confusing. Were it not for her hatred of what he represented, she was afraid she could desire him.*

And then her father would win once again.

She pushed at him abruptly as all the hurt and anger came flooding back. There was no way she would lie with him willingly. Not after what he'd done. What he'd taken from her. It mattered not that he'd had no more choice than she. It mattered not at all! Wedding-night or not, she would fight her imprisonment to the death. Her father had every right to force her to marry the guard as a punishment for her actions, but she would never give him the satisfaction of liking it!

"Jewell! Get up! We have to go!"

Jewell awoke abruptly, momentarily befuddled as her gaze darted from one corner of her room to another. Gone was the colorful netting hanging from the ceiling. Gone was the extremely large, round bed covered by pillows made of the finest Egyptian linens. Dressers her father built replaced the tightly woven papyrus shelving. Highly polished hardwood replaced hand-woven rugs that had covered a bricked floor. And gone was her dream-self's lover.

She crawled from her bed slowly as her head still spun with the images, the feelings, and the sexual desire that even now had her aching and wet between her legs. More than a little disoriented, she made her way to the bathroom to splash cold water on her face but was startled at her reflection as she stood before the sink's vanity.

Her heart pounded wildly as she took in the swollen lips, the disheveled hair, and what looked suspiciously like a hickey on her collarbone. Jewell shook her head, wondering how she'd bruised herself, knowing the man in her dreams couldn't have actually left the mark on her when he'd stopped at that one particular spot to suckle at her skin.

"Jewell! Are you up?"

Startled into jumping, Jewell nodded even though she

knew her sister couldn't see her. There was no way she could speak as she stared at the reflection of her swollen nipples and the tiny bruises he'd put around them with nibbling nips of his teeth while he'd breached and readied her core with his long, skilled fingers. Her knees buckled as her body reacted to the memory of his passionate onslaught, and she had to capture the edge of the vanity's sink to keep from falling completely. With a shaky breath she pulled herself back up.

"Jewell? Come on! You promised to go with me! We've got to do this before Sapphire finds out I broke those dishes!"

Though she couldn't gather her thoughts enough to remember when she'd promised anything, Jewell nodded again and then shook her head in an effort to clear it. She tried to respond, had to clear her throat when her voice barely worked, then took a deep breath before trying again.

"I'm coming, Dia. Five minutes. Ten tops."

"Okay!"

Jewell smiled at her sister's happy response, glad she had Dia to keep her grounded in reality. The small bruising on collar and breasts were obviously the result of her running into something, sometime, without her being aware she'd hurt herself. What she was feeling was lust, pure and simple, and a result of the erotic dream. True, she hadn't seen his face, had for some reason resented being with him, but the passion and desire on her part, and the erotic onslaught on his, had felt just a little too real to ignore. And the aftermath still did....

She laughed at herself as she turned on the shower. Boring, dependable, studious Jewell Cavanaugh-White... Passionate? Adventurous? Desired by a man with a killer body? "As if!"

Jewell took one last shaky breath, determined to put the dream behind her and get on with her day. Of course she couldn't help but wish that kind of passion really existed.

Chapter One

The explosion was ear piercing. Pictures shook, flapped against the wall, and hung sideways. Glasses and plates fell from behind banging cabinet doors to shatter on the hardwood kitchen floor. The drink Sapphire had sitting on the end table beside her wobbled, then tilted, but before she could grab the glass, it tipped over and emptied on the arm of the couch. She looked over at Jewell with lips pushed firmly together, her sapphire-blue eyes sparking with fury.

Jewell ignored her sister's silent outrage and hit the floor at a run to go to the room specially built to protect the rest of the house from just such a disaster. She threw the thickly padded door open and stopped cold as she took in the scene.

Dia's blond-white streaked hair was tinted with charcoal, her forehead, cheeks, and chin as well. The overlarge goggles that swallowed a good portion of her heart-shaped face were so thickly covered with soot Jewell couldn't even see Dia's ice-blue eyes. But Diamond Cavanaugh-White was still standing, and as far as Jewell could tell, blood wasn't squirting from any body parts, so she figured Dia wasn't hurt too badly.

"What happened...this time?"

Dia's white teeth seemed even whiter when she flashed Jewell a smile.

"I almost got it right that time! Just a little tweak and I think I can turn this wood into gold!"

Jewell sighed, wondering why Dia was still trying to make gold when they had more than enough wealth to sustain many generations to come. But she knew that wasn't the point. Poor Dia, she wanted so badly to conjure.

Jewell smiled back at her sister, always wanting to

encourage rather than discourage, but even *she* was getting tired of shopping for new housewares. Especially since they'd just bought all new dishes, again. That didn't matter; Dia worked harder than anyone she knew trying to attain her goals. "Well, good for you. Keep up the good work."

"Are you *kidding* me?" Sapphire demanded, as she stopped just behind Jewell in the hallway. "Don't you think it's time we put our collective foot down? This house is a mess, *again*, and I'm not cleaning it up this time!"

As Dia removed the goggles, Jewell could see the hurt in her amazing eyes. But Dia wasn't looking at Jewell; she was looking over Jewell's shoulder to their older sister.

"Who asked you to? I'll clean up my own mess. You don't have to do a thing, Sapphire *Cavanaugh* White!" She threw the goggles on the table she used for her experiments. Those experiments were, in fact, her quest to perfect a magic she believed was hers by birthright, but had never worked quite right.

"It isn't like *you* help *me* do *anything*," Dia continued. "You're so busy being *normal* that you refuse to use the powers that come so easily to you. It makes me mad that you got what I want, and you don't even want it for yourself."

"I would help you if I could," Jewell put in quietly. "But I didn't get that particular gift. It's too bad our grandmother isn't alive. Mom says she was an incredible white witch. Of course Mom is pretty amazing herself, but she rarely practices anymore since she's often in the public eye." millennia of Cavanaugh

Jewell stepped to the side when Sapphire placed a hand on her shoulder, and gave a little push. Their oldest sister stopped just inside the doorway. She surveyed the mess, with tightly clamped lips, before turning to glare at Dia.

"Does it ever occur to you that it isn't yours to have?" Sapphire asked, angrily.

Jewell gasped. "Sapphire!"

"No! It's time *someone* said it."

Jewell watched as the youngest of them looked so

crestfallen she might cry, before turning her attention on Sapphire. "That isn't nice and it isn't necessarily true. Mom says we can have more than one gift."

Sapphire turned to Jewell, her voice laced with contempt. "She also said the hereditary gift chooses us, *not we choose the gift*, and the others don't come until later if at all. Just because her generation got more than those who came before doesn't mean you two will." She turned back to Dia. "It's about time somebody got that through her thick head." With that, Sapphire pushed past Jewell and left the room.

Jewell didn't bother to correct Sapphire. There was no use in pointing out she, too, was included in what magic they all had to look forward to because it would only start an argument, and Jewell never argued if she could avoid it. She sighed, as she looked first at her disheveled younger sister, then at the debris that would take hours to remove.

"Let's get this cleaned up as quickly as we can. Kevin is coming over later to take me out to dinner tonight."

Both girls jumped as the front door slammed, and Jewell sighed again before moving forward to pick up what she thought may have once been a picture frame, or...something else. *Who knew?* "It isn't that she's angry at you, you know. She's mad because she doesn't want to be a Cavanaugh."

Dia nodded and smiled wickedly as her eyes sparkled with all the colors of the rainbow and then some. "That's why I always say our last name when I address her. To remind her of who she is."

"All that does is make her mad." Jewell lifted and studied a small piece of twisted metal she thought might actually be gold. She slid it into her jeans pocket to check out later as she continued to gather the remnants from the explosion. There was no use getting Dia's hopes up unless there was a reason to.

Dia grinned as she rose to carry both hands full of what was now garbage to the large trashcan across the room. She turned back to Jewell, satisfaction clear on her face. "I know."

Jewell had to bite her lip as she continued cleaning up Dia's mess. Though polar opposites in some ways, Diamond and Sapphire were more alike than either of them would have wanted to admit. If anything, Jewell always felt like the odd one out. Both of her sisters were wildly passionate, though one was always happy, and the other always angry, where she was the most even-keeled of the three.

There were times she wished she could be more like Dia and look at the world through rose-colored glasses and times when she wished she could hold a mad over something like Sapphire did. Jewell knew she was always too quick to forgive and often had to suffer the same insult or injury again. People didn't do things to anger Sapphire, well, except Dia, because Sapphire wasn't one of those people who let things go. Ever.

"Look! I think I might have something here!"

Jewell glanced over at her sister. Dia was smiling as her eyes did that spinning kaleidoscope thing they did every time she got excited. "What?"

Dia advanced on her to hand over another small lump of what looked like gold. Jewell took her time examining it, then handed it back. "I think we should have that tested," she said, not mentioning the one she'd found. She would give that one to Kevin and ask him to find out if it was gold or not. But in the meantime, she smiled at Dia encouragingly. "If nothing else, you've created something!"

Dia nodded and an unusual frown lowered the edges of her lips. "Yeah, that's true, but I need it to be what I'm trying to make it be. What if it is something weird and we have it tested, and then there are questions about its origins?"

Jewell sighed. She hadn't thought of that. "Good point. Maybe we can ask Mom to look at it instead."

Dia nodded, the seriousness of her expression so out of character that Jewell wished she could think of something to say to bring back her baby sister's normal smile. "Well, let's get this place cleaned up. If Kevin gets here before I wash all this dust and dirt off, I'll have to lie to him about why I suddenly look like a chimney sweep. And I suck at lying."

Dia's expression held a hint of devilment. "Maybe I'll just try turning him into a golden frog."

Laughter exploded out of Jewell before she could stop it. "I've told you not to be mean to him. He's been a good friend. And you'd likely kill him!"

"A friend, huh?"

Jewell sighed. "Yes. He's just a friend, and you know it. Now help me, or I'm going to go all Sapphire on you and leave you to clean all of it up by yourself!"

"One of these days, I'm going to be able to wave a magic wand and everything will clean itself up."

Jewell grinned. "If that ever happens, you'll make Sapphire and me the happiest two sisters on the planet!"

Forty minutes later, Jewell faced the full-length mirror her parents had loving designed together, and her father constructed for her eighteenth birthday. She finished drying her long red hair, thrilled with the useful piece that enhanced the rest of the room's decor. Her parents had worked together to create a unique mirror for her two sisters as well, and each had something to do with the names they'd been given at birth.

Her eight-foot tall mirror was a work of art. She treasured it for the craftsmanship as much as the love that had gone into its making. The perfectly carved Egyptian Hieroglyphics had been her mother Rayne Cavanaugh-White's idea, and as he always had, her father did whatever he could to please her. Knowing his wife so well, Garrison White never questioned the design choice but simply did as he was asked with the same extraordinary workmanship that had made him a famous furniture maker worldwide.

The design spelled Jewell Cavanaugh-White across the top, and the remaining figures all the way around the mirror told the story of the *original* ancestor who began and cursed the mystical line within a span of minutes.

Queen Nefertari didn't curse the triplet daughters she gave birth to on purpose, as far as the family knew. She cursed their father, the man who had proclaimed to love her above all else when Nisu Ramesses the Second, who had ruled Egypt from 1279 BC to 1213 BC, declared the triplet children had to be killed and their hearts sacrificed to preserve the Egyptian Dynasty. From what her mother could deduce when studying the hieroglyphic inscribed papyrus now locked away with the many other Cavanaugh Diaries, the Queen's anger had brought down a storm that empowered her children and their future line, while cursing their chances at love. Love had failed the Queen miserably.

From Jewell's earliest memories Rayne had taught her and her sisters that no one outside of the bloodline must ever know of the gifts they would inherit when they reached puberty. Even though Rayne believed she and her sisters, Destiny and Haven, had broken the curse by finding men who accepted them, gifts and all, that was no guarantee the history of disasters that befell women of the Cavanaugh bloodline wouldn't come back to haunt them. Mystical gifts were still considered taboo by many, and Rayne didn't want her children or their cousins to suffer the consequences of exposure.

The only exceptions to that rule were her father and her Uncle Logan. Uncle Tom already knew about the Cavanaugh gifts before either her father or uncle, since he too was a mystic, who had actually summoned her aunt Destiny from across the country all those years ago.

The stories of their parents' beginnings were precious to Jewell and to Dia, but Sapphire had made it clear whenever the subject came up that she would have been just as happy if no one knew anything about any of it, including herself. *Especially her,* Sapphire had emphasized more than once.

As hard as it had always been for Jewell to understand why that would also include the man she would one day fall in love with, Jewell, her sisters, and her cousins still had sworn to uphold the pact that her mother and aunts made so many years ago.

Jewell turned her attention from her family's history back to the mirror. She loved the elaborate carvings with their secret story. But the thing she liked most, was the way her father set a small number of the vast Cavanaugh precious stones collection, within the dark walnut frame. Because of Garrison White's way with a chisel, the jewels radiated prisms of colorful light whenever the sun reached that side of her room or when the reflected light of the moon did the same.

She looked from them to her own reflection while she pulled her hair up into a messy bun. Reflected behind her was the large room her mother had designed with other original Egyptian artifacts after her father and uncles finished construction on the house.

The three-bedroom four-bathroom house had also been a gift, though this time it was meant for the three of them to share until they decided where they wanted life to take them. The college graduation gift was an amazing surprise when they'd all returned home with their degrees, and it still was, but living with two adult sisters, who always seemed at odds, was turning out to be a bit more problematic than Jewell had anticipated.

And she was sure her sisters felt the same way.

Poor Diamond. If she didn't get some control over her magic soon, Jewell was afraid living together wouldn't be an issue. Either Sapphire would move out and leave the two of them to their own devices, or Dia would burn down the house and none of them would have a home.

She knew living together was more of a burden for her sisters than it was for her. She loved them both no matter what, but it would make her life easier if one would get herself under control and the other would have a little more compassion. She hated always being in the middle of their fights.

Jewell sighed, as she often did when thinking about her sisters, so she turned her thoughts to the night ahead. The light summer dress she'd bought for her date made Jewell feel totally feminine. She loved that it swirled just above her knees when she spun around in circles. It reminded her of when they were very young and she'd always wanted to be the fairy princess of the kingdom. That had been fine with her sisters. Sapphire always wanted to be a knight of the Realm, and Dia inevitably chose to be the court jester whose foolishness made them laugh.

Well, made her laugh, Jewell remembered. Sapphire, even then, could be a stick in the mud when it came to Dia's pursuits.

She stopped spinning and reminiscing and quickly applied a light coating of makeup to enhance the gifts of her genetic inheritance. As she applied a little mascara, Jewell was thankful again she'd been the one to carry the Cavanaugh emerald green eyes and deep auburn hair.

Until her generation all the green-eyed triplets up the long family line had come from only one of the three identical redheaded females born. The other two identical sisters were resigned to only being aunts who would use their maternal instincts in assisting in the upbringing of the next generation unless they chose to live a life on their own, which her mother told her was rare until after the next generation had grown into womanhood.

But somehow things had shifted in the universe because of something Jewell's mother and aunts did before she and her sisters had even been conceived. Now not only did she and her sisters have different eye and hair colors, Aunt Haven's girls didn't even look alike or possess magic, and Aunt Destiny gave birth to boys. So instead of their just being three there were nine to carry on the bloodline. And instead of all of them being identical, there was an interesting hodgepodge of now young adult children.

The fact she didn't have to worry about not being able to bear children just because Sapphire or Dia *could* was a burden Jewell was thankful not to bare. And in truth, though they were identical in every other way except for their eye and hair colors, she was comfortable with people not knowing that they were, in fact, identical triplets.

Concerned for them following their births, Rayne Cavanaugh-White had them thoroughly checked out. The genetic testing proved they did indeed share identical DNA, and though confused by the knowledge, the doctor who delivered them confirmed they were delivered from the same fertilized ovum that, at an early stage of development, separated into the three independently growing cell aggregations, eventually developing into the three individual baby girls she gave birth to. From what her mother had told her, the poor doctor had spent the remaining years of his practice researching how that could have happened, dying years later without the answers he sought.

The most important thing to her mother was that they were all healthy, and once that was confirmed as well, Rayne went about being the best mother any child could ask for, and Jewell was grateful for her. And for her adorable father as well.

The sound of the doorbell pulled Jewell's thoughts away from her family. She took one last look in the mirror knowing Dia or Sapphire would get it if she didn't immediately appear. When it rang again, she remembered Sapphire was probably still out working through her irritation, and Dia was likely locked in her lab, creating something else to explode.

She grabbed her clutch from atop the bed and hurried from her room. Jewell made it to the door as the bell rang continuously as if someone was holding down the button. Burying aggravation at Kevin's impatience, she slapped a smile on her lips and opened the door.

"Well, I was beginning to think you had forgotten our date and weren't home."

Well, hello to you, too! "No. Actually I was running a little behind, and I couldn't get here in the ten or so seconds it took you to ring the doorbell three plus thirty times."

He studied her for a second, and smiled. "Sorry. Bad day. Hi."

Jewell relaxed and smiled back. "Hi. Sorry about that. Our resident mad scientist blew up her experiment and I had to help clean it up."

Kevin peered over her shoulder, looking into the house, then back down at her. "So, your sisters are home?"

Jewell nodded, just as she would have even if she were there alone. She and Kevin were into their fourth month of dating, although she really thought of it more as hanging out. While she liked him a lot, there was something holding her back from letting that deep *like* slide into more. Because she was afraid Dia would do something crazy, she hadn't invited him into the house since moving in the month before.

"I'm ready," she said, holding her clutch up so he could see. "We can go. I know you have a reservation for eight." *Since you reminded me of it at least ten times over the past week.*

"Hi, Butt Face."

Jewell turned to glare at Dia, but stopped short of a reprimand since her still unwashed face made it look like she wore a raccoon mask in reverse. "I thought you were done cleaning in there."

Dia smiled. "I am. I was just heading to my room to shower. But I saw you standing here talking to Butt Face."

Jewell glared again. Though she spoke quietly, she was afraid he was close enough to hear, anyway. "I asked you not to do that."

Dia smiled at her and spoke just as quietly, but it was clear she was mocking Jewell. "I know. But I couldn't resist."

Jewell closed her eyes and counted to ten, before she smiled and spun around. "Sorry. My sister has no manners. Let's just go."

Instead of turning away as she expected, Kevin stepped closer. Since she didn't budge from blocking the doorway, he looked over her shoulder. "Just what is it about me that you don't like?"

Jewell groaned inwardly. "I really want to go."

Kevin looked down at her, his expression very serious. "It's important to me. If we are going to have a future together, I need to know what it is that I've done to cause your sisters to hate me."

Kevin's choice of words surprised her. "They don't hate you. I've never even heard Sapphire say anything to you."

He shook his head as if he couldn't believe she didn't get it. "And you don't think it's strange that we've been dating for all these months and one sister calls me names and the other won't pull her nose down out of the air long enough to acknowledge my existence?"

Jewell swallowed. He was right. She turned around to Dia one more time. "That is enough. I don't want to hear you calling Kevin anything but *Kevin* from here on out. Clear?"

Dia's normally amused eyes went flat, as they sparked in warning. "Clear." She pivoted and walked toward the hallway leading to her room. Jewell turned back. "It seems tonight is about nothing but apologizing. I'm sorry for the way my sisters are treating you. I don't know why, but I *will* find out and address it."

Kevin leaned forward slightly and kissed her closed lips. "Thanks, because tonight isn't all about, or *only* about, apologies. Let's go to dinner and start the evening over."

Jewell blew out a breath as she walked with him to his sedan. He opened the door and she got in, and put on her seatbelt as he closed the door and rounded the car. By the time he was settled behind the wheel, she was ready to put all thoughts of family behind her for the rest of the evening. As they were pulling away, she thought she saw a flash of light and fleetingly wondered if Dia had returned to her lab, and then realized that whatever she'd seen came from the corner of the house where hers was the only room.

She almost told Kevin to turn around, but she clamped her mouth shut instead. Even if her sister had blown up her room, there was no way she could let Kevin know. She just hoped Dia hadn't hurt the mirror their father made, or there would be hell to pay.

They drove in silence giving Jewell time to wonder just

what it was that her sisters objected to. Kevin was a nice guy, though a little sedate, but that meant he was steady and dependable, too. Of the two of them, she was always the one to forget to acknowledge their acquaintance anniversary each month, probably because she hadn't really thought they needed an acquaintance anniversary reminder. Sometimes Kevin was a little awkward, and those times he made her nervous because she was certain he was about to kiss her, or do something equally ridiculous like ask her if they could start actually dating. As far as she was concerned, things were perfect just as they were.

"We're here!"

Realizing she'd been lost in thought, Jewell looked up and could only stare. They were sitting outside her parents' cabin. She turned to him in confusion. "What are we doing here?"

Kevin smiled, his eyes awash with delight. "I wanted to meet your parents so I looked up your father's business address and gave him a call. I told him I was the guy you've been dating for the last four months and asked if would be okay to come by. He said sure and to bring you too as they never see enough of you."

Jewell didn't know if she was more angry or mortified. Kevin had no right to jump over that hurdle until she offered to introduce him to her parents, and her father and mother were probably sitting inside waiting to bombard her with questions. She had never mentioned Kevin in theory or in fact even though she had visited them *often* since returning home.

There was nothing to do but get out of the car when he came around to open her door. She allowed him to take her hand as her stomach plummeted more and more with each step they took. Once they reached the large front porch, Jewell decided she'd have to address his little surprise before they faced her parents. But before she could speak, the front door opened and her father stood looking at the two of them with an assessing gaze.

A heartbeat too late Garrison White smiled, and Jewell

knew the night was going to be a very long one. She struggled to find a smile of her own. "Hi, Daddy."

Garrison's smile fell into a more natural lifting of the lips, and Jewell realized she'd stopped breathing once she started again. It didn't make a dirt's worth of difference that she was an adult of twenty-three. When she was in her father's presence, she was still ten years old and Daddy's little girl.

"Hi, baby. Why don't you and *your young man* come on in?"

Said the spider to the fly....

Chills ran up her spine as they moved forward and Garrison moved back. Kevin stopped to allow her to enter the cabin in front of him so she sent him a frown, hoping he hadn't gone and done one of those stupid things she'd been thinking about. Feeling as though she'd stepped into the twilight zone, Jewell fleetingly thought about shutting the door behind her before Kevin could follow. Just what had Kevin said to her father? She sent him an awkward smile and then saw her mother walking forward from the back room. The relief she felt was short-lived.

"Jewell! I'm so happy you two could come for dinner tonight. I even had your Uncle Logan make us one of his chocolate cakes!"

Jewell accepted her mother's cheek-kiss as she glanced over to where the sinful confection sat beneath the dome of the glass pedestal dish. Since the calorie count was atrocious and the cake to die for, they only had one made when there was something big to celebrate. She looked at her mother with a frown as the chills took a one-eighty and raced back down her spine. "You didn't need to do that."

Kevin moved toward her father as her mother headed to the stove to stir whatever it was that smelled so delicious. He extended his hand to Garrison. "Hello, Mr. White." Kevin glanced over to her mother with a nod of respect. "Mrs. White. It's so nice to finally meet you both."

"It's nice to *finally* meet you, too," Garrison said with a quick glance at Jewell, before accepting Kevin's handshake.

He walked behind the island to stand by his wife, but it was several seconds before he turned around. Jewell watched as her mother slid him a warning glance before she turned back to smile at Kevin. "I'm happy you came."

Jewell took in her father's demeanor once he did turn, and she wondered at his defensive pose. With his arms crossed so that his massive biceps bulged beneath the short-sleeved shirt and his stiffly clamped jaw ticked away just above the massive muscular neck, he looked like a boxer just waiting for the bell to ring.

Jewell glanced into her mother's eyes, but all she read there was concern and confusion. "I'm sorry we've imposed. I should have called and made the arrangements for you all to meet Kevin, myself."

"Yes, you should have," Kevin and Garrison said at the same time.

Rayne moved forward and took Jewel's hand before staring very deeply into her eyes. "Are you sure?"

Sure of what? Before Jewell could voice her question out loud, Kevin moved to stand in front of her at her mother's side. He dug in his jacket pocket and pulled out a small box. As denial rang in her head and nausea churned her stomach into powder, he popped the box open and a small diamond sparkled at her as it reflected the cabin's bright lights. Kevin knelt before her and held out the ring, and she looked from it to the adoration in his eyes.

"Jewell Cavanaugh-White, would you do me the honor of becoming my wife?"

****

"This doesn't smell right!"

Rayne Cavanaugh-White turned from her husband, to take in the rest of the large room. After seeing Jewell and her fiancé out the door half an hour earlier, she'd cleaned up the dishes and Garrison had taken out the trash. "I don't smell anything."

Garrison looked over at her, his face unusually irritated. "I'm not talking about our house! I'm talking about our daughter and *that* boy!"

Rayne turned away slightly so Garrison couldn't see her smile. Although she was as concerned about Jewell at the moment as he was, watching Papa Bear emerge from the gentle Teddy Bear she normally abided with was something to behold. "That boy has a name."

"Well... So what?"

Taking pity on him, Rayne crossed the room and nestled into his massive chest. It still amazed her all these years later that the lanky man she'd first met and fell in love with had changed so drastically. Even to this day Garrison mourned the loss of his murdered older brother, Grey, and Grey's wife, Joy, and the nearly yearlong traumatic kidnapping of their son Gavin. Fortunately that had ended on a positive note, and from that point on, his health and attitude about life had been nothing but joyous. He'd not only filled out to magnificent proportions, she believed he might have even grown an inch or two.

And not just in height.

Rayne bit her lower lip to keep from smiling again as she realized what a trial it was going to be for Garrison now their daughters were back home in Mystic Waters. After four years of college and the three months abroad, he'd have to face the reality that, as women, they were sexual creatures.

She had no doubt that was the problem as Garrison had gone all *protective-father* on that poor young man. But she had to give him props. He'd held everything negative inside until Jewell and Kevin left the cabin.

"You are going to have to accept him if she does."

"Says who?"

Rayne laughed and pulled his face down for a kiss. She released his lips but not the grasp she had on his jaw so he kept his attention on her. "I do. You don't want to hurt your relationship with Jewell just because she is old enough to enjoy sex."

Garrison winced and looked like he was going to throw up.

"Seriously, don't ever say that to me again about one of

our daughters."

Rayne laughed again and released him. "Well, I'm done cleaning, and I'm old enough to enjoy sex. Do you want to hear *that?*"

For the first time in their twenty-four years of marriage, Garrison hesitated in responding, and Rayne knew her daughters were in for a time. But now that the idea had taken form, she wasn't going to let him get out of it. She unbuttoned the dress she wore for the engagement gathering and let it fall to the floor.

Garrison's eyes blazed when he saw the new black lace bra and panty set she had bought that morning in the little downtown shop she loved. Without hesitation he moved up against her.

"You can have your way with me this time, woman, but I'm warning you, if you ever use one of our daughters' names or even refer to one of them generically in the same sentence with the s-e-x word again, then I'm cutting you off for good."

Rayne's laughter turned to giggles as he lifted her and threw her over his shoulder before heading to the king-sized bed in the room that had once been his office, then his orphaned nephew's bedroom.

Chapter Two

Jewell endured the ride home in silence, but Kevin was oblivious, as his excited chatter seemed without end. She tried to listen to him now and then, but her mind was stuck in neutral. She tried to figure out how a friend-date had turned into a meet-and-greet with her parents that resulted in an engagement.

Southern manners aside, Jewell knew she should have just said *no*. But Kevin's look of anticipation and adoration, and her parents' looks of curiosity that she hadn't even told them about the American she'd met in Italy and subsequently hung out with exclusively, made saying yes the easier option because that was then the end of that.

Only it wasn't.

Now her mother was planning a wedding. Her father was envisioning his baby girl with a penis stuck up between her legs, and Kevin was talking dates and the sooner the better.

And all she wanted was to get home and take another shower and hit the sheets. Not that she really expected to get any sleep.

"Please. Can you just stop talking a minute?"

Kevin turned to her, clearly surprised by her tone. "What's wrong?"

Jewell shook her head, losing the courage to hurt his feelings when he was on such a high. "I just have a really bad headache. You kind of threw me for a loop tonight."

Kevin turned back to watch the road. "It was meant to be a good surprise. I was happy to finally meet your parents face to face. When I first called your dad and told him that I was asking his permission to marry you, he acted like he didn't have any idea who I was.

"After your reaction when I proposed and after talking

to them through dinner, I could tell that was actually the case." He slid another brief glance her way before pulling into her driveway and parking.

Kevin sighed. "I guess I should ask if you want to reconsider."

Jewell looked down at her hands and then shook her head. "I don't know. I just need more time. We both just graduated from college. I haven't even gotten my feet wet in the business world yet, and even though you work for your dad, you haven't either."

Kevin laid his head back against the headrest and stared straight ahead. "Okay. That makes sense. But what I don't hear is how you feel about me."

Jewell shrugged. "I really enjoy your company."

Kevin's chuckle held no amusement. "That's it?"

"I just wasn't thinking past getting back to the states, getting moved into our new house, looking for employment, and spending time just getting acclimated to being back home after so many years away. I'm sorry. I'm really fond of you, but marriage is the furthest thing from my mind.

"Once everything settles…."

Kevin turned his head to look at her. "So you *were* thinking we would be together in the future?"

Again Jewell shrugged. "I guess I just assumed we would be best friends forever. I didn't really enjoy being in Italy until you got there. We've had so much fun together and since you are only twenty miles away I thought we could meet each other's friends and just keep on having fun together."

Kevin reached out and took her hand and held it in his on the console between them. "I can work with that, for now. But I need to know if you just don't have *any* feelings for me, Jewells."

She looked at him and decided honesty was required. "Of course I have feelings for you. I just don't know yet if it's a good idea to move beyond friendship. If becoming…*more* doesn't work out, for whatever reason, I don't just lose a boyfriend, I lose a really good friend too. I'm not sure it's even worth risking."

Kevin's head fell back onto the headrest. "I thought making friends with you first was a good idea. Guess I miscalculated. I should have tried sweeping you off your feet from the get go. At least if you knocked me down from the start, I'd know where I stood."

He shook his head. "A guy knows better than to let himself fall into the *friend zone*, it's too hard to get out of. I can't believe this. I feel like an idiot."

Jewell felt like she was kicking a puppy, but that wasn't fair to either of them. Kevin was a great guy; good looking in a very neat and tidy way, hardworking—even though she knew from conversations they'd had over the last months his dreams were being overshadowed by his father's plans for him to take over the family business—kind, and she really liked everything she knew about him. There was just something missing from her side. And though she hated to admit it, she knew exactly what it was.

There was no passion.

At all.

Jewell sighed. "We've never had a fight."

Kevin turned to her, confusion lifting his brows. "You want to *fight?*"

Jewell smiled at how dumb she sounded. "No. But I think that's the problem."

"I don't get it."

"I guess we're too comfortable. At least I have been. You're so easy to get along with, and though you annoy me at times, it's never anything big.

"And see? If we were…something *more*, I would be afraid to tell you that you annoy me sometimes because I'd be afraid to get something started that wouldn't end well. And I know I annoy you sometimes, too. I saw it earlier tonight when I stood between you and the threshold to my house.

"But as long as we are just friends, I know you'll just have to deal with it because it's my house and I can do what

I want. But I'm sorry about that, too. I didn't want to admit it to either of us, but my sisters don't like that I spend time with you. Although I really don't know why, it's their house too."

"*Wow!* Just so you know, I'm pretty *offended* right now," Kevin said, looking away.

"That's what I'm talking about. If you just thought of me as a friend, then you'd be annoyed maybe, but not offended. You wouldn't care what my sisters thought."

"I don't give a hoot what your sisters think. I'm offended that you think I'm so boring!"

Jewell cringed. She hated hurting anyone's feelings, especially his. "I'm truly sorry. But again, you're making my point for me. Now you're getting angry over something I didn't say. That's what a boyfriend, *or girlfriend,* does when their emotions control the relationship.

"You aren't boring at all. You're witty and thoughtful and love to do the things I love to do. I thoroughly enjoy our time together. You're a great guy and I love you in so many ways."

"But you're not *in* love with me. And you make me sound like a pair of comfortable old house-shoes you like to wear because I don't pinch your toes."

Jewell lowered her head because that analogy was too close for comfort. "I'm sorry."

"Please stop apologizing. I'm tired of it."

Jewell's head came up sharply. "Excuse me?"

Kevin turned to her then, his expression one she had never seen before.

"I'm not your bunny slippers. And just because we always do the things you like to do doesn't mean I like to do them, too. It just means I like to please you. And I *am* a man, Jewells, although you've succeeded in cutting off my balls tonight.

"I need to get home. I've got work tomorrow. And I need some time to think."

Knowing that was her exit cue, Jewell nodded. "Okay." She almost apologized again and then stopped herself. "I hate this. This is exactly what I was talking about. We've never parted before with one of us angry."

Kevin didn't even look at her. "Please just let me leave."

Jewell nodded and opened her door, but before she stepped from the car, she took the ring off her finger and held it out to him. Kevin looked at it a moment and then at her face. "So that's it? We're done?"

Jewell's eyes filled and her throat nearly closed. "I hope not. But I thought you'd want it back."

He studied her, and Jewell remained silent. He finally took the ring. "I'm taking this for now. But our relationship changes tonight one way or the other. We both have some thinking to do for the next five days. When I call you on Friday to see if you want to go out, say yes, if you're willing to give me a chance, but say no, if I don't have any chance of being more than a friend."

Jewell nodded and stepped from the car. She walked to the front porch and unlocked the door before turning back and sending a small wave. He returned it before starting the car and backing out as Jewell entered the house.

Feeling sick to her stomach for hurting him, Jewell sighed. She wished she felt something more than friendship for Kevin, but she just didn't, and she knew it wasn't his fault. She'd never met a man yet that sparked a fire within her. She was beginning to wonder if one ever could.

Dia was sitting on the couch eating popcorn and watching a horror movie. As Jewell hated zombies and needed time alone anyway, she said, "Hi," and started back toward her room.

"Mom called."

Jewell stopped and turned back. "Why?"

"Said you and Butt Face got engaged."

Not up to having a discussion about her relationship with Kevin right now or her sister's lack of memory regarding the name-calling, she nodded. "Yes."

"Dumb move."

"Dia, I'm not in the mood for this. I'm going to bed."

Dia muted the television and turned to look over the back of the couch toward the wide hallway where Jewell stood. "He isn't right for you."

Jewell turned and began walking. "I said I'm not in the mood." She got to her door and Dia was right behind her.

"I need to tell you something."

The flash of light from her bedroom window came back to her, and she turned to face her sister. "Were you in my room earlier?"

Honest surprise registered on Dia's face. "No. Why would you ask me that? We don't go into each other's rooms unless invited."

Jewell relaxed. "Sorry. I thought I saw something when I was leaving earlier, but…never mind. Listen, I need to get ready for bed. It's been a very long day."

Dia studied her for a minute and then nodded. "Okay. And I'm sorry. Are you okay?"

Jewell nodded. "Yes. But why do you ask?"

"Mom said you looked a little pale when you left their house tonight. She was concerned. And since Buu…Kevin proposed, and I don't see a ring on your finger, and you were outside for a long time, and it wasn't to make out…."

"You were *spying* on me?"

Dia shook her head quickly. "No. I just looked out when the car pulled up to see if Sapphire had made it back yet, then I saw it was you so I came back to watch TV. But when you still hadn't come in ten minutes later, I just peeked out to see if everything was okay, and with the floodlight Daddy put in, it was clear you two weren't, *you know*, all over each other."

Jewell couldn't get mad over her sister showing concern so she nodded. "Yeah, I know. And no, we aren't in a good place right now. I didn't know Kevin was going to propose or that he had pre-arranged it with our parents."

"Ouch! That must have been awkward."

Jewell nodded. "To say the least."

"So you guys are more than friends?"

"I…don't know."

Dia's brows drew together as her gaze sharpened. "You don't know?"

Jewell opened her bedroom door. "Come on in. I guess we can talk while I get ready for bed."

Dia followed her and looked around the room. "Good grief! This room is a sterile as a hospital. Don't you ever drop your clothes on the floor? Or let a dust bunny move in for company?"

Jewell took off her earrings and placed them inside her jewelry box then did the same with the bracelet Kevin had gotten her before they left Italy. "Why would I do that?"

Dia smiled. "Yes, why would you? "Anyway... *give.* What's the deal with you and...Kevin?"

"He wants to be more than friends, obviously, but I just never think of him like that."

"You mean you guys spent all that time together in Italy and you didn't make out or have hot Italian sex?"

Jewell glanced over before pulling her dress off to hang it with the others she needed to launder. "Well, we made out some, but it was just for fun."

"As in friends-with-benefits?"

Jewell shrugged. "Not *too* many benefits."

"So no sex."

Jewell took off her bra and panties and put them in the hamper as she walked into her bathroom. Dia followed, stopping at the door. "Oh, my gosh! This room is even cleaner. Do you have a maid?"

Jewell stepped into the shower and turned on the water. "Of course not."

"And no sex?" Dia persisted.

Jewell rolled her eyes knowing Dia couldn't see. "No sex."

"That's good. I was afraid he'd gotten you pregnant and you had to get married... Hey, why are you taking another shower? Didn't you do that right before you left?"

Jewell looked around the curtain. "No, I'm not pregnant and if I was, it wouldn't mean I'd have to marry him. And yes, I'm taking another shower because I'm getting into bed. You know I can't be dirty and get on my sheets."

Dia laughed and sat down on the closed lid of the toilet. "So you're saying Mom and Dad's house got you dirty?"

"Don't be ridiculous."

"So it was Kevin's car."

"Dia!"

"Hey, I'm not sure I'm the one being ridiculous. You showered less than three hours ago. You went to the parents' house which I know is clean, though probably not as clean as your space here, then you rode in Kevin's car twice, and as there was no bodily fluids exchanged between the two of you, just how is it that you think there is any *dirt* to wash off?"

Jewell turned off the water and opened the curtain as Dia grabbed her towel from the bar. She held it out to Jewell and looked at her with a great deal of assessment in her gaze. "I think your tits are bigger than mine."

Jewell took the towel and patted herself down before wrapping the towel around her and securing it just above her left breast. "I doubt that my *breasts* are any different than yours. We have the same genetic makeup, remember."

"I don't know if I believe that's true. I know Mom had us all tested when we were babies, but maybe they made a mistake. You have the Cavanaugh emerald eyes and red hair. Sapphire has sapphire eyes, of course, and that black hair. And I'm practically an albino."

Jewell heard the hurt in Dia's voice. "You aren't. You just have white-blond hair and really amazing eyes. When you're tanned like you are now, you look like you should be on the cover of a magazine wearing someone's designer activewear. You are so beautiful.

"And you don't need to doubt your connection to any of us. The DNA is accurate. I had the samples pulled back out and retested when we were in high school. Mom took me because I questioned it too."

"Thanks, and maybe...if I wore sunglasses so I didn't look like an alien. But how do you explain the different hair and eyes between us if we are actually identical?"

Jewell smiled. "*Magic*. And we are."

The light in Dia's irises glittered and changed anytime she experienced emotion, and any time the subject was magic Dia got extremely emotional. Her eyes went from the lightest of blue to looking like the finest opals the earth had to offer up. The opaque almost white background cradled chips of blue, green, pink, and purple, and their magnificence nearly took Jewell's breath.

"Do you ever practice? I've never see you, but you don't talk like it's a curse the way Sapphire does."

Jewell shrugged. "I haven't for a while. Not like when we were new teens and it was fun and I was more curious. But the first day I was in Italy something happened that made me feel like I shouldn't wake up the magic inside of me. I haven't told anyone about it, but it was strange."

Dia's eyes settled and returned to pale blue. "Strange how?"

"After I got checked in to my hotel, I wanted to take a walk just to check out the city and the people. But about an hour into my stroll there was this man, only I'm not sure he was *just* a man. He was huge. Not fat…I mean like seven feet tall and all muscle, and he had the most perfect face I think I've ever seen. But what was weird was the way he looked at me. I think he knew I wield magic because as he was approaching me—and all eyes were on him, as you can imagine—he was looking right at me. When we were side by side, I swear he sniffed me. His nostrils flared and he inhaled deeply."

"That *is* weird."

"Not the weirdest part though. As he sniffed me, I *inhaled* him and oh, my, gosh! He puts out these pheromones and everything inside of me woke up. Not just the fact that I was a woman, but the magic too. I could feel power popping and crackling inside of me."

"What did you do?"

"Nothing. He kept walking and I kept walking in the other direction, feeling a little drunk."

"Why didn't you stop him?"

Jewell shrugged, curious about the tone in Dia's voice. "I don't know. Fear I guess. It freaked me out a little at the time. And what could I have said?"

Dia shrugged and said nothing, which was surprising. If Dia didn't have an answer to something, she usually made a flippant remark. Jewell picked up her blow drier and looked at her sister expectantly. "Do you mind if I finish getting ready for bed?"

Jewell turned it on and started drying her hair as Dia rose and walked the short distance to the door before she turned back around. "I've seen him."

Jewell's brows rose and she turned off the blow drier. "What?"

"I've seen the man you're talking about."

Jewell frowned. "That isn't possible. You were in France."

Dia nodded. "I know. He was there the first day I arrived, too."

Jewell frowned. "We all got to our summer retreats the same day. Describe him."

Dia pulled her cell phone from her back pocket and moved closer to Jewell. "I can do better than that." She slid the ring on the touch screen that woke her phone up and pushed the Gallery icon. Immediately block after block-filled pictures came up.

Dia scrolled down then hit the screen with her thumb before handing it to Jewell. "I got him from the side, because I didn't want him to see me taking the picture. I still think he knew because he suddenly turned and looked at me. His eyes did something, but it happened and was over too quickly for me to catch exactly what it was that they did."

Jewell stared at the picture of the man who was head and shoulders above all the men walking close to him in the snapshot. He had the same curly blond hair and square jaw, and though she couldn't see his face in its entirety, she was certain he was the same man...or *his* identical twin. "This isn't possible."

"What isn't?"

Jewell and Dia looked up to see Sapphire standing at the opening of Jewell's bathroom. Jewell waved her in. "Hi. Come here. I want to ask you if you've ever seen this man."

Sapphire entered the room and took the phone and then looked at Jewell quickly. "Yes. In England." She frowned and looked again while the hand holding the phone began to shake. "It was the day I arrived. I remember him because I got…*agitated* as soon as we made eye contact."

Jewell and Dia exchanged a look before turning their attention back to Sapphire. Jewell took the phone when Sapphire handed it back. She gave it to Dia. "I think we need to show that to Mom."

Dia nodded. "I agree." She started poking at her touch screen in a rapid succession while Jewell caught Sapphire up on the conversation they'd been having. Sapphire agreed that their mother needed to know too.

After she finished sending the text message to their mother, Dia looked over at Sapphire. "When you say agitated, do you mean you felt the magic?"

Sapphire hesitated then nodded. "Yes."

Jewell was torn between telling Sapphire magic wasn't anything to be ashamed of and telling Dia to stop goading her. But neither seemed agitated with the other at the moment so she didn't say a word.

Sapphire looked at one and then the other. "Did he…*speak* to you two, too?"

"No," Jewell and Dia said together.

Jewell frowned and put the hair dryer down. "Let's go back to the living room. It's too crowded in here."

Sapphire, followed by Dia and Jewell, led the way to the living room. While Dia and Sapphire settled on the couch, Jewell took the large comfy chair facing them. She caught the falling towel and re-tucked it while looking from one sister to the other.

Though their bone structure, wide full lips, and body

masses were identical to hers, the contrast between Sapphire's deep sapphire eyes and black hair and Dia's nearly translucent eyes and white hair made a startling difference in their appearances, and Jewell realized she hadn't *really looked* at either of them in a very long time, and certainly not side by side.

As they'd spent nearly every day of their lives together before the college graduation presents of the trips abroad from their parents, Jewell was faced with the reality that she treated Kevin the same way as she did her sisters. They were just there, sometimes a joy in her life, and sometimes an aggravation, but mostly just there.

And she would have to pay more attention to all of them.

"What did he say to you?" she asked, wondering if her sister was in danger.

Sapphire's agitation was apparent as she picked at her fingernails. "He didn't actually speak. But I heard music radiating at me and somehow knew what it meant."

"What?"

Sapphire turned to Dia. "He was looking at me…no, *into* me. And everything inside of me felt light and airy, if that makes any sense." She shook her head. "I don't know how to explain it, but it was like a chorus of soft voices singing songs of worship, and it felt like it lifted me. I was floating even though I was still standing on the street corner."

Dia looked from Sapphire to Jewell and then back. "Why do you think the music was coming from him? Maybe you were walking by a church or something and you were so distracted by him you didn't notice?"

Sapphire looked at her hands again. "Because all of a sudden the song stopped and I *felt* him say, 'Mystic Waters.'"

A chill went through Jewell again, and she shifted in her seat. "What does this mean?"

Sapphire shook her head. "I don't know." She sent an apologetic look to Jewell and then to Dia. "I've been sick with worry about it ever since it happened, but I didn't say anything because I was afraid maybe he was after me because I refuse to use magic. I guess I figured if I didn't acknowledge him to anyone, I would just forget about it. *Eventually*."

"That's why you've been so angry since you got here."

Sapphire shrugged and then grinned. "Well, yes, and the fact that Dia keeps blowing our house up."

Dia made a face. "I'm trying to do something that is really important to me."

Sapphire nodded. "I know. And I'm sorry. But maybe we can get Dad to build you something somewhere else where it won't be so annoying."

"I think that's a great idea," Jewell put in, hoping Dia wouldn't start a fight. With the strange man a possible threat to them, the last thing they needed was to fight amongst themselves. As a thought suddenly entered her mind, she stood and walked to her room. Jewell returned seconds later with her cell phone in her hand and a nightgown hanging on her body. "I need to text our cousins. Soleli, Luna, and Celestia were sent abroad too. I wonder if they saw him."

"You need to ask the boys too," Sapphire added. "With the genetic combination of Uncle Tom's abilities added to Aunt Destiny's, if anyone was after magic, they would target them first."

Dia frowned. "I wish I had been one of their kids. The magic in them is crazy strong."

Jewell hesitated before texting their cousins. "Maybe we should just have Mom call a meeting at Aunt Destiny's house. We need to get together and hash this thing out."

Dia's phone sounded with the heavy metal music she'd set up as their mother's ringtone. "Speak of the devil." She pushed the screen. "Hi, Mom.

"Yes, we need to talk to you. But we think we might need everyone to meet at Aunt Destiny's house.

"Yes.

"Oh, okay, let me check." She looked at Sapphire and

Jewell. "Mom said both her sisters just called her and they wanted to meet, too, but she doesn't know if it's about this or not. I'm available. Can you two meet there tomorrow morning around nine?"

Sapphire hesitated. "I have a job interview in the morning, but it isn't until ten-thirty so I can as long as I leave by ten."

Jewell nodded as her stomach started to hurt. "I'm in." She put her hand over her abdomen hoping the pressure would help, wondering if nerves were getting to her.

Dia hung up and looked at them, concern pulling at her normally happy eyes. "I feel really bad about this."

Jewell nodded. "Me too. But I have to go to bed. This has been a really long day and I'm not feeling too well."

Sapphire agreed. "I'll see you guys in the morning. I'm taking my own car so I can leave when I have to."

Jewell nodded and turned to Dia. "I think I'll drive too. I need to take care of something as soon as the meeting's over."

Dia shrugged. "Then I guess I'll take mine too. It's a good thing they cleared the area in front of the cabin or we'd all end up parking on the road."

Chapter Three

Jewell settled between cool, butter-soft sheets and tried to clear her mind. The pain in her stomach had eased some but was still there as a reminder there were too many things going on that could alter her life and the lives of those she loved, possibly for the worse.

Not only had she had to endure the concern of her parents and her own shock when Kevin surprised her with the meet and greet followed by a proposal of marriage, now she was afraid someone, or *something*, was looking into their family.

Hoping she was wrong and that it was nothing, Jewell turned onto her side and noticed her mirror as the moonlight reflected off the jewel at the top of the wooden frame, as well as the others spread throughout.

Her mother said the moonstone was the stone of the goddess Diana, and that its power was strongest on the night of a full moon. It was supposed to bring her good fortune, assist in telling the future, enhance intuition, promote success in love as well as in business matters, and offer protection on land and sea. And it was supposed to reunite lovers who had quarreled.

Jewell shook her head, wondering if it was all just foolishness. The moon was full tonight and she hadn't had any intuition where Kevin's feelings were going or a premonition that he was going to propose. And she certainly wasn't on board with delving into a love-life with him, at least not until her feelings manifested in that direction, if they ever did, so she wasn't sure there was any reuniting necessary. As far as protection, now that she was faced with the possibility that she and her family were endangered, maybe it would help in that regard....

Her mother and aunts, even her great-aunts, put great

store in the crystals and rocks the earth provided in abundance. As she was taught, each Cavanaugh was chosen by one or more of them, rather than the Cavanaughs choosing which ones would impact them. She had to consider, like Sapphire told Dia earlier about the gift of conjuring possibly not being hers, maybe the moonstone wasn't meant for Jewell either.

But it *was* very pretty, and that was something.

As the largest of all the jewels worked into the frame, the pale milky white stone with the single black vein running through its lower right side illuminated even more. Jewell had to remember to thank her mother for insisting it be the crowning jewel of the piece as it set in the center at the very top of the artwork her father had carved.

She looked at it for some time and then thought it twinkled. Her eyes became so heavy they closed, and her body relaxed and slid into slumber.

The warmth of the sun caused her transparent linen dress to stick to her skin even though her slaves kept her shaded with the large ostrich feathered fans as she walked through the thigh high flax plants being harvested to make new linens. Though she knew her father would be angry with her for disobeying him, she couldn't help herself. She knew Jacob would be among the slaves sweltering in the heat, and she couldn't pass up the opportunity to see him, even if only from afar.

She pretended to head to the bank of the Nile as she searched the faces of each Jewish slave she passed, but Jacob's sun kissed brown skin and nearly bleached hair was not among those working so hard in her father's fields. She glanced back to see if the overseer had noticed her yet, but he was busy at the far end of the field. From the shouting she surmised yet another slave's life was in peril. Knowing the overseer could turn at any moment, she stepped down from the bank into the cool water. Her slaves followed as they always did.

"Put those down," she commanded of her fan bearers, certain they were all now well hidden. They immediately complied, and she took a moment to lower herself until her shoulders were submerged and her body had cooled. When she stood again, her dark nipples were pebble hard and showed clearly through the thin white linen, but she didn't care. It was the way of her people to celebrate the human body, and

although she knew the slaves were sometimes offended by her lack of modesty, she knew not a word would be said.

The only opinion, slave or Egyptian, she cared about was her own, and she had wanted to have Jacob celebrate her body since they'd first accidentally met the year before. At fifteen she was considered too old to still be unwed, but her father had doted on her over and above all his other children and he had given her a chance to choose a husband of her own.

But what he didn't know was that she was in love with someone he would never approve of, and though she wasn't entirely sure of Jacob's age, she believed him only a year or two older than herself.

"Greetings, Princess Anippe."

The name startled her for only a second before her mind accepted it. She turned to see Jacob's wet head emerge from the water only feet away, and her heart kicked up a beat. Anippe ignored the uneasy glances from her slaves as their disapproving eyes bounced off Jacob and then were lowered to stare as if something amazing had entered the Nile at their feet.

"Greetings, slave."

Jacob smiled, his brown eyes filled with mischief and merriment as he moved closer. His gaze spoke of his love, but she knew he wasn't comfortable in proclaiming it publicly, which was just as well. Neither could she. Should any report reach her father, he was a dead man for sure and she had no idea if she could sweet talk her father out of the reprimand she was sure to be forced to endure. But for once she was more concerned about another over and above herself. Just being in the Nile at the same time as she, could cost Jacob his sight as her father had a mean streak and would take pleasure in watching as the slave's eyes were burned with a branding poker.

"You risk much," Anippe stated sternly, hoping her slaves took her tone for authority rather than the fear it was. Jacob's smile didn't alter and her fear for him grew since he refused to hold any for himself.

"I ask your forgiveness for trespassing, Princess. I meant only to cool off a moment before continuing my work. Please forgive me."

They both knew he was lying through his teeth, but it was the only way they could speak to each other with eyes watching and ears listening. As much as she wanted to trust her servants, she knew there were always those who sought to advance their own position by *delivering damning news to the Nisu.*

"I will ask your forgiveness again, Princess Anippe. May peace be with you, always." Jacob looked from her eyes to her chest, then into her eyes again. He smiled slightly before submerging and swimming away.

Anippe exhaled with relief as she watched and waited until she saw him climbing up the bank a great distance away. She marveled at the hunger that swamped her as she witnessed the bunching of sinewy back and bulging arm muscles as he pulled himself up the much steeper bank than the one she had used to enter the Nile. She had already marveled at his ability to hold his breath for so long beneath the river that sustained her people.

"Excuse me, Princess. It is best that you come out now."

Startled, she glanced up to see the overseer looking down at her breasts instead of her face. The lust in his eyes had Anippe lifting her chin as she crossed her arms over her chest. Fear that he'd barely missed catching Jacob sharpened her tone even more than normal. "Look away! Or I will have my father deal with you."

"Your father is the one who told me to keep an eye out for you, Princess. You should go back now."

The derogatory tone of voice irritated her, but the knowing look in his eyes sent a chill up her spine that had nothing to do with the coolness of the water. It hardened her nipples even more, all the same. Anippe didn't know if he knew she'd been entertaining the forbidden or if she was just being paranoid.

She hurriedly returned to the shore, her heart still beating painfully. She ignored the hand the overseer offered and crawled her way up the muddy bank until she was at his side. Her slaves hurried to follow her as she ignored the man her father had picked to oversee his papyrus fields and the slaves that worked them, to head straight for his chariot. His shout of indignation when the four of them took off in it without him didn't fill her with the satisfaction it normally would have.

Knowing she was in real trouble if the overseer knew, or thought he knew anything about the clandestine meeting, Anippe hurried to their palatial home in the hopes of gauging her father's mood. If he acted as if everything was fine, she'd do whatever she had to do to keep the overseer out of her life. Even if it meant lying through her teeth to the point of having his head chopped off.

She jumped from the chariot as soon as it stopped and threw the reins at the waiting guard, not caring that she'd thrown wide and they landed on the ground. "Tell my father that I need to see him as soon as I've changed. His overseer has insulted me for the last time!"

The guard nodded and bowed before retrieving the reins and jumping into the chariot to take it to the stables. Anippe glanced at those meant to serve her, only then realizing what a mess she must look too. "One word from any of you against me and they will be the last words you ever speak!"

In spite of the mud-damp dress trying to tangle with her ankles, Anippe ignored their bows and ran up the many stone steps leading to the vast Residential Palace, nearly out of breath by the time she entered the breezy open-ended throne room.

She stopped when she realized a massive crowd had gathered. Fortunately, all were turned toward the throne and had yet to realize her presence. Curious as to the gathering and embarrassed in earnest to be seen looking like she had fallen into a mud-pit, Anippe started to turn away but was stopped by a young guard she didn't recognize who pointed to the area where her father would be holding court.

Stunned at his audacity, she turned back to find those who had gathered parting as if a line had been drawn down the center of the massive room. Realization dawned as the only one remaining in the center of the room was some stupid slave who had gotten himself in trouble. For him to have been brought before her father proved his offence was grave, as would be his punishment.

Anippe took only a second to take in the slave's blood- soaked back, the way in which he was shackled, and that he seemed to have been dipped in liquid. She tried not to shudder as she'd once witnessed the process of torture the guards used to get information from a rebellious offender, knowing the oil coating his skin would soon remove it from his muscle.

Well, she had her own problems to deal with. Anippe dismissed him from her mind as she moved forward, already trying to come up with an excuse for her appearance and her absence from the palace. When she was even with the slave, she glanced over and then stopped dead as her heart stuttered and stalled, as this was no mere slave.

Jacob was on his knees with his hands tied behind his back. The same thickly woven papyrus rope ran up his back to circle his neck and down over his bottom to hang loose until it encircled his ankles.

Relieved he didn't glance her way, Anippe looked from him to her father as fear for them both choked her. She moved forward more slowly now, knowing her disheveled appearance before such an audience would shame the Nisu, though not nearly as much as her love for a slave would.

Anippe approached the many shallow steps leading to the platform where the solid gold throne was occupied by the man she now feared as much as she had always loved. She bowed. "Father."

"You have defied me again, I see."

Anippe was afraid her bowels were going to give. "I do not understand."

The Nisu looked at her with irritation. "Do you deny that you and this slave have been cavorting with each other?"

Anippe's head jerked up as she looked at her father in horror-filled confusion. "We have not. I have never disgraced myself."

The Nisu's eyes flashed with doubt for only a second before he looked at her shrewdly. "So you have not met this dog in secret?"

Anippe couldn't keep from trembling now. That her father was questioning her so publicly did not only bode ill for Jacob. She had no clue how to answer. If he'd only found out about the meeting in the Nile that happened moments before, she could claim it was an accident, but if he somehow knew of the other times....

"Have you nothing to say, Daughter?"

Anippe took a deep breath and nodded. "I'm sorry. I…only found him an interesting diversion, and though our encounters have been rare, I have sought him out a few times…because he fascinates me." She cringed, not knowing why she'd said what she'd said, just knowing it was required that she say something, and that damning information was more truth than lie.

The Nisu settled back into his throne as his addressed the room at large. "It is of no consequence. Out of love for my disobedient daughter, Anippe, known by all as the Jewel of the Nile, I will remove the object that causes her to sin against her Nisu and her people. The slave will be put to death this day, and my daughter will be wedded and bedded by the man of my choice this night." He indicated the man standing to his right and a cheer went up and reverberated around the cavernous room.

Her half-brother, and heir to the throne, Horus, looked at her with distaste though she knew it was because of her appearance and that she had chosen a slave over his attentions. That she was still a virgin was no thanks to him as she had fought him off more than once when he had invaded her rooms.

Anippe looked away from him and shook her head, though she knew no one was looking at her. Cheers and words of praise for the Nisu echoed throughout the room and she looked at them all, wondering if they would be so cheerful if they were the target of her father's wrath.

When the furor died down, she struggled to hold her tongue, but she could not allow her father to condemn her into eternal enslavement with a man so cruel.

"I beg of you, Father. Please reconsider. He is my brother!"

The Nisu nodded. "Yes. And you shall have children with royal blood flowing in their veins. Not! The! Blood! Of! A! Jewish! Slave!"

Anippe winced as each word was shouted at her. Even though she knew that there were endless generations of inbreeding in her family, she had always expected to be joined with a distant cousin. Until Jacob. Then she'd wanted nothing or no one else.

Falling to her knees, sick that this was so much worse than anything she could have imagined, Anippe's eyes leaked tears of fear and heartbreak. Her father had loved her above all! Had spoiled her rotten and enjoyed that she was the product of his making. How could he treat her thus now?

"I beg of you, Father, please, choose another. And please let this slave go. He never pursued me. The fault is all mine. I was simply toying with him and I swear will never leave the palace again…. But please do not put murder on my head by killing him for my sins."

The Nisu looked from her to the slave, and then at his favorite son as the room silently awaited his response.

"As your brother seems displeased with my choice of you as his first wife, I may reconsider to whom you will be wed, but the deed will be done. As to the dog, I will not allow him to remain a temptation you seem unable to deny. He will die this night as the sun sets."

She heard Jacob's gasp and knew that he didn't fear death, but that it would come when he was to say his evening prayers to the God

44

of his fathers. She wanted to beseech her father to change the time as well, but to say anything on Jacob's behalf would only get him killed sooner. But more importantly, it would only make him angrier with her.

"You have nothing more to say, my daughter?"

She shook her head. "No Father, my Great and Mighty Nisu."

"Well, maybe you have learned after all.

"You will go and wash that mess off of you now, and you will allow my concubines to prepare you for your nuptials to…whomever I decide. Then you will wait in your rooms until you have been summoned."

She bowed her head again, knowing there was nothing more she could do for either Jacob or herself. "Yes, Father."

It wasn't unexpected that his sergeants at arms followed her and her servants after she stood and headed to the bathing room. Nor that they remained there with their backs turned to guard her while she slipped off the single shoulder strap before stripping the muddy dress from her body. She glared at a young one when he turned to look back and fumed when all she got for her effort was a grin.

Anippe's servants entered the large marble pool of water behind her, carrying the oils and the alkali used to wash her hair and body. She dunked her head under the water and then walked over to stand in the shallow end while they cleansed her from head to toes.

A silent procession of more than a dozen of her father's concubines filed into the room carrying towels and decorated clay jars as well as other oddly shaped items wrapped in linens, which were hard to identify from her position in the pool. Once she was rinsed off, she walked to the steps leading to the end of the room where they had assembled, curious as to the number of them as well as the purpose of all they carried wrapped and hidden within the linens. She had witnessed an older sister's wedding preparations and only a handful of people had been present to prepare her, and nothing was ever held from her sister's view. She swallowed and turned to the one in charge.

Her father's oldest concubine Tawaret was quite old at forty or so years, and though she had once been a beautiful woman, the weight of her service to the Nisu showed in the lines of her face and in the loss of her teeth. She smiled sympathetically at Anippe. "Come, child, we must prepare you as the Nisu commands."

Anippe allowed herself to be led toward the back of the room where a wall hid the toilet, relieved the guards did not follow this time. Unlike the rest of the structure, it had no roof so it was open to the elements. Two much younger concubines stepped forward at Tawaret's signal and made a pad of several linens and placed them upon a short block of granite. Tawaret indicated the pile of folded cloth. "Please get on your knees and lean down for your cleansing. The Keeper of the King's Rectum will be here soon to examine you. Once we have purged all from your bowels he will examine you front and back, inside and out. And upon his approval, we shall finish preparing you for your wedding night."

As colon cleansings were a part of her everyday life, Anippe did as instructed and assumed the position with her bottom up high and her head lying on her folded arms. Knowing the eyes of her father's concubines were on her exposed parts and that she was being judged, not only for her sins against the crown but for whatever flaws they might find in her physical makeup, was difficult to endure. Only two of her own servants ever assisted her in the ritual cleansings, and it was always in the privacy of her rooms with her toilet box handy for her to expel the liquid and any toxins from her body.

She turned her head away as humiliation washed over her. She was a princess and the daughter of the most powerful man alive. For so many, of such low rank, to be able to look upon her genitals was a clear indication of how far she had sunk in the eyes of her father.

It surprised Anippe that she was being granted the privilege of one of the Nisus' personal physicians for the nuptial examination since she had fallen so far. She knew it was probably more to assure her future husband she was a virgin still and had not contaminated her womb by consorting with the Jewish slave.

Anippe flinched when Tawaret touched her to rub warm oil in and around the opening then endured the deep probing of her long finger as it went further than her own servants ever dared to lubricate her for the reed that would soon be pushed inside.

"I feel nothing. Bring me the reeds. The Nisu commands we go deep in the cleansing to expel the demons that possessed Princess Anippe to sin," Tawaret declared, before additional oil was drizzled over Anippe's bottom.

Though she had felt no ill will from Tawaret, the old concubine was much rougher than the servants who usually served this need, and when she finally pulled her finger out and then slid two back in to spread her opening painfully, tears smarted Anippe's eyes. What followed was so much worse than anything she could have imagined. She was held down and filled beyond what she felt her body could endure and then forced to expel the toxins from her body. As if that were not enough to both shame and punish her, Tawaret had her flipped over for more torture.

"You must be very still. Your father has instructed that we know that all the demons inside of you are completely expelled," Tawaret repeated, this time directly to Anippe. "You cannot lay with your husband until you are purified and your virginity has been verified. This is the decree of the Nisu, and so it shall be."

"And so it shall be," all those present, save Anippe, responded.

The woman stepped back, and Anippe was certain she heard Tawaret whisper an apology. Anippe knew those words did not bear her good will, but she had no idea what was in store beyond the cleansing. Seconds later her fear exploded into panic. A cloth was stuffed into her mouth, and strips of material were wrapped around her wrists before they were pulled so that her arms were forced to remain beside and slightly over her head. Visions of those her father condemned, and commanded hung from crossed wood as a means to a slow and hideous death, had her fighting the bonds, but there was no escape.

Anippe's heartbeats increased and she shook her head as the physician took a long object from one of the linens a young concubine held. He lowered himself until he was eye level at the apex of her thighs once they were pulled wide and held still with fingers that bruised her flesh. Not able to take the strain of trying to watch him as everything inside of her was still cramping and everything upon her surface screamed in pain, she forced her muscles to relax. But as soon as she gave in and laid her head against the cloth-covered slab, it jerked back up while her muffled screams broke the silence of the room.

Tears were endless and as blinding to her sight as was the pain of having her maidenhead so brutally torn, and Anippe knew, with no doubt left, that her father now hated her, and he had instructed them all to treat her with a brutality normally reserved for criminals.

The physician rose, holding the marble stick now covered in blood. He wiped it on the linen before handing both over to Tawaret. "Take this to the Nisu. She is yet pure."

Tawaret took the cloth-covered stick and left the room in a hurry. The physician turned back to Anippe before a vase filled with frigid water was thrown upon her. Her screams were muffled by the cloth still stuffed into her mouth, and each attempt to cry-out only closed off her breath even more. More of the shocking water came at her as if she was a slab of meat to be washed down. The lack of oxygen, blessedly, took her to the edge of blackness.

"Enough! Be done with this before you kill her!"

Nearly unconscious, Anippe couldn't make out who had ordered them to stop, but it was a male, and not the physician, which meant others were now witnessing her humiliation. The cold bath stopped, but her shivering legs were pulled open and up, again, waking her from the stupor she'd fallen into. She screamed into the choking cloth and thrashed her head back and forth as another guard approached, carrying an iron rod with a glowing red tip.

Several hands covered her body and encircled her legs to hold her down and immobile so her feeble struggles made no difference at all. As her heart pounded and sweat poured from her pores, the iron was placed on her inner thigh and excruciating fire seared her flesh.

Unimaginable pain threw Jewell into a sitting position as she screamed and fought the hands holding her down.

"Jewell, stop! It's a nightmare! Jewell, stop! Wake up!"

The hard slap brought her attention to Sapphire's horrified expression and made her realize she was back in her own room, that the hands holding her down now were those of her sister.

Chapter Four

Jewell sat in her aunt Destiny's cabin as family members arrived and chatted while they awaited the last of Haven's daughter's to arrive. She was still reeling from the horror of her dream and wasn't up to making light conversation. Fortunately, her sisters were keeping her mother occupied, and Rayne wasn't aware that her middle child was on the verge of falling apart.

"Hey cuz, what's up?"

Jewell tried to smile naturally at Heracles. Uncle Logan and Aunt Destiny's youngest along with his older brothers, Zeus and Apollo, had all flown in to make the meeting. She doubted their arrival had anything to do with the concerns she and her sisters had, but then again, just because she, Dia, and Sapphire *just* discovered each one of them had seen the same strange man, at virtually the same time in different countries, it *had* happened months ago.

"Not much," she lied. "How's life for the hottest model to hit New York in decades working out for you?"

Heracles grinned. "Fantastic! The money is great but the ladies are even better. The snots are probably jealous I'm heading to Greece next week for a shoot." He laughed. "Really original of the magazine isn't it? But hey, I'm all over getting a free trip abroad so it's all good."

Fortunately Jewell didn't have to respond to what was undoubtedly their most vain cousin. The child named after their revered grandmother, Celestia, entered the door and everyone immediately took a seat or settled on the floor.

Rayne, Haven, and Destiny were still as identical and as beautiful in their early fifties as they had been when she was a child, and Jewell could only hope she and her sisters aged as well. As the oldest, Destiny Cavanaugh stood in the middle of the three with a look of pride at the family and concern for whatever they'd assembled for warring on her face.

"Thanks, kids, and my love, for coming. We called you all here for one thing, but it seems there is now more we need to talk about. But first we'll let Haven tell you all why we originally called you here." She looked encouragingly at her sister.

Haven moved forward and took a moment to look each of her daughters in the eyes. Then she looked at everyone else. "Yeah, thanks for coming. I know this all seems a little melodramatic and cloak and dagger, but the truth is that something has happened, and I know you all love us and we love you, but...."

Rayne put her arm around Haven, and Destiny did the same.

Haven nodded her thanks and then continued. "My daughters, as you all know, didn't inherit magic at fifteen like the rest of you. And although it didn't matter to me, it has always mattered to them. But something happened on their, *and your* last birthdays, and between then and now we thought we'd just wait and see what was what and wait until the Whitehawk boys could make it back before saying anything.

"Congratulations, by the way, Heracles."

As everyone's attention was turning to him, Heracles smiled his thanks with the same flash of teeth that was making him millions.

Haven turned her attention to her daughters again and smiled, and they smiled back at her. "It seems Luna, Soleli, and Celestia have had a...transformation. We don't know yet what is to come for them, but the big change is they now have silver in their veins instead of blood."

There was not a single sound in the room as everyone looked to the young women then back to their mother. Haven was obviously waiting to see if anyone had questions, but Jewell figured they had no more of an idea of what to ask than she did.

"Well then. Okay. Girls? Is there anything you would

like to add?"

All three of the Cavanaugh-Hansen sisters shook their heads before looking at each other. "Okay. I know we are all very curious as to what this means. The girls and I, along with my sisters, are scouring the family diaries to see if this has happened in the past, and we'll keep everyone informed as things develop.

"Now Rayne has something she wants to bring up, too."

Rayne hugged Haven and then looked at her own daughters. "Well, as you all know we sent the girls to different countries as graduation gifts. I just found out last night they each encountered a man who was in all three countries at the same time.

"Of course being a triplet from a long line of triplets, I don't discount the possibility it was three brothers. However, the girls are fairly certain this is the same man, and he is looking for someone in Mystic Waters."

The attention of everyone in the room sharpened, and murmurs were heard between cousins. Jewell still felt too fragile to say anything so she stayed silent. After a moment the room was quiet again as everyone settled before her mother continued.

"Sapphire seems to have had the most serious encounter with him, although I understand he had a connection with each of the girls. I've asked Diamond to pull up the picture she took of him and to send it to you all. So, I guess the next logical thing to do is ask if anyone else has seen him or had any type of communication with him."

The room filled with the differing tones when the cell phones received the multimedia text message. As each member of the family received theirs, they opened it to look. Jewell was waiting for one or all of them to confirm a sighting too, but her cousins were all shaking their heads.

She glanced over to Sapphire, but she was talking to Dia, and then they both looked over at her with concern. As she didn't know whether it was because no one else had seen the man, or if it was because they had been terrified for her this morning when she awoke from the dream of torture covered in sweat and crying hysterically, Jewell lifted her brows questioningly.

Dia shook her head sharply before turning to listen to something else Sapphire was saying. Jewell sighed as Destiny once again stepped between her mother and Aunt Haven. "Is there anything else anyone needs to bring up while we are all here?"

Tom Whitehawk stood and stretched, smiling at the assembly though his eyes held confusion and concern. "I think both of these things are significant in their own way, and as we all know, there are forces both human and mystical always at work around us. I want to tell my boys, as well as my nieces, to be very careful and alert."

As the three sets of triplets nodded, he continued. "There were stories my grandfather told me when I was very young about people with the silver blood. As a child I would eat the stories up, but as I grew older I assumed they were just a different version of fairy tales other children were told.

"Since we now know this is a reality, I need to revisit the stories as best I can. But I was just a toddler at the time so I fear my memories may be distorted. But the one thing I do remember right off is the men with the silver blood he spoke of were celestial beings, and what we have always known as the mythical unicorn carried the silver blood too.

"As the horned horse is considered a fictional animal, I discounted all he said about those with silver blood as another of my grandfather's stories. He was a very good storyteller and always kept the children of my people occupied while they worked or hunted, or when the adults wanted private time to themselves.

"I will speak to my father about this. Though he is very old now, his mind is still sharp, and I am certain my grandfather told him as a child all the things he imparted to my generation."

Jewell sat in wonder as Uncle Tom took his seat again. Again there was quiet talking throughout the room, and she wished she could get over her own mental roadblock to engage with her cousins.

"That's cool."

Jewell looked over at Heracles and smiled in spite of the lethargy claiming her. Gorgeous as he was, he wasn't the brightest bulb in the lamp and hadn't picked up on her need to be left alone, as everyone else seemed to. "It is. But kind of scary, too."

As if he hadn't considered that, he slowly nodded. "Yeah, but just think, how cool would it be if there were actually unicorns?"

Jewell shook her head. Only Heracles would look at today's gathering as something fun while everyone else acknowledged the possibility it could also mean danger. As silly as it made him seem, she liked that about him. He always saw the sunny side of everything even if it meant danger might be coming. Jewell looked back up as Destiny Cavanaugh-Whitehawk crossed the room and her husband stood and opened his arms.

Destiny went into them without breaking stride, kissed him lightly on the lips, and then turned back to face the room. "Thanks, honey. Is there anything anyone else has to say?"

Heracles smiled and stood, and all eye turned to him. "Yes. Can we have some of Uncle Logan's cake now?"

As expected, everyone in the room laughed, but interest sharpened in the eyes of the late Celestia Cavanaugh's grandchildren; they had all been raised on the heavenly confection. Since Jewell hadn't been able to eat the slice she'd been offered the night before during the fiasco of an engagement dinner, and hadn't felt up to eating anything since awaking from the nightmare, she stood, too.

Sapphire stepped forward from the corner she and Dia were huddled in and smiled at the room at large. "It's great to see everyone, but I have to go. I have a job interview, and I'll probably be late as it is. I hope I'll get to see you all again before anyone leaves town. Kisses!"

She grabbed her purse and hurried to the door as

everyone yelled goodbye.

"She is one hot-looking lady."

Jewell turned to Heracles and frowned. "She's your cousin!"

He shrugged. "Didn't say I wanted to bed her, Jewells," Heracles said with a laugh. "But that black hair and those eyes... I bet she would make it big as a supermodel."

Jewell turned back to watch as Sapphire sent one last wave before walking out the front door, and she had to admit Heracles was right. No matter how late her sister was for the interview, it was likely she'd land the job because no man in his right mind would say no to her lovely face.

Dia walked up to the two of them and punched Heracles in the arm. He didn't flinch but grabbed her in a headlock and made a fist to rub into the crown of her head as he spun her around in circles. Heracles laughed when he stopped spinning and so did Dia as she stomped her high heel down onto his booted foot.

Jewell watched the two of them tussle with grunts and laughter a few minutes more before they broke apart and smiled at each other. She and Sapphire never had understood Dia's tomboy tendencies, but the silliness between Dia and Heracles had been ongoing since Jewell and her sisters, the Hansen triplets, and Heracles and his brothers had all shared the same thick blanket on the floor of one or the others parents' homes as infants and toddlers. By the time they had all started elementary school, Dia had accumulated as many black eyes and busted lips as Heracles, and though his father had punished him for hitting a girl, their father had laughed and cheered Dia on, much to their mother's consternation.

"Hey, Skunk Breath."

"Hey, yourself, Sissy Boy! How ya been?"

Jewell walked away from the two of them, knowing the insults and probably more wrestling would continue for some time to come. She approached the three sisters on whose behalf the meeting had been called and smiled at Celestia, Luna, and Soleli. They were each as much a

Cavanaugh as any of Celestia Cavanaugh's grandchildren, but there was nothing about their appearance that could be considered physically identical, though they too were identical triplets as science decreed it.

While meditating within the confines of his sweat tent—his way of tuning into the universe—Uncle Tom foresaw the Hansen pregnancy dilemma. The possibility of a scientific investigation that could have destroyed their lives in general and that of Logan and Haven's girls in particular. And, as every Cavanaugh was warned from early on, the danger of snooping noses regarding even one Cavanaugh, or Cavanaugh descendent, endangered all of them. In essence, it could have been one giant disaster.

As being forewarned allowed her to be forearmed, Aunt Haven had rather nonchalantly informed her doctor weeks before the birth of her children that it was so funny: she and her sisters had looked nothing like each other at birth, but that they had grown to look more alike as the months went on. In turn, once her girls were born, and handed off one by one, the doctor had laughingly stated it was a really good thing she'd told him what to expect or he would have been very confused.

That bullet dodged, Aunt Haven had used different pediatricians in several distant towns for the physicals and immunizations needed until the girls were nearly two. After that she just told the local pediatrician that they were fraternal triplets and that had been that. Which was a good thing as their features changed even more as they grew. They ended up being a combination of both their father *and* mother, unlike her and her own sisters who totally had Cavanaugh written all over them.

Celestia Cavanaugh-Hansen was a young platinum blond version of Aunt Haven though her eyes were more hazel than emerald, and she was of slightly above-average height like Jewell and her sisters. Because of her need to save animals and children from those who would abuse or neglect them, Celestia often put herself in the line of fire. She would often be found picketing and rallying against injustice.

Soleli's features and coloring were more like Uncle Logan's. They both had rich mocha-brown hair and tall, statuesque physiques. She also had her father's serious nature and was continuing her education to be a doctor who specialized in heart surgery, like her dad.

Luna was a variation of both parents and actually looked like neither one. Her strawberry blond hair was in long curly ringlets she'd never mastered taming, which complemented the heavy splattering of freckles covering her face and body. Her shy nature was reflected in her inability to talk comfortably with people or look them in the eyes. Her incredibly long lashes accommodated her shyness by hiding her large brown eyes whenever she glanced downward.

Unlike her sisters and millennia of Cavanaugh women who had come before, it could be said Luna was *plain*, although Jewell felt she was pretty in her own way and believed if Luna would just come out of her shell, people would see she really was a beautiful soul.

And then there were the boys. The *Sons of Cavanaugh*, as Aunt Destiny had decreed her identical sons at birth, looked just like their father, who was still a man who turned the heads of women young and old. This explained why women swooned at Zeus, Apollo, and Heracles' feet on a regular basis. But of the three, Heracles seemed to be the only one who noticed and took advantage of their Native American good looks.

"Hi, Jewell," Luna said quietly before quickly looking down.

"Hi. How are you doing with all this?"

Luna shrugged and then glanced up quickly before her lashes were once again shielding her eyes. Celestia gave a little shoulder lift and smiled before giving Jewell a hug. "Hi! Thanks for coming. I really don't know exactly what to think. We've been talking since Uncle Tom spoke up, and we're hoping that there is something he'll remember from his grandfather's stories."

Jewell nodded. "I hope so, too."

Soleli grinned. "Thanks. We're excited but nervous about it. I don't know exactly what we're going to do if we need to give a blood sample now, but I guess we'll figure it out as we go."

Jewell grimaced, realizing what a dilemma the three sisters would have any time the issue of blood came up. "Let me know in advance and I'll give you some of mine."

Soleli nodded. "Thanks. If it's possible I will. Otherwise I'll have to steal it from a patient at the hospital. I'm doing my residency here in Mystic Waters while I'm studying for my Boards, which is a relief. I was afraid I was going to have to stay at Chicago General, but Daddy pulled some strings. I just hope all this doesn't complicate things too much."

Luna grinned shyly. "Me either."

Jewell grinned back, relieved Luna was interacting at all. When they were younger, she didn't unless forced, and then it was obvious to all just how much pain it caused her. Though the rest of them had attended public school, Luna had been home schooled. In second grade a teacher had forced her to recite a poem on Parent Night, and it had traumatized her so much she disappeared for three days. Even as young as she had been at the time, Jewell still remembered how franticly the family had searched the mountain, and the relief they'd all felt when she turned up, wet but well.

"Hi, guys! I'm so excited for you! I can't wait to find out what this means for you!"

Dia's bubbly enthusiasm made the cousins smile even more and reminded Jewell of why she loved her younger sister so much. Unlike herself, Dia had a passionate nature that made a room seem to expand when she was in it, and even though there was an element of worry in her eyes, Dia never let it pass her lips especially since it concerned Celestia, Soleli and Luna.

The overly protective feelings for the Hansen cousins had started the day they all turned fifteen. The families, minus her own father and Uncle Logan—who bowed out any time mystical things were in the making—had gathered the evening before their birthdays at Uncle Tom's historic family cabin. Once together, they'd hiked further up the mountain to an area where the land plateaued and was naturally cleared of the trees that had completely covered the remainder of the mountain before mankind interloped.

Since their mothers had already experienced the *ascension* and knew what was needed and what to expect, Rayne, Haven and Destiny planned an overnight camping trip for their children. The mothers made more than enough food for the celebratory picnic, which was to sustain them all for the upcoming event. Uncle Tom busily prepared the land to his wife's specifications. When his assignment was complete, he kissed Destiny on the mouth for long moments then her sisters on the cheeks and had a few private words with his sons. Then he left them all to hike back down into the trees to wait until Destiny called him to return. The remaining group waited for the full moon to reach its mark and for the clock to strike midnight.

Jewell remembered the night like it was yesterday. All nine of them had been giddy with excitement. The Whitehawk boys had eaten enough for twenty people. They then stripped naked and had run around and wrestled with each other like fools, which was completely normal.

Even though she, Sapphire, Dia, as well as Celestia, Luna, and Soleli had grown up seeing their male cousins in the buff, just as they had seen all the girls save shy Luna from infancy on, that night it suddenly became uncomfortable. Jewell had recognized that it was because they were no longer going to be children.

Since every generation before hers was comprised of only female Cavanaugh children, it was expected they would, as had every generation before them, remove all clothing so there was nothing between their bodies and the magic that would come upon them from the sky. But this time each child was given a white robe to adorn their bodies until the first strike of the midnight hour when they would be required to open and drop them to the ground.

Even that night, before they'd arrived at the site and the boys actually stripped down, Jewell hadn't foreseen nudity being a problem. She had expected it. But as the time approached and the mothers began undressing to put on their black silk robes, and as her sisters and female cousins, save Luna, began undressing, Jewell suddenly felt a moment of panic.

She ran to Rayne and hugged her hard so she would stop taking off her clothes. Rayne had hugged her back and whispered in her ear. "It is fine, my love. They do not know this night you become a woman, just as they do not know what is in store to bring them to manhood. They are so full of themselves right now they will not see you any differently. Boys mature mentally at a slower rate than girls, then after, as their blood must be sacrificed also, they won't even know for a while that the rest of us are here.

"Once it is all over, you will all be a little disoriented, but you will feel the power of womanhood within you. And all that you experience this night will be worth what is to come."

Her mother knowing her concern, without Jewell having to voice it, eased most of her distress, but knowing part of the ceremony was directed at the blood flow that each of the girls would experience for the first time still rested heavily on her, and she expressed those feelings to her mother.

Rayne had smiled at her again. "As soon as the ascent has happened, and you are returned in your new body, I will do as I have told you and your sisters. It will not hurt, nor will it take but just a second, and I can assure you the boys will not see."

Jewell had nodded and returned to the circle. As everyone but she and Luna stood naked beneath their robes in the moonlight, she hurriedly undressed and pulled on her robe. Luna did the same at a much slower pace. In a way it had given her comfort knowing she wasn't the only one bothered by their situation, though she knew for Luna it must have been much worse.

As oldest, Aunt Destiny walked to the center of the circle they had formed. She lifted a large leather-bound book above her head. Jewell recognized it as one of the ancient diaries she and the others had been shown on rare occasions throughout their childhood.

Destiny began an incantation, and everyone followed along and turned in the proper direction with her each time she acknowledged the four elements of earth, wind, fire, and water. As storm clouds rapidly gathered and lightning crackled within their graying folds, a fire shot up from the five-foot-tall white candles placed in the direction each element was honored. Even though they were placed twenty paces away from the circle, their heat was instantly felt, but because Jewell and her sisters had been briefed about the ceremony by their mother the day before, she knew they symbolically lit the way for the magic to find them.

When they were all once again facing each other, Destiny placed the book next to an unlit scarlet candle atop a long stone table that looked natural. Jewell had wondered at the time if Uncle Tom was responsible for settling the large flat stones into the ground on their sharper ends and then somehow managed to place the long one across the top as an altar for the ceremony. She was certain he was responsible for the candle, as she'd seen him place it there.

As Destiny's chant continued Rayne and Haven walked forward, each one carrying a stack of three sauce-size milky-white bowls in their hands, and both had three folded hand towels draped over their forearms atop their robes' sleeves. They approached the altar, but instead of standing by Destiny's side, they each stood at opposite ends of the long surface.

Destiny, Haven, and Rayne, with the ceremonial precision of practice, lifted and placed their towels in a vertical row on the surface before them. And again, as if they had counted out the beats of silent music, their choreographed movements had them lifting then placing each bowl atop the towels, and finally the three reached into the large pocket of their robes to pull out the devices Jewell had feared most.

The wind picked up and clouds swirled in angry circles as Jewell's hair beat against her face and, as they all dropped their robes one by one, against her shoulders and back. She had no time to worry about her growing modesty. Jewell was certain her cousins were as preoccupied as she was just remaining upright as the pressure of the air increased in a downward spiral.

Though she and her sisters were told what to expect, her heart went crazy and her knees began to shake. The quickly conjured lightning was as wild as the beat of her heart that night, and the sky was alight with a magnificent though terrifying show of power.

She'd barely heard the command to raise her hands to the sky and looked to see her mother and Aunt Destiny were also fighting to lift their arms, whereas Aunt Haven seemed unaffected by the wind at all. She was the one controlling the elements. The approaching lightning rained down on the ground around them and harmlessly pelted trees in the distance.

Jewell's eyes had stung and watered from the wind smacking her hair against her face, but she hadn't allowed herself to shut them as she watched the bolts of lightning draw closer like tentacles searching for a victim.

Her body suffused with heat, and every inch of her shook unmercifully as the storm moved first to the opposite side of the circle where her male cousins stood. She nearly cried out as a lightning bolt hit one after the other in the center of their chests before lifting them off the ground.

By the time it moved across, taking everyone else, she had been torn between courage and cowardice. She'd stood her ground and when she was struck, and rising into the air, too, she realized she'd had nothing to fear.

There was no pain, only a magical wonder as energy

engulfed and caressed her. She'd felt the *changing* to the marrow of her bones and in each and every organ. Heat filled her womb and she felt it swell as it filled with the blood that carried magic. All too soon it was over, and she was being lowered to the ground and placed upon the pallet her uncle had prepared.

Things got a little foggy after that, but she knew her mother eventually came and covered her body before moving on to her sisters. It was a short while later that she felt her legs being lifted and held open beneath the robe. Her mother quickly slid the narrow small-headed spoon just inside her vagina, only enough to recover a small portion of the blood from her first menstrual cycle. Then Rayne placed one of the hand towels there and lowered Jewell's legs. Rayne covered Jewell with the edges of the robe again before walking back to the altar.

Though her head still hadn't been clear, and she had not the energy to sit up and watch, she knew her mother would put her and her sisters' blood into the individual bowls lined with frankincense and a few drops of the oily myrrh then light them with the scarlet candle.

As the flames burned and the sacrifice of blood was complete, each girl's magic would be sealed for the duration of their natural life and thereafter. And though they'd been told it could take many years before they reached mystic maturity, the idea that she was now magically enabled had been enough for silent celebration.

Her peace and tranquility was soon shattered by the hysterical screaming and crying of her cousins. It hadn't been until later that day, when she had mostly recovered, that she learned the boys' blood sacrifice was captured as they were circumcised by both her mother and Aunt Destiny, as her female cousins were being frantically consoled by their distraught mother. Although the lightning had claimed them, not one of the Hansen girls had been infused with magic, as they hadn't produced *The Blood of Continuation.*

The trip back down the mountain had been a

completely different experience than the trip up. Not only had her male cousins cried a good portion of the walk, her female cousins had, too. By the time the group made it back to the cabin, the boys were whining in earnest and the girls were totally silent.

Within a week the boys had recovered, but her girl cousins never did. And because of that she and her family as well as the Whitehawks had always treated them with kid gloves. Jewell sometimes wondered if they hadn't all done the girls a disservice.

Dia's face appeared close to hers and Jewell jumped back. "Jewell! Hey! Finally! Where did you go? I said Mom needs to talk to you."

Realizing she'd gotten lost in thought, Jewell slid a glance to their mother. Hoping the conversation was about anything but *Kevin*, she quickly hugged each of her cousins and turned to Dia with a *What's up?* look. Dia only shrugged.

Jewell looked over at her mother again and blew out a breath of relief. Rayne was in the process of cutting and serving cake to the Whitehawk brothers, and she surely wouldn't mention the awful engagement dinner of the night before in front of them.

Given the share-fest the family had just had, Jewell was thankful no one had mentioned it. It was bad enough she was going to have to tell her parents what had actually happened; it would have been mortifying to have the entire clan know. But then again, there were very few secrets within the Cavanaugh families.

Jewell approached the table and smiled at Zeus and Apollo, who were waiting for Heracles to get his piece and move on. As usual he wanted seconds before anyone else had had firsts, and because he was such a spoiled brat, he usually got what he wanted.

As the Whitehawk boys were identical in every way except for personality, Jewell had always thought that, in spite of their gender and their father's equally strong genetic makeup, they more closely followed the historic family line. Not only were they drop-dead gorgeous and a testament to what the Whitehawk and Cavanaugh genes were capable of doing together, they'd wielded well-controlled magic very soon after their ascension all those years ago, unlike her and her sisters. But they had been free to do so, too. Since Uncle Tom was as mystical as Aunt Destiny, there had never been any constraints placed on their using the crafts with which they'd been gifted.

They smiled at her now with their megawatt smiles, and Jewell understood what Heracles meant about Sapphire. Related or not, beautiful was beautiful.

"Hey, Jewells," Zeus said, smiling, though his eyes were assessing, as always.

She grinned at him. "Hi." She turned to acknowledge the middle Whitehawk brother.

"Hi, Apollo."

"Hi, beautiful. What's this I hear about you getting engaged?"

And there it is... Jewell glanced at her mother, who shrugged.

"Well, you know I had to tell my sisters."

Jewell nodded. Of course she did. "Yeah, well, it didn't work out."

All eyes immediately went to her bare finger, and Jewell stood still even though she wanted to squirm like a naughty child caught doing something she shouldn't have.

"That's too bad. Are you okay?" Zeus asked, real concern in his eyes.

"I'm fine. There was just a little confusion on my friend's part. And I really don't want to go into it now. Today is about other things."

"Do we need to break his face?" Heracles asked before stuffing a large forkful of cake into his mouth.

Jewell grinned at him. He really was cute with those devilish eyes and that megawatt smile. "Nope. He's a good guy. I just guess he thought we were more than I even thought about. He surprised me last night by bringing me to the house," she added, looking at her mother. "Now I have to figure out what to do. I like him a lot, but there's just no...."

"Passion," all four of them said at the same time.

Jewell nodded. "Yeah. Well, if that's all you wanted, Mom, I need to get on home. I need to get busy and look for work. I just can't seem to find anything I like."

"Wait!" Rayne turned to her nephew. "Zeus? Would you get you and your brother some cake? No more for Heracles, though, or no one else will get any." Rayne smiled at Heracles apologetically, but he just grinned in response.

Zeus nodded and she smiled at him before stepping around the table. "I'll walk you out."

Knowing something serious was coming, Jewell said goodbye to the boys and the rest of those still milling around talking. After stepping out onto the front porch, she turned and waited until Rayne closed the door behind her. "What's up, Mom?"

Rayne looked her over, concern clear in her eyes. "Are you really okay? Dia said you woke up this morning screaming."

Jewell relaxed. "I just had a really bad dream, Mom. It's nothing. I guess I was just upset last night because I ended up hurting my best friend's feelings."

Rayne bit her bottom lip and then released it. "Okay, but if you have more bad dreams, please don't keep it to yourself. There are Dream Spinners in our lineage. And if you are one, you have to be really careful."

Jewell shook her head, certain that it was nothing. "Okay, but what's dangerous about having a bad dream?"

"Your great, great, great-aunt Eufaria had dreams. She detailed them in her diary and then detailed what happened when she awoke."

"Like what?"

Rayne gestured for Jewell to join her at the corner of the porch where it began to wrap around the side of the cabin. She took a seat that was obviously a Garrison White piece and Jewell took its twin.

Rayne sighed. "Her diaries actually scared me so much

that when you girls were little and one of you would have a nightmare, I'd actually check your body to see if you had an injury anywhere. I was very relieved I never found one, but that's what happened to Aunt Eufaria."

Jewell swallowed. "So if she dreamed something...whatever had happened to her body in the dream actually had happened when she awoke?"

Rayne nodded. "Were you harmed in your dream in any way?"

Jewell knew she could never tell her mother what she had experienced so she shook her head. "No. I'm fine."

Rayne nodded, the relief evident in her sudden smile. "I'm so glad. I was terrified."

"What happened with Aunt Eufaria's dreams? Did they eventually go away?"

Rayne shook her head. "No. Her sisters, Eugeni and Euther both wrote diaries too. In both each sister detailed how many months they awoke to their sister's screams. They were terrified for her as each one was more tormenting than the last.

"Eufaria wrote close to her last entry that she felt like each time it was harder to get back. That she feared sleep because once the dreams started she had them every night. She was terrified of them because she was convinced she was reliving a past life that had turned out tragically the first time.

"Her last entry was very short. It said, *They will not let me go. I will never escape the horror. If I can't make it back, please never let another child dream.*"

"Her sisters each had an entry the next day. They wrote that the gown she'd worn to bed that night was on the bed just as if she were lying on it, but Eufaria was gone. No other possessions of hers were missing. And they both recorded they sat together for three days reading her diary, only then realizing she had known she was being trapped, but she hadn't let them know as there would have been nothing they could have done to stop it.

"The very last entries the other two sisters wrote were

about the loss of the other or others. They never heard from Eufaria again."

Jewell felt chills up and down her body. "You're scaring me, Momma."

"That's why you can't keep these things to yourself. If you have any more dreams that terrify you so you wake up screaming, you have to let me know. We know more now than those who came before because, although they detailed their own lives and kept the diaries of their ancestors, they didn't study them. There is so much that can happen to us that has nothing to do with this realm."

Jewell was shocked. "But you all never told us any of this! You only warned us about people finding out about our magic."

Rayne nodded. "I know. And we need to rectify that. I'll talk to my sisters. Each of us has studied so many over the years, but none of us have studied them all. There are just so many!"

"I want to read the ones you're talking about."

Rayne looked at her with compassion. "Then I'll ask you again, Jewell Cavanaugh-White, were you harmed in the dream?"

Jewell hesitated and then nodded. "Yes."

Rayne reached across the small space separating them. "Did you awake to any marks on your body?"

Jewell shook her head slowly. "I don't think so, but I was in such a hurry this morning. I was so tired from staying awake so late I didn't look, and I didn't feel anything except a sore throat from screaming.

"Did Eufaria feel pain when she came back to reality?"

Rayne shrugged. "I don't know. She never mentioned it either way. But will you look? Or let me look?"

There was still no way Jewell could hurt her mother by telling her how she had been molested and abused, and the fact was she was embarrassed her mind had gone to such places in her dream. "I still don't think it was anything, Mom, but I promise I'll look when I get home."

Rayne nodded although from the look in her eyes,

Jewell knew her concern had only increased. They both stood and Rayne placed her hand on Jewell's arm.

"Sometimes there is more than one reality. Don't discount a dream as something your mind has made up. If Eufaria was correct in the conclusions she recorded, the other side was just as real."

Jewell nodded, truly afraid, but she couldn't let it show. She smiled and gave her mother a hug. "I'm sure everything is fine. But I promise I'll check just as soon as I get home."

Chapter Five

Jewell studied the area on her leg where she'd been burned with the poker in the dream, and, much to her relief, nothing was there. She sent her mother a quick text message and then went to the cubby where her desk sat.

Within minutes she was searching the Internet for job opportunities in the immediate area. She'd majored in education with history and subsequently anthropology being her main focuses. She'd even gone so far as getting a teaching degree. But, by the time she had, and after three summers of more than fulfilling her teaching internship, her interest in standing in front of a room full of entitled brats had run its course.

Which meant she had an education she had no interest in using.

Yay!

Now, the question was where did she go from here? She wasn't the least bit interested in working in a factory as a night shift supervisor, and fast food was a joke. There were at least ten or more advertisements for nurses, and truck drivers, and of the two she'd rather smell diesel all day than empty bedpans. She wasn't qualified for either, so it wasn't an issue. Some of the ads were work-from-home opportunities, but every one of them had a warning below it to proceed at your own risk. The paper that produced the daily online news and want ads hadn't put it that way, but a girl could read between the lines.

And that was it. "Great options."

Jewell closed down her browser and looked around her room for something to clean. What Dia didn't understand about her, beyond the fact that she was indeed a germaphobe, was that since moving into the house, her extreme tidiness was due to the boredom of a life that had no real direction, or purpose.

She wandered to the living room and considered turning on the television, but she really wasn't much of a watcher. Jewell looked through the cupboards in the kitchen. Since the dream of the night before, she just hadn't had much of an appetite.

The really aggravating thing was, any other time she'd been bored, all she'd had to do was call or text Kevin, but now that he'd made his manly stand he had ruined that option, too. Which totally sucked.

Jewell pulled her cell phone from her hip pocket and scrolled through her contacts. There were the girls she'd been friendly with in high school. She hadn't contacted them for years—even though she should have once she'd come back home to stay. Then there were the ones she'd made at college, but she hadn't gotten as close to any of them once she outgrew the bar scene. And then there was her family, but that was family, and they already knew enough about her.

It was aggravating to realize, since Kevin first came into her life, she had let everyone else go. Now she had no one to complain about him to other than her sisters, and they would enjoy it more than she would. So what was the point?

Of course, if she did complain about him to them, then decided she wanted his sorry ass after all, they would never let her hear the end of it. Not even when they celebrated their fiftieth wedding anniversary.

Jewell smiled at the thought of her and her sisters being little old ladies, but it was eye opening to realize she didn't see Kevin in the picture at all. She needed to make a to-do list starting with laying the law down with him. He could be her friend, and they could continue to have fun together, or she would have to find a new best friend.

Next on the list was a job of some kind. As much as she appreciated not needing one to live, there was no way she was going to break the tradition of Cavanaugh women by becoming a slouch. That decided, Jewell went to her room and grabbed a sexy blouse, her finest jeans—which made her butt look amazing—and her new push-up bra and matching panties. Even though Kevin wouldn't get to see what was underneath, it made her feel powerful just knowing how she looked in them. And, yes, she was going to make him suffer just a little for ruining their friendship.

Thirty minutes later her hair was shiny and styled, her make-up perfect, her body perfumed and moisturized, and as she looked in the mirror, she was quite satisfied with her reflection. She started to turn from it to leave the room, but movement other than her own caught her eye and she quickly turned back.

And fell to her knees.

It was *he*... Jacob...from her dream. Her heart thundered and her body suddenly hurt as if she had been violated and beaten, and as terrifying as that was, she couldn't take her gaze from his translucent form or from the form of the guard at his side. He was the same one who was there while she'd been tortured!

Jewell tore her gaze away from the guard and looked at the man Anippe loved. Jacob seemed to be propped against something as he slouched in a sitting position, but his head was back as if he'd fallen asleep or passed out atop what looked like soiled straw or, possibly, dried reeds. A pile of dung and the distinguishable tips of a camel's toes were visible just inches away from his hip, but that was all she could see of the animal as the mirror's frame ended the scene on the left side. It was clear they were in a stable or barn of some kind.

Jacob's face was battered, his right eye swollen shut, and his body covered with marks of torture and filth. Jewell wanted to escape from the scene as her mother's words came back to her, but it wasn't about self-preservation. She couldn't stand the horror of seeing someone brutalized like that. Escape didn't seem to be an option though, as something held her to the spot.

She shook her head trying to break the hold, determined to remember she didn't really know him or love him. But while her mind was screaming for her to run, her heart was demanding she save Jacob somehow.

Dizziness and nausea forced Jewell to hold her stomach while she closed her eyes and leaned forward to rest her head on the cool reflection glass. Slow breathing and determination kept the need to vomit controlled until it eased. When she was finally certain the moment had passed, and she was once again in control of her body, she opened her eyes and froze.

"Oh, no!"

Her heart dropped and she shook her head in denial as she took in the gauzy netting draped over the pillow-covered bed she kneeled upon. As there were no sounds, she quickly pushed away the netting and fled from the large bed as if it was capable of biting her.

She looked around frantically and then forced herself to calm down. In the last dream she'd had, she hadn't questioned her surroundings or her recognition of everything about the life of the woman she had stepped into. Not sure why she knew she wasn't dreaming this time, Jewell said her name many times in the hopes of holding onto her identity. Doing so didn't help her. She had no idea which way to run. But Anippe did.

With fear of losing herself, Jewell swallowed and whispered the woman's name. Nothing happened. She took a shaky breath and repeated the name, but still nothing. Determined to force something to happen, she cleared her tight vocal cords and stated with a loud, firm voice, "*I am Anippe... This is my room. And my bed. And my life.*"

Immediately the room looked, and more importantly *felt,* familiar. She took a deep breath and didn't allow herself to think about the life she wanted back *immediately.* Instead, she embraced the life she'd never lived as memories that were not hers filled her head.

The layout of the Nisu's grand palace developed in 3-D drawings and became as clear as a blueprint in her mind. Relationships both immediate and extended flashed like word document after word document of the princes and princesses who were her brothers and sisters. She knew each and every one by sight and by name. The death of her mother, the adoration of her father, and every other childhood memory of the Princess Anippe washed through her like a movie at warp speed. She inhaled sharply and stood in confusion for only a moment and then headed for the two large doors that had been framed and installed since the last time she'd been in her other-self's room. She stopped before pushing at them, knowing they were likely blocked in some way on the other side and guards would be standing sentry.

Otherwise there would have been no reason to put them there in the first place.

Using Anippe's memories, as Jewell's faded away, she turned and ran to the area where cubbies had been fashioned to hold the laundered linens the servants used to remake her bed each morning. She dug down to the bottom of the lowest stack and reached as far back as she could before she grasped the kalasiris her personal servant Hesta had hidden there at her request.

Though lower quality than her own dresses, the close-fitting dress of the Nisu's female servants would give her free access throughout the palace as the women went mostly unnoticed. For a guard to look upon one as anything but the Nisu's property would cost him his life. The only other men in the palace were the eunuchs, whose testicles had been removed so that their desire for a woman was eliminated. They were assigned to guard and protect the females of the palace, from within their private rooms and baths. With such intimacy there was familiarity, so she would have to be particularly careful if she came upon one in her effort to escape.

It was a stroke of luck she'd had the forethought to have Hesta's head shaved to fashion the black wig. Anippe now felt a moment of regret for ordering Hesta to lose her locks the month before. Anippe had thought to use the disguise to sneak out of the palace and find out where Jacob dwelled. She hadn't gotten up the nerve to give it a try until now, though, which probably worked in her favor. She hadn't known her father was already having her watched.

Since the Nisu commanded all the women serving him would be identical in size, coloring, and adornment, all Anippe needed now was the hammered brass collar each female servant wore to allow her to blend in. She regretted not having Hesta get her one sooner. But Anippe had her own made of solid gold, and if no one looked at her too closely, they wouldn't notice the difference.

She was really depending on no one looking too closely.

That gave her a moment's pause, as she had no idea how much time she had to get away. It was already starting to darken at the high open-air windows and the arch leading to her balcony. She quickly shed her wedding dress and pulled on the kalasiris, securing it with the gold-braided rope servants and women of higher rank wore. The sound of voices approaching did not bode well at all though, so she quickly stuffed her dress beneath the linens and placed the wig made from her servant's hair over her own hair.

In spite of his disfavor, her father had insisted his concubines braid Anippe's hair close against her head so she could wear the wedding headdress befitting her royal station. It took little time to hide her deep auburn tresses beneath the shoulder length wig, and as little to garner and attach the gold collar. She took a deep breath and listened intently but the voices were no longer audible.

Relieved, Anippe glanced around quickly, trying to decide what she needed to take with her. Short of stealing the bejeweled gold pieces given to her throughout her life, which would get her killed quickly if she was caught and thought to be a servant, there was nothing except the water jar she could carry out of the room. It would not be obvious to others that something was amiss.

Afraid she was delaying too long, Anippe stopped looking and again headed to the stone balcony her grandfather, the previous Nisu, commissioned, designed and constructed even before her father's birth.

The wood required in constructing additional floor levels, as well as the support beams required to hold them in place, was not readily available along the Nile. Desirable commodities not common to the area were purchased within the vast system of trade her grandfather had established with other nations.

It was her misfortune the newest additions to the palace were not a series of brick and stone rooms within rooms, as was the custom throughout the history of the Nisu's residences. However, the master builder concealed the wood to make it look as though the customary materials were exclusively used. Even now all those who saw the tall Residential Palace marveled and wondered at the ingenuity of the Egyptian people.

It was too high for her to jump from her balcony to the cobblestone alley below. There was another wing, built a level below hers that belonged to her personal servants. They'd been instructed to leave her once the preparations for her wedding had been made, and it was quite likely they were in their rooms now lounging around and eating fruit, or getting their backs scrubbed, or their rectums purged by one or more of the eunuchs.

The female slaves pulled from the Jewish settlements worked in the fields, scrubbed and cleaned the palace, as well as laundered clothing, prepared meals, and when forced, serviced the guards sexual appetites before returning home each evening. The personal servants of the royal household were lowborn Egyptian women whose beauty caught the eye of the Nisu when he paraded through town or were the daughters of distant relatives whose lives were greatly improved once the sacrificial lamb was moved into the palace, for the Nisu's personal pleasure. Though often as not, those chosen by the Nisu included pretty sons as well.

Sometimes the personal servants were required to serve the Nisu's wives' and concubines' sexual desires if they were so inclined as well, but most of their time was spent in service to the royal children. When daily duties were fulfilled, however, they were free to enjoy the benefits of residing in the palace for the remainder of their usefulness.

Each woman, no matter her past, served at the pleasure of the royal family. All others throughout Egypt treated them with deference, as they were personally vetted by the Nisu's most trusted seer and thus chosen by the Nisu, *himself*. They were fed well, cleansed inside and out daily as was the custom, and always wore freshly laundered clothing. They also had access to the royal physicians when they were ill, though that was because the Nisu feared illness touching his household, and more importantly *himself*.

Anippe knew even though Hesta had fashioned the wig as well as the dress she now wore, she couldn't depend on or even trust her servant to assist her further. There was a very wide river between appeasing the silly requests of a favored daughter of the Nisu and helping a disgraced one escape his command.

She glanced up the stairway that continued past her rooms and saw her only other option was to climb upward and hope no servants dwelled in her father's private rooms. She knew he would be about the business of preparing for her wedding, and as he had a tight rectum about such things, he would be managing every tiny detail for the purpose of further shaming her.

With one last look back at the room she had grown up in, Anippe took the stairs at a run. The steps were built outside of the structures they led to. Anyone could walk out on a balcony, or one of the servants could carry refuse out to the alley, and then she would have to face consequences far worse than before.

She stopped before stepping through the netting that was fashioned as his door and listened, but she heard nothing. She stepped inside. As no alarm had yet been raised, she hurried through the many rooms to the other side. There the balcony led to the private gardens he never walked.

"Girl! Come here!"

Anippe stopped as her heart figuratively hit the floor. She lowered her head and waited to be smacked as she turned to face one of her father's servants. But he thrust a wide-mouth pot into her hands instead.

"You are late! I sent for you some time ago!"

Anippe kept her head down and exhaled in relief. She'd forgotten she'd donned a disguise. Knowing the protocol of their household, she was relieved not to have to respond. She nodded and quickly hurried to carry the offensive smelling bodily waste in the direction she'd already been headed.

Since all Nisus were considered gods, her father's excretes were too valuable to be disposed of in the normal fashion, as well as it being too dangerous to allow his bodily fluids to fall into the wrong hands. Because her father's waste was always buried at the farthest reaches of his private gardens, Anippe felt the fates were smiling upon her. The smelly jar was her ticket to freedom. She hurried to the far side but was careful not to allow the slop to splash onto her. When she reached the small bush with the golden shovel, she pretended to go through the motions of prayer and servitude before digging a shallow hole. She poured the contents into it and replaced the soil. Then, as was required, and more importantly, in case anyone was watching, she placed the shovel at the next little bush before heading to the little building known as a water shed where the pot was to be cleaned before returning it to the Nisu's toilet room.

Though the outer wall to the royal grounds was very tall and considered impregnable, as a member of the royal household she knew of the hidden escape option built within the stone wall. It required her to round the small building, which was something a servant would never do. She could only pray her father's manservant was too busy to be watching her.

Anippe hurried to the backside of the building and was relieved when again no one shouted an alarm. She pushed the loose bricks and nearly had the last one released when a movement to her right caught her eye.

Expecting to be hit, she flinched. She then realized the movement wasn't close but that of a camel walking out of a stone shed a hundred or so paces away. Her heart kicked into gear again, and she looked to the sky. The sun was about to set.

Torn, Anippe lost precious moments debating her chances but then closed her eyes in defeat. She couldn't save Jacob, even if they'd put his poor tortured body in that close a building. On the off chance he hadn't already died from what would have been done to him, she knew to attempt a rescue would surely only get her killed as well.

"Princess! Stop!"

Anippe closed her eyes and placed her forehead against the wall that should have led to her escape. She drew in a harsh breath, wishing she hadn't wasted valuable minutes. Now, she would be put to death just like the boy she'd never even gotten a chance to know.

"You must come with me now."

Anippe opened her eyes and turned to look up at the tall guard. He was young compared to most of her father's guards, and though she couldn't believe she even noticed, he was pleasant to look at. His facial features were what her people considered ideal. His broad, sinewy shoulders, his massive hairless chest, and the rippling abdominal muscles, which went into hiding when they met the loincloth required of her father's guards, were perfection. Rather than the angry expression and sharp weapon she expected to see pointing at her, he held out his hand, and Anippe's heart slammed against her chest-wall.

"I do not know you."

He frowned at her with distaste. "I am called Amen-ra, as the earth shook at the moment of my birth. My father says it was a sign from *Ra* that I was born with the power of the universe at my disposal. I have been your personal guard for weeks now. I was commissioned by my father to watch you from afar, but not interfere, as you confirmed suspicions the Nisu had about your behavior. You have disgraced yourself by proving those suspicions to be truth."

Anippe jerked her hand away as her head lifted so that her nose was in the air. "Who is your father? What right have you to spy on me? You are nothing!"

With a heavy sigh, Amen-ra shook his head. "I asked to guard you when your father suspected you of misdeeds. As my father is Asim, the Nisu's most trusted protector, I was granted the privilege. I will pay dearly for it as your disobedience will fall upon me."

Anippe stared at him for a moment as realization hit home. "You! You are the one who turned me into my father!"

Amen-ra nodded. "It was my duty."

Fury replaced fear. "You have condemned my love to death! And now me as well by stopping my escape. Get away from me or kill me, but do not stand in my presence one second more!"

A hint of amusement tilted the corners of his charcoal-lined eyes. "You are no longer in a position to command, *My Princess*. I will take you back to your rooms now. You can either go like the princess you are, or you can be carried kicking and screaming, which will call attention to others that you have once again disobeyed your father, the mighty Nisu. But either way, you will go."

Anippe silently debated her chances of pulling the last brick from the wall, hitting him in the head with it, and then running through the maze of secret stone tunnels to attain her freedom. It angered her further the size and strength of Amen-ra made it more than apparent her chances of success were zero. She squared her shoulders and faced him fully before giving him a look she was certain would put him squarely in his place. "Move back and allow me to pass!"

Though his bow and the sweeping of his arm were mocking, Anippe held her head high as she passed him. She trembled as much with anger as fear. She headed toward the small barn where she'd seen the camel depart, though she couldn't for the life of her remember why she needed to head that way.

"You are going the wrong way, Princess. You must turn back now."

Anippe ignored him but was aware his steps had increased along with hers, propelling her to walk faster.

"*Please,* turn back now."

Anippe refused to pay him heed and took off at a run. The pounding step coming up behind her pushed her harder, so she was breathless and surprised to make it to the barn before he caught up with her.

"Stop! Do not go in there!"

Anippe glanced back at him as he came to a stop only a few feet away from her. "I am not trying to escape. I only wish a moment."

Amen-ra shook his head, which she expected, but his eyes held compassion, which she did not. She almost wavered, but flashes of a woman, who was her yet who was not, looking into a reflection glass that closely matched one in her own room, disoriented her. The camel she'd seen leaving this dwelling earlier clashed and collided with the image in the reflection the other woman saw. Anippe gasped and held her stomach, dizzy with it all.

"Jacob! He is in there, isn't he?"

Without waiting for Amen-ra's response, she moved quickly into the darkened barn.

"Jacob!"

"Anippe! What are you doing here? You must go now! They will come for me soon." Jacob struggled with the linen binding his wrists. "Please, I cannot bear what will be done to you. Go!"

Ignoring his protests, she quickly worked at the knots keeping Jacob tied to the iron ring attached to the barn's stone wall. "Can you run?" she asked, frantically working the complicated array of knots.

"You will stop now, Princess."

Anippe jumped at the sound of Amen-ra's voice and turned his way. "He will be killed!"

Amen-ra looked from her to Jacob and back again.

"Yes. The Nisu has commanded his death."

Anippe moved closer to Jacob and put her arm around his waist. "I will not let that happen. If you were humane, neither would you. Come, please help me help him."

Sadness and a shaking of his head preceded Amen-ra advancing on her. "I am a servant of the Nisu, as are all. I cannot help you in this matter. Neither can I allow you to get yourself killed by assisting this man. I am sorry, but you will go with me now."

Anippe stepped back, shaking her head, belatedly realizing she'd trapped herself in a corner. "I will not go with you! You will allow me to help him even if you will not help!"

Amen-ra pulled a roughly woven papyrus blanket from the stack sitting atop a bale of straw. "Please do not make me mishandle you, Princess. You must go to your rooms now!"

"Anippe, my love, please heed him and go. I will go into the next life filled with love for you, but I cannot see you harmed in this one before I do. Please! Do as he says!"

Anippe shook her head and charged Amen-ra, hoping she could surprise him. But he quickly caught her, pinned her arms at her sides, and spun her in the blanket so that she was immediately suffocating. Her muffled screams to be released went unheeded as she was lifted and thrown over his shoulder.

She couldn't hear the exchange between Jacob and Amen-ra before his jarring steps were causing her lightheadedness to increase to the extent she was floating in and out of consciousness. With her innards still suffering from the earlier abuse, intense pain overtook all other thought until she finally blacked out.

Chapter Six

"Jewell!"

She awoke with a start. It took several seconds for her to figure out she was back in her house, in her room, lying before the mirror on her hardwood floor. Only now there was a pillow beneath her head and a blanket covering her body.

"Sapphire! Call Mom back in here! Jewell is waking up!"

She tried to sit up, but her arms were too weak to push.

"Don't move. We were so afraid to move you!"

Seeing Dia's face only inches above her own made Jewell wish she had even an ounce of strength. She wanted to kiss her sister in celebration of making it back in one piece. But her mind wouldn't relinquish control to allow her to dismiss what could be happening to Anippe or Jacob. When she was there, she *was that young girl* and eventually had forgotten all about herself. Now she was back where she belonged, she still *felt* Anippe's feelings and fears. "I need Mom," she said, before bursting into tears.

It took some time for Jewell to catch her breath as her mother petted her. She was settled with a blanket and pillows on the couch once she'd had the strength to move. Within an hour all the women in the family arrived in groups or alone. The fact all of them brought food eventually made her laugh through her tears. But she appreciated their support and tried to answer their questions as best she could. Eventually, she shared everything she remembered.

"Thanks, guys. I don't know what to say. Except I'm terrified of going back and terrified of what will happen to Anippe and Jacob if I don't." Jewell frowned. "Although I guess there isn't really anything Anippe can do to save him now."

The day was nearly over, but everyone settled in to munch on paper plates filled with food. They talked about possibilities and promised to search for answers. As her mother and both her aunts brought over the family diaries each held in keeping for the entire family, there was a roomful of fascinated women scanning pages and pages of the delicate documents to see if there was any indication of an ancestor who had experienced reincarnation before. With more than three thousand years of diaries to go through and many in the language of the country the Cavanaugh women of that time lived, it was almost impossible to find any one issue unless one of the moms had already read about them in their studies, or one of the rest just lucked out and ran across something.

"I think I have something!" Luna looked up with excitement in her plain brown eyes, and Jewell's assumption that she was beautiful when lively was confirmed.

Rayne rose and walked over to her niece. "Where, sweetheart?"

Luna smiled at her and put her finger on the page as she lifted it up for Rayne to take. "Here."

Rayne looked at the passage and then looked to Jewell. "Let me read this to you all.

"June 27, 1525. Today was a bad day. Something strange is happening to Kecea. My sister has been having terrible dreams, but we aren't sure they are dreams. Angcea and I are trying to help her, but we don't know what to do as she refuses to tell us about them now, but if they are as horrible as the ones she first told us about, then I fear her heart will fail."

Rayne kept her finger between the pages as she allowed the book to close on them. She looked at those assembled. "We need to find out if Kecea wrote her own diaries and if so, we need to find them. That means we have to look through every one of them that are similar to this." She held up the cloth-covered book and the material and pages bent with her movement.

Everyone placed the one they were scanning down and

walked to the stacks and stacks of journals Destiny, Haven, and Rayne brought and unloaded onto the kitchen table. They each chose a stack and looked for a softbound book about the same size and make to pull out and look at the name and dates.

Haven looked up and held up a book. "I have one. Let me look and see how far it goes." Everyone stopped and waited as Haven looked first at the front pages and then went to the back. "It looks like she was in her early twenties here. But it ends a year before the date of the one you have," she said to Rayne.

Rayne nodded. "Okay. Let me review it while you all keep looking to see if there are more. There is no telling how long this goes on or how it ends, and we need to know."

Everyone agreed and resumed the search as Haven handed over the book. Jewell glanced from her mother to the others, so thankful for their love and support her eyes filled and spilled over. When Rayne saw her, she immediately was at her daughter's side pulling her into a hug.

"We're going to fix this, baby. I promise. Somehow we are going to fix this."

Jewell nodded. "I know. If it can be fixed, I know you will all do everything in your power to make it happen. That's what brought me to tears. I just love you all so much and I'm so grateful to everyone for being here."

As the entire room was focused on them, many eyes filled, and smiles and air-kisses were sent her way. Jewell knew whatever it was she was facing didn't have a chance of taking her from so many gifted, loving women.

Everyone resumed the search as Rayne pulled Jewell over to the couch. "If you need, we can go outside or to your room, but I need you to tell me every detail about both trips you made to your other life."

Jewell cheeks heated, but she nodded. "We can stay here, but I will talk quietly.

"The first one started with me walking in a field of

thigh high papyrus plants that went all the way to the Nile. There were hundreds of Jewish slaves out harvesting it to make the different things needed at the palace. I was looking for one particular slave who I am in love with, or I guess I should say Princess Anippe is in love with." Jewell looked into her mother's eyes. "But when I was there I was her, and I felt her love for this man. It is like nothing I had ever dreamed of feeling for someone outside of the family." She frowned. "I have finally come to accept I am not like the rest of you. I feel I have no purpose, no passion. About anything, or anyone."

Rayne shook her head. "I hope you don't believe that is true. You just haven't found your passion in life or love yet. The first, only time will tell. But loving a man who is meant to be yours goes so deep it is nearly inexplicable. There is only one other type of love that goes even deeper, and that is the overwhelming love you feel the first time you see your newborn child." Rayne's eyes filled as she looked at Jewell adoringly. "I will kill to keep you safe and I will die to keep you safe. I promise you, we will find a way."

Jewell hugged her mother and was enclosed in Rayne's warm embrace as well, and they just stayed that way until Jewell pulled back so she could resume her story. "Jacob… He's about my age I think, but Anippe is only fifteen." Jewell shook her head. "It's so strange because she, I, we… were glad that our father, the Nisu, hadn't married us off yet.

"This is so hard. I don't even know who I am!" Jewell said, her voice high.

Rayne took both her hands. "You are Jewell Cavanaugh-White. But if it makes it easier to tell, say I instead of her or we. It's okay."

Jewell nodded. "Okay. I'm only fifteen and my father loves me, or I should say loved me, more than all his other children because I was his favorite wife's only child. I have close to a hundred siblings, which is strange that I know this, because while I was there I only met one face to face."

Rayne nodded. "So you have all her memories even

though you haven't physically, as Jewell, lived them."

Jewell nodded. "Yes...but I don't have my memories while I'm there after I become her. At least I don't think so...although when I first got there the second time, I still had my memories of being Jewell. The first time I was just suddenly her."

"This might be a good thing. If you can remember who you are here while you are there, you should always be able to find a way back."

Jewell hoped her mother was right. "I had to make myself be her, so I would know how to escape from my room in the palace." Stark fear slammed into her. "Momma, do you think I could lose me and become her forever?"

The concern in Rayne's eyes was answer enough, but she shook her head. "I won't let that happen. I won't lose you. But I have to know everything so we can figure out a way to stop this."

Jewell nodded. "Okay...I was in my room at the palace the second time, and I realized I was going to be forced to get married within hours. I knew I had to escape, but because I was still thinking like Jewell, I didn't know how.

"I made myself stop panicking and told myself I was Anippe, and that it was my room, and then everything became clear after I became her again. I knew how to get out, and to make a long story short, I basically dressed like an Egyptian servant and made my way out to a place where there is a secret escape from the palace grounds."

"So you escaped?"

Jewell shook her head. "No. There was this, well, unbelievably gorgeous young guard named Amen-ra, who stopped me. It took me a second to realize he was the only male present when I was being...cleansed, before the other came and burned my inner thigh." At the look of fury on her mother's face, Jewell hurried on. "I know. I was mad too, but I think the torture would have continued if he hadn't stopped them, and he looked really upset when they branded Anippe."

She had to take a moment as the fears she'd experienced as the princess resurfaced to take her breath. Her mother took her hands and held on until Jewell could continue.

"When Amen-ra stopped me from escaping the palace grounds, I think it had more to do with his sense that he had to, rather than he wanted to. He wasn't exactly nice, but I think it was because Anippe had offended his sense of protocol by having a relationship with a slave, and of course he'd caught me trying to escape the palace grounds, red-handed." She shook her head, not sure if she was right or not. "Regardless, he wouldn't let me leave. He told me my father the Nisu, which we now call a Pharaoh, had him following me for weeks, and he was the one who had turned in Jacob and me.

"I was so angry I ran from him and ended up where Jacob was being held in the little barn I'd seen in my mirror right before I was transported back to Anippe's life."

Jewell let out a shaky breath. "Mom, I wouldn't want to hurt Dad's feelings, but I think I'm going to have to get that mirror out of my room. I think it had something to do with me going there the second time. Maybe even the first."

Rayne nodded. "It won't hurt his feelings, honey. If you think that has anything to do with it, then we'll burn the damned thing."

Jewell shook her head. "Please don't. I love it, and I love that you designed it and Dad made it. It's just a thought, and I'm not even sure it has anything to do with it. I'm just guessing because I can't think of anything else to blame."

Rayne's expression reflected that she was processing all Jewell had told her. She raised her brows. "You might be right. We'll have to check into that. You've told me about the second time, but not much about the first. I know something happened that you are holding back, but I really need to know if you are harmed in some way."

Jewell sighed. "I'm okay, Mom. But I will tell you."

By the time Jewell finished giving her every little detail,

Rayne was doing her best to hold back her tears. It was obvious she was distraught over the humiliation and pain her daughter had suffered as Anippe. Then she looked at Jewell sharply. "You said you don't remember you are Jewell while you're there, but you remember everything Anippe experienced once you're back here. Does she know her body was abused or was yours the only conscious mind there through all of that?"

Jewell squeezed her mother's hand then released it. "I don't know. It's so confusing because it seems like I'm experiencing it as me, but I have her thoughts, and I'm not in control of her actions. At least I haven't tried to take control and keep it yet."

Rayne looked at Jewell with resolve. "Then the next time you go back, you keep control if you can. I'll see if there is a spell in my books that will assist you. Our history is long, and there have been many spells created by our family. If there isn't one in the books, then I'll figure one out. I just hope we can put this all together before you leave us again."

Me too!

"I found another one of hers!"

Jewell and her mother glanced over to Dia, who was quickly crossing the room to stop in front of them. She handed the book over to Rayne and sent Jewell a look of support. Jewell nodded and saw her mother was already studying the book.

"This is good. This is the year we are searching for." She quickly kissed Jewell on the cheek then stood.

"Hey everyone, let's call it a night. Just leave the diaries. We need to search more I'm sure, but I'll look these over tonight and get with Jewell then all of you tomorrow. Thanks so much for coming."

Jewell rose and rejoined her female relatives and hugged and kissed each before they took their leave. After her sister's went to their rooms, she walked her mother to the door. "I can read those, Mom. I'm an adult, you know."

Rayne smiled at her. "I'm sorry. I'm still treating you

like a baby. But I've read so many of these, and I've come to understand the subtext of some of them, if you know what I mean, the words that aren't spoken."

Jewell nodded. "I didn't mean anything. It's fine if you want to read them. But I'm afraid to go to sleep. Since I plan to stay up, I'll need something to do."

"I'll stay here with you tonight."

Jewell shook her head. "That isn't necessary. Besides, what would you say to Dad?"

Rayne smiled. "Your father never questions me about things that are questionable. Although he has always treated me with unconditional love, he pretends we are all normal. He doesn't see some of the rather odd things we all do. But sometimes I think he sees and knows more than he lets on."

Jewell smiled, too. "He's really smart."

Rayne nodded. "And he loves you to death. We'll let him in on this only if it's necessary though. It would kill him to know one of his babies was dealing with all this, knowing there was nothing he could do to help or to stop it. Men aren't like us. They can't take what they don't understand as easily."

"Well, go home to your man, and my dad, and just tell him that I send my love. I'll be fine."

Rayne shook her head. "I can't. I need to be here in case you leave again. I need to see you are okay and see if there is anything that can be done to bring you back."

Jewell hadn't thought of that possibility. "Okay, if you're sure. I have to admit it makes me feel better that you're staying. But what if it doesn't happen tonight? Then you've stayed for nothing. And you can't stay with me forever."

Rayne took her into her arms. "I'll be here one way or another until we figure this out."

Jewell hugged her mother again, thinking she hadn't been hugged so much since she was little. They stepped apart and Jewell sighed. "I must look horrible. I was getting myself fixed up before this last...."

Her heart thudding, Jewell grabbed her mother's hand and pulled her toward her room. "I need you to look at this, and tell me why you chose this design for my mirror."

Rayne allowed herself to be led and stood by Jewell's side in front of the mirror. She looked at it and then at Jewell. "Do you really think this mirror has something to do with what's happening?"

Jewell shrugged. "I don't know. But you had Daddy make this one especially for me. You chose what he put on it, and you chose which jewels to use and told him where to put them, right?"

Rayne nodded. "Yes. I did." She shook her head. "If I've caused this to happen…."

"No, Mom. Don't think like that. Just help me to understand what all these hieroglyphic symbols mean."

Rayne nodded. "Well, you know the ones across the top spell out your name, and because the writings of the original papyrus the mother of us all used was written from bottom to top and right to left, that's how I had your dad carve the rest of them."

Rayne stooped down and put her fingers on the picture at the bottom and read as she slid her fingers upward. "It reads: *The Jewel of the Nile, so lovely of face with a heart so black, began her journey here and then back.*" Rayne stopped reading as she studied the mirror's frame.

"Your dad didn't make a mistake. But this isn't what I had for him to put on here!" She looked at Jewell, then at the mirror again. "We have to get this thing out of here!"

Jewell's heart pounded. "Why? Tell me why?"

Rayne's eyes filled. "It was supposed to be an incantation of protection. But it's not. That isn't what I gave him, and I read it all after he finished it! This isn't the mirror your dad made!"

Memories that were not her own crashed and banged within Jewell's head, and she swayed as she felt her mother's arms catch her. Fearing she was about to be transported back in time, she struggled to remain conscious. When her head cleared and she was still in her room and her mother was repeating her name hysterically, Jewell opened her eyes and they both sighed.

Rayne pulled her closer and held her tight. "I thought I'd lost you. I thought I'd lost you!"

Jewell held just as tightly. "Me too, but I'm still here."

"Tell me what just happened. *Exactly* as it happened."

Jewell sat up, but they both remained sitting on the floor. "I was listening to you and you said it wasn't the mirror that Daddy made, and all of a sudden memories, *Anippe's memories,* just came all over me and I got confused and dizzy."

"Is there anything that you remember in particular?"

Jewell nodded. "Yes. A mirror. There's one in her room that looks identical to the one Daddy made. But I never read it while I was there, but now I know she did at one time." Jewell looked up at the black onyx at the top center. "That jewel, where did it come from?"

Rayne looked up, and then stood to look closer. "It isn't the one your dad put there... Oh my God! This one was in one of the treasure chests that has been handed down in our family for generations. I never pulled it out when I was choosing the jewels for you and your sisters."

"Are you sure?"

Rayne nodded. "Yes, I remember it particularly because every time I was about to lift it, something stopped me. I thought maybe it was one of those that would only allow the one it chose to touch it. Some of them are very stubborn like that. Especially if they had already bonded."

She looked down at Jewell. "It must have been Anippe's. Their bond must have been as strong as my mother's Celestial Divinity Crystal bond was with her. To this day my sisters and I know better than to touch my mother's diamond. We rarely even remove the necklace it's placed in from the case where it's been housed since her death."

Jewell sighed. "What about you and Aunt Haven and Aunt Destiny? Are your crystals as particular?"

Rayne shook her head. "We have the magical uses of

many, but none of the three of us ever had one particular crystal that chose us to the extent that it was our only power source. When that happens, it can be miraculous, but it can also be very dangerous. Because choices are taken away from the one it chooses.

"If this one has chosen you, it must mean that you will be able to use its power in a mighty way. But it also means you have a quest to fulfill and something to conquer. We have to figure out what it is that you are supposed to do."

"Is this what happens to the Dream Spinners you spoke of?"

Rayne shook her head. "No. I don't think so. This isn't dreaming. From what I remember of a diary I read years ago, long before you were born, I think this is reliving a past life that should have turned out better."

"Maybe we *should* just burn it."

Rayne shook her head. "No. If we try to destroy it and it holds its own purpose, there could be grave consequences. It could possibly take you with it and leave you in its past where it is still a living thing."

Jewell looked at it and chills covered her skin. "Is there anything we can do?"

"I don't know yet. I need to call your great-aunts and get them both here as quickly as possible. They are both filled with knowledge of the mystical world past and present. Surely they, my sisters, and I can find something that will help us. But the first thing is we need to read more diaries. I need to know if this ends on its own or if we can cast a spell to end it. Hopefully, at least one of our ancestors experienced this and found a solution we can replicate."

Jewell heard what her mother wasn't saying, and she knew one of them had to. "But if they didn't find a solution, then I may leave and never come back."

Rayne shook her head hard. "No! I told you, I won't let that happen. Every spell has a counter-spell. We just have to figure out what it is if they didn't.

"I'm calling your dad to tell him I'm staying and then

we are going to get busy reading. Okay?"

Jewell smiled, although it was nothing more than bravado. "Okay."

Chapter Seven

It was well past midnight, and Rayne had fallen asleep on the couch with the book opened to the page she'd been reading. Jewell knew she wasn't going to last too much longer herself, but she was so afraid to go to sleep and was doing her best to stay awake.

So far neither of them had been able to find anything significant, and that worried Jewell. She'd really hoped for a quick solution so she wouldn't have to live in fear of disappearing at any moment. She placed the diary on the table to her side and went to the kitchen to get water to drink. She reached for her cell phone where she'd left it on the counter hours before.

There were thirteen missed calls from Kevin, and Jewell had to smile at his inability to give her until Friday to let him know how she felt about things. But so much had happened since she'd last seen him that she really wanted and needed the humdrum of normal. She looked at her text messages and saw he had blown it up too with even more messages than calls.

She opened the oldest one and worked her way down.

I'm sorry.

I'm REALLY sorry.

Please don't ignore my calls.

Come on Jewells, I said I was sorry!

Now you are just being a bitch.

I'm sorry for calling you a bitch.

Damn Jewell! I said I was sorry!

Jewell read a few more, but it was more of the same. Kevin was sorry, then he was mad, then he was sorry for being mad, and on and on it went. She sent him a single text just so he'd stop making a fool of himself.

I'm sorry, too. Didn't mean to ignore you. Large family gathering, personal family stuff going on. Would love to get together Friday if you want, but I still need time to consider going beyond friendship. I know that's hard, but it is what it is. My life is a little complicated right now and I need a friend more than a lover. Text me and let me know if you still want to get together.

Jewell read over her text then grimaced at the word *lover.* She erased the word and replaced it with *boyfriend.* Satisfied, she hit *send* and put her phone down. To her surprise, it immediately rang.

Seeing Kevin's picture on the screen, she almost hit the *deny* icon. She hadn't expected to have to deal with anything more than a text this late at night. But she didn't want her mother to wake up, so she answered as she quickly left the room. "Hi," she said quietly.

"Hi. I'm glad you finally responded. I was about to get in my car and come over, but then I remembered you wouldn't let me in, so I was getting ready for bed."

Jewell tried not to roll her eyes. Why did Kevin suddenly seem so annoying? "I'm sorry, but like I said, I've had a family crisis and things are a little crazy around here."

"What's going on?"

Jewell frowned. How did she tell him it was none of his business and not say it was none of his business? "Private family stuff. I'm not at liberty to discuss it."

There was a long pause. "Oh, okay. Well I guess that puts me squarely in my place."

"Kevin, look. It has been a really long day, and I didn't text you so we could start fighting. I'm sorry you are feeling…whatever it is you are feeling right now, but I'm not able to go into this."

"Okay. Sorry. But what about the other. We have been dating for months now. Exclusively. Why all of a sudden are you backing off?"

Jewell bit her lip as she tried to think of a way of telling him what she had already told him, but in a way that wouldn't hurt his feelings more. She had nothing. "Kevin, please. Let's get together Friday and hash this out. I'm exhausted and I don't want to lose my temper because I'm tired and may say something both of us will regret later. Just let me have tonight. Okay?"

"Fine. I'll pick you up at seven."

"Okay. I'll see you then." Jewell turned off her phone, not wanting to deal with him if he suddenly decided he had more to text or call about.

"Is everything okay?"

Jewell swung around at the sound of her mother's voice, surprised to find herself back in her room. She had wandered in there without thought while trying to be quiet. "I'm sorry. That was Kevin. I didn't mean to wake you."

Rayne stretched and yawned. "I didn't mean to fall asleep on you. I wasn't going to say anything until you did, but is there anything I can do to help?"

Jewell shrugged. "It's a long story, but I never expected what happened the other night. Kevin misunderstood my feelings."

"And yet you are still talking?"

"I don't know exactly what we are doing. The truth is, I don't know with everything else going on if I need to keep him in my life at all. What if I leave and don't come back? With the exception of him, everyone else will understand what's happening."

Rayne shook her head. "Not everyone. What about your dad, your Uncle Logan, and your other friends? But that isn't the issue is it? You don't love him, plain and simple."

Jewell honestly didn't know. "I thought I was headed into it. You know we have so much fun together and he's a great guy, and until after his proposal, we had never fought. I thought that was the problem, but now I just don't know. I don't want to fight with him. And I don't want to marry him, at least not right now. But I don't want to lose him either."

"You have no karma connection with him. Come on, let's go back and sit in the living room."

Jewell frowned and followed her mother. "I didn't think you read Karma."

Rayne took her seat and waited as Jewell joined her. "Not like Destiny does. But over the years, I've gained knowledge as well as a little skill in that area, just like Destiny is able now to cast and conjure but not at my skill level. We all have our strengths, but we also have a variety of gifts at our disposal if we take the time to develop them."

"I'm not sure what my gift is."

Rayne's eyes turned introspective, and she lifted the diary she was reading before she fell asleep. "I found something here I want to read to you."

Jewell nodded. "Okay."

She turned a few pages then held the book a little closer to her face. "*I went there again. I can't talk to my sisters about this anymore because I'm afraid they might think I have lost my mind, or worse yet, they will believe me and fear me. If they read my diaries after I die, or leave to go there for the rest of whatever life I have to live on the other side, I want them to know it is fine. Mostly. I'm still afraid, but now I know the Dark Witch must be defeated.*"

Rayne stopped and looked up at her daughter. "She describes the Dark Witch in an earlier passage. The woman is hideously ugly as her soul has rotted from all the dark magic she spent her life performing. And where the soul goes, so goes the body."

"Who was the Dark Witch?"

Rayne frowned. "She was a member of our family. She was this young woman in an earlier life."

Jewell shook her head. "I don't understand. I thought the women of our family only practiced White Magic."

Rayne took a long slow breath. "So did I. Until now."

"But what made her turn dark?"

"Greed. Resentment. Envy. And finally hatred."

"I don't understand."

Rayne set the book aside and turned to face Jewell fully. "Reincarnation is a chance for the soul to come back into a new body and do things better than it did the time before, in its old body. And, from my understanding, and I'll talk to Destiny about this to make sure, when a soul is reincarnated it has a chance to reconnect with the souls of others who it had a bad karma connection with in the past. To correct those mistakes allows that soul to be rewarded in the future with a better life in the life to come."

"I think I'm more confused than ever."

Rayne shook her head and Jewell could tell the action was self-directed.

"Okay, look at it like this, let's say you and Kevin had a bad connection as people in a past life, and you did something mean to him as Anippe that ruined his life back then, but now, as Jewell, you have a chance to do right by him and undo the sins of the past."

"So are you saying we are all repeatedly reincarnated? And I need to marry Kevin to make up for something my soul did when it was someone other than me?"

Rayne laughed as she shook her head. "Heavens, no! I was just trying to make an example. I think Kevin is too new a soul to matter in this equation. But you are an old soul. You always have been.

"Let me try again. If this ancestor was a dark witch in a previous life, she became that way because her soul was unhappy to begin with. If she can find a way to go back and change her previous-self's ways before she became the dark witch, then she can have a happy life in the past and in the present, depending on which life she ends up living out, or maybe even both. Like I said, I need to study this with my sisters, and hopefully with my aunts."

Jewell tried not to react. Her brain was on overload, and she couldn't follow enough to figure out what point her mother was trying to make. But she needed to know at least one normal thing… "So, what did *you* think of Kevin?"

Surprise at the change of subject lifted Rayne's brows. "I don't know. He seemed nice enough. But I didn't see any chemistry from your side. That never works for long. You didn't look at him with love shining from your eyes. There was never that unconscious reaching for each other just because you were standing close."

"Yeah. I know. But I don't think the problem is Kevin. I hate to admit it, but I believe it's me. Maybe that kind of relationship isn't mine to have. You and Daddy, *and* the aunts and uncles, came from a generation where passion meant more... *Maybe*? At least I hope it isn't just me..." Memories of her dream lover came back and Jewell frowned.

"Oh, I hope not, honey. I want you to know rapture in a man's arms. Don't ever settle for less than everything. We Cavanaugh women are a hot-blooded lot." She grinned. "Sex is too much fun to settle for bland."

Jewell looked at her mother for a moment before speaking. "You are such a beautiful woman. It's no wonder Daddy was never able to keep his hands off of you."

Rayne laughed. "And I've never been able to keep my hands off of him either. But have you looked in the mirror, my love? You are me twenty years ago."

Rayne and Jewell frowned at the same time as the mention of a mirror brought them back to the reason for the impromptu sleepover. Rayne sighed. "Sorry. But now that we are back on the subject, I think I'm going to have your dad come pick the mirror up after daybreak and take it to our place."

Jewell nodded. "Okay. Thanks, Mom." She shrugged. "But what if it isn't the mirror? What if I go back to ancient Egypt anyway?"

Rayne took Jewell's hands into her own. "I don't know. This is still out of my range of understanding to a great degree, but, if nothing else, it will eliminate one possibility."

Jewell nodded. "Okay."

"Don't give up hope, honey. I can see defeat in your eyes. We'll talk to Destiny tomorrow and to Aunt Soleli as soon as we can get her here. They know more about this kind of thing. I think you are like them. You have the gift, or in this case it seems to be a curse, to transport your spirit, but in a different way.

"It's like this...in each generation of Cavanaugh triplets we have had these repeating mystical themes—the

Enchantress who is capable of casting or conjuring, the Regulator who is capable of controlling all natural elements, and the Divine whose spirit is free to discover truth—though for each subsequent generation the individual gifts are distinctly different."

Jewell nodded. "I know, you've told us that since we were kids. But this is different. Aunt Destiny and Great-Aunt Soleli transport their spirit by their will. This is happening against my will!" Jewell felt emotions building, making her chest tight.

"I know. But that's how it happens at first. When I first started seeing and hearing ghosts, it terrified me. But as time went on, through trial and error, I learned to control which spirits could approach me and which ones had to stay away. And when I don't want to have them around at all, I know how to stop them altogether."

"So you think I can stop this?"

Rayne nodded, though cautiously. "I think it's possible. Eventually. But first something needs fixing, or this gift wouldn't be manifesting right now. I knew you girls had magic, but unlike my sisters and I, and the generations before us, your specific gifts didn't really become defined the day you turned fifteen.

"Destiny, Haven, and I think that has to do with things that happened when they and I chose to change the course of our own history by marrying and staying married to the men we love. It's also why you and your *identical* sisters have different eye and hair colors, Aunt Destiny had boys instead of girls, and why Haven's genetically identical girls are so physically different from each other people wouldn't even suspect them of being related, much less all of us Cavanaughs."

Jewell looked at her mother curiously. "The three of you broke a three-thousand-year-old curse that started with the mother of us all, yet I am going back about the same time period when you believe our lineage began. There has to be a reason for that. Don't you think?"

Rayne shrugged. "I have no idea, honey. But I do know

you girls and your cousins need to start studying these diaries. Although I have chronicled the lessons of many of the earliest ones, as well as my sisters doing some of the first ones written in English, there are still so many to go through. After you kids were born, we kind of let the studies go to raise you. But there is still so much for us all to learn, and so much for us to document for coming generations. I should have had you girls doing that all along," Rayne said, sorrow in her eyes.

"I have written a journal almost since leaving home for college. But there isn't much up until now that was worth reporting."

Rayne shook her head. "I bet you're wrong. If you go back and read them now, you may see something you thought nothing of when you wrote it. I know that sounds silly, but a lot of the day to day chronicles of our ancestors seemed boring until something they wrote means something more later in their life."

Jewell frowned. "Like what, for example?"

Rayne settled back and looked away and Jewell knew she was searching her memories before she suddenly smiled.

"Okay, there is an ancestor that travelled across the United States with a wagon train when the country was still young. I can't remember her name right off, but she and her identical sisters took the family treasures with them and used many of the lesser pieces to create jewelry when they reached California.

"But while they were still on the trail there was an incident of a raid by bandits from the state that is now Texas, though at the time it was still a part of Mexico. The men wore cloths to cover their faces and had belts of bullets to fill their guns and rifles."

Fatigue fell away and Jewell sat up straighter on the couch as she listened. "So they were robbed?"

Rayne nodded. "Of everything the bandits thought valuable. But one of the sisters had chronicled pages and pages in her diary when she had to have a bowel movement, and she always recorded what they looked like and how much there was, as well as how many days they were into the long journey. Though there was no map, *per se*, by detailing these things she was committing the sense of place to her diary's memory."

"Ewww!"

Rayne laughed. "Yeah, I know. That's what Haven thought too because she was reading that one when we were trying to figure out how to find your cousin Gavin when he was kidnapped.

"But anyway, it wasn't until years later that I picked up that diary and started reading it. Once you got past months of her detailed toilet recordings, the robbery came up. But what was significant wasn't that they took all the family jewels, although the incident makes for some exciting reading, it's what came afterwards. When the sisters got to California, they still had all the jewels, and the men who got back to Texas to divvy them up had a trunk full of her poop."

Jewell smiled. "Are you serious? How?"

Rayne laughed. "This is the really good part. All our ancestor had to do was get her sisters to go with her. They snuck away from the wagon train for a night. She pulled out her diary, which had the *locations* of all the places she, well, *pooped*, and over it they created a *Spell of Transposition* that sent the jewels back to them, and sent all those piles of poop to the men responsible for the hold-up. But the sisters didn't just do it for themselves. They did it for the others in the wagon train as well. I'm sure there were a lot of very confused people at the end of that trip!"

Jewell shook her head. "That's wild!"

Rayne laughed again. "Yes it is. But the Cavanaugh ladies weren't just getting their stuff back. They made sure the ones who set up the robbery got what they deserved, by making a statement."

"No doubt... 'Steal from a Cavanaugh and all you'll end up with is a pile of shit.'"

Jewell and Rayne burst out laughing together.

"What are you two doing in here?"

Jewell looked at Sapphire's bed head and marveled that she looked like a hot mess instead of just the mess Jewell knew she was when she awoke. "Hi! Sorry. Mom was just telling me a story about one of our ancestors."

Sapphire smiled. "It must have been a good one." Her expression settled. "But have you found anything to help you?"

Jewell looked at her mother. "Maybe. Mom, you tell her."

Rayne scooted to the edge of the couch and patted the seat between her and Jewell. "Come on over here and sit with us, baby."

"Can I join too?"

They all looked up to see Dia with her nearly white hair standing straight up as if she'd just put mousse in it. "Come on," Rayne said, scooting even further.

"She can have my seat. I need something cold to drink. Anyone else?"

Since everyone wanted bottled water, it only took a minute to get the drinks while Rayne went back over what she and Jewell discussed. Dia listened intently then turned to smile at Sapphire. "See I told you! I will be able to make good magic one day, one way or another. But if that isn't my particular gift, I wonder what is?"

"I think you are going to have to wait and see," Rayne said, her eyes filled with concern. "Now that Jewell has had this...*thing*, happen to her, I'm thinking it's possible that your generation may have to take a wait-and-see attitude.

"I know from talking to my sisters that Destiny's boys seem to have no trouble conjuring, but none have a particular talent otherwise...yet. And I know you three have always been able to do a little magic, but minimally. And to be honest, I thought the changes in our family dynamics might have diluted the magic in your generation. I see now that is definitely not true, but I don't know where this leaves any of us."

Dia flashed her megawatt smile and put her arm around

her mother as she had wedged herself between Sapphire and Rayne rather than taking the seat Jewell vacated. "Don't worry, Mom. We'll get it all sorted out. Why before you know it, Jewell will have this time-travel issue under control and I'll be making gold out of…whatever!"

Sapphire said nothing. Jewell knew it was because she was more than satisfied to leave magic out of her life. And at the moment Jewell had to agree. "So…I guess the next step is for me to try to go there on purpose and see what is what? And then see if I can come back?"

Rayne shook her head. "Not yet. We need to have a family meeting again, at least one that includes my sisters, and hopefully my aunts. If you can keep from going back until we are all gathered, maybe we can pull you back if you can't make it yourself."

"And if I'm forced to go against my will?"

Rayne looked at her, her eyes filled with anger. "You fight it with everything you have. If you go there and can't get yourself back immediately, then try to figure out what it is Anippe needs to do differently than she did the first time."

"But I have no idea what she did the first time. I don't think I've gotten that far into her life yet."

"I know. But I'll go back home at sunrise and pull out the papyruses. There has to be something that I missed."

Sapphire turned to her mother then, her eyes burdened. "And what if she never made a diary or had someone record one for her? Or what if she did, but it is one of those lost to time and deterioration?"

Rayne was silent for a few seconds, before she looked back at Jewell. "Then you write your own story and you make it her story. Don't allow yourself to forget who you are now. As long as you can hold onto the present even while you're there, then you can change the past."

Everyone was as silently as she was, and Jewell could only surmise they, too, were mulling over the possibilities. Exhaustion finally hit Jewell full on; she blew out a breath. "I'll try, Mom. Believe me. I'll try. But if anything ever happens and I can't get back, I will hide my writing somewhere where it won't deteriorate. I'll find a way to get a message to you. I promise."

Tears filled Rayne's eyes and she stood to walk over to her child. "It won't go that far. We won't let it."

They held each other for a moment, and then Jewell stepped back to look at each one in turn. "I don't know why, but I feel like time is important. I'm not sure we can wait for everything to be in place. If I can't manage to stay here tonight, I'll just have to figure all this out on my own."

At Rayne's whimper, Jewell turned so she was only facing her mother. "I am your daughter. And I am a Cavanaugh. Nothing will ever defeat this family. You told us that when we were little, Momma. Please, don't doubt it now."

Chapter Eight

The morning was beautiful, the air crisp and invigorating. Jewell sipped her tea as she stood on the wide porch her father had insisted every home needed. She had to agree with him as she watched her mother pull off to head back to the cabin that was once her childhood home.

It was a relief to have made it through the night without another trip back to Anippe's life, although the girl who'd once housed her soul and the boy she'd loved were never far from Jewell's thoughts. She turned to reenter the house her father and uncles built and glanced around at the simplicity of the living room, thinking the differing shades of beige needed more splashes of color. Immediately the soft pastels, bold reds and gold that decorated the different rooms inside the Pharaoh's palace filled her mind, and a wave of dizziness washed through her.

A shiver went through Jewell. She forced her thoughts from that place to her home, her parents' home, and the woods of Mystic Mountain that had always been home. She went into the kitchen and turned on the faucet just to make the water run and then added more to the teakettle on the stove. She flipped the light switch to the right of the sink to turn on the overhead light, not because it was dark, but because electricity was a modern convenience. She moved to the gas-burning stove and turned the knob, sighing in relief when the low hum turned into red, yellow, and blue flames. She sat the teakettle down upon it and sighed.

These were normal things. Modern things. Things she would turn to when her mind started to wander to the past.

"Hey, Sis. I'm glad to see you're still here."

Jewell turned as Sapphire made her way to the preset coffeemaker she'd bought a couple of days before. As most of the Cavanaughs drank tea, the new appliance sitting on the counter looked out of place.

"Why are you drinking that?"

Sapphire grabbed a cup, poured the coffee and then turned to her with a smile. "Cops drink coffee. I got the job! I start this evening and I can't wait!"

Jewell grinned, happy to see Sapphire so happy. "That's great, Sis! Why didn't you say something last night?"

Sapphire shrugged. "It didn't seem as important as what was going on with you."

Jewell shook her head and moved forward to pull her sister into a hug. "Of course it is! You worked your butt off to get the education and training! I'm so happy for you! This has been your heart's desire for as long as I can remember. So you'll be working nights?"

Sapphire nodded, her smile so big nearly all of her even white teeth showed. "I will. I can't believe it was so easy. I went in, I interviewed, and poof! I'm hired." Her brows drew together and then smoothed back out. "You remember Captain Grammar?" At Jewell's nod, she continued. "He was there when I arrived, visiting the new captain from what I understand, and the weirdest thing happened."

Jewell leaned against the counter. "What?"

"He stopped talking in the middle of a sentence and walked over to me and gave me this look... I don't know how to explain it. And then he said, 'Celestia.'"

Jewell tilted her head as she thought that was strange too. "Why would he say our cousin's name? You don't look anything like her."

Sapphire shrugged again. "I know, and I don't know. It was weird because he's old as heck, and I had the feeling that he wanted to hug me. In fact, when he said her name it was like he was caressing it with his voice. I know that sounds strange, but it's the only way I can think to describe it."

Jewell's lips twisted at the thought. "That's creepy. He knows Dad and Mom, and they think a lot of him, but that's just creepy."

Sapphire nodded. "It was. But that's not all. After he says her name, he blinks, and it's like he doesn't even know where he is. I'm glad he's retired. It would be really uncomfortable to be around him if he acted like that all the time."

Jewell nodded. "Yes. I'm sure it would. Maybe we should say something to Celestia."

Sapphire glanced at the big black watch on her arm. "Maybe. Well, anyway, enough about that. I'm glad you are okay and are still with us. I've got to get to town and pick up my uniform and gun, and badge!"

Jewell's lips lifted again at Sapphire's enthusiasm. "I guess it's a good thing you got Dad to teach you to shoot when we were kids."

Sapphire nodded. "I knew I would need the training, even back then, so I'd have a leg up going into the academy. Being a cop is all I've ever wanted to do."

Jewell knew that had been her sister's dream since they were kids, though she personally didn't see the appeal of a job where you hung around with criminals all the time. "I know. And I'm glad for you. Just be really careful when you're on duty."

Sapphire walked to her and gave Jewell a hug before stepping back. "I will, sis. You too. I'm afraid for you. And I hate having to start my new job when you need me to be here."

"There isn't anything you can do. But thanks. I'll be okay. I'm going to try to do what Mom says, and if I go back before we can figure all this out, I'll try to remember I'm me while trying to find out what it is that is going on with Anippe."

Sapphire nodded before heading to the door. She turned back. "Text me, or have the family do it, if anything important is happening. I'll leave immediately and come home."

"You don't have to do that. You just got hired."

"I'll give up this job before I'll give up you."

Tears sprang into Jewell's eyes, but she choked them

back. "I love you, too."

Sapphire smiled gently before her gaze turned into a glare as she looked past Jewell. She turned quickly and walked out, closing the door quietly behind her.

"I love you, too. So I'm thinking we need nourishment."

Jewell turned and smiled at Dia, understanding Sapphire's parting expression, wishing her two sisters could just get along.

Unlike Dia's scary hair and sleep-disheveled appearance during their midnight chat, she was now much more put together than usual. Her lanky, sloppy *stay at home* attire was replaced with a formfitting jacket that covered her silk blouse and the top of her low-hipped jeans. Her hair was not only brushed for a change, she actually had it styled into loosely flying curls. Jewell wondered if her youngest sister had finally used the hair-straightener and curling iron she'd bought for her three Christmases before.

"Are you going somewhere?"

Dia nodded as she headed to the refrigerator. "Yes. Dad texted that Uncle Tom said I could live in his little cabin up the mountain, since none of his boys want to right now. They think it would be a good idea for me to have somewhere more secluded to practice and build my magic." Dia grinned. "And blow things up."

Jewell's brows rose. "You are moving out?"

Dia glanced over as she pulled a small vegetable drink out, sympathy in her eyes. "Only a dozen or so miles away by road. Once I learn the spell to fly, I'll be able to get back here quicker. But if you don't want me to go, with everything that's going on with you right now, I won't."

Jewell shook her head as the suctioning sound of the closing refrigerator door filled the silence of her hesitation. She swallowed then spoke quickly, "Of course I want you to do what you want to do." Although she suddenly felt very alone, Jewell didn't want it to show so she smiled conspiratorially at Dia. "Think how happy Sapphire will be."

They both laughed before Dia's pale blue irises shifted like a kaleidoscope, making changing patterns of many different colors. "That works both ways."

Knowing the subject of her warring sisters wasn't something she was up to, Jewell turned to the stove and remembered she hadn't turned the burner off. She did so quickly. When she turned back, she was relieved to see Dia's temper—and eyes—had settled. "Well, enjoy your outing. And tell Daddy I say 'Hi.'"

Dia took a deep breath and looked at Jewell hard. "I can stay here. Seriously."

Jewell shook her head. "No, you can't."

Dia's brows rose. "So now you're throwing me out?"

Jewell laughed, wishing they were all still children. Even with her sisters fighting, life had been so much simpler for them all. "No. I'm pushing. But only because I know it's what's best for you. How amazing will it be not to be locked up in some little room to practice your craft? You will have the earth and the sky at your disposal. I think it's really cool Uncle Tom would allow you to use what he considers sacred ground."

"I know. He's always been such a cool uncle to have. Maybe he'll even stop in on occasion and teach me a thing or two. Now *that* would be really amazing!"

Jewell smiled again, although it felt like her heart was breaking. There was no way she would let any of her family know that in some way, however small, the fact they could go on with their lives, when hers was in shambles, hurt. And it shamed her to even think it.

"Go. Meet with them and make plans. I'm good. I'll start looking through the mountain of diaries that are still on the table and wait for Mom and the aunts."

Dia nodded. "What if I'm gone and you go back? No one will know."

"Mom said she'd be right back, and since Dad is meeting you and Uncle Tom, they've already parted company. It should only be a matter of minutes before she gets here. Besides, I can't have someone babysitting me every minute. You all have lives, too."

"Okay…if you're sure."

Dia hesitated a second longer and then headed to the front door. She glanced back, her white-blond brows raised in question.

"I'm sure! Go!"

"Okay… I'm going. But don't *you* go anywhere!"

Jewell shrugged but was trying to be positive. "I'll try not to."

Once the door closed behind Dia, Jewell remained where she was for silent moments and made her breaths even and slow as she pondered her situation. The truth was she wasn't in the mood to read. That required her to sit still and she felt antsy. And she wasn't about to go back into her bedroom. The mirror she had always loved wasn't the mirror her father made, and the one in there was an object to be feared. She poured more steaming water in her cup and snagged a new tea bag from the tin she kept in the spice cabinet. After steeping it she took it with her to the front porch. Standing at the railing, Jewell focused on the green leaves that danced like silent ringing bells in the soft breeze. She listened intently and tried to decipher the species related to the numerous birdsongs filling the air. She closed her eyes and concentrated on the musical trickle coming from the little waterfall that sat several yards from the house. The tiny vein had only recently developed from the much larger flow on up the mountain. It was something she needed to remember to speak to her father about. The last thing they needed was for an underground well to take out the side of the mountain right next to the house.

But for now, she just wanted to enjoy the symphony surrounding her home, the warmth of the breeze, and the knowledge that she was still Jewell, and she was still in Mystic Waters.

"I'm sorry to bother you, but—"

Jewell screamed and dropped her cup as her eyes flew open. She placed her hand over her racing heart as she took in the man standing before her. She kept her eyes on him as she backed up, glanced down quickly at the broken cup and wet porch, then looked back up at, and then past, him. There was no car to be seen between the cabin and the end of the drive, and her heartbeats increased. "Who are you? How did you get here?"

A flutter of a smile touched his lips before they settled into seriousness. "I'm sorry I scared you and caused you to spill your drink and break the cup. I've…lost my dog, and I followed his trail this far." He studied her with concern. "I should warn you, he's sick…really sick, maybe even rabid, and I need to find him. Please be watchful when you're outside. He's very dangerous."

Jewell nodded, wishing he would just go. She'd heard about men who lured children away claiming they'd lost their dog, but so far this one wasn't advancing on her or asking her to help find it. "I haven't seen any dogs. And I'll be careful. I'll ask my family. They're inside fixing breakfast."

Again that slightly mocking smile touched his lips, and Jewell was afraid he knew she was lying. But he nodded and backed away. "No problem. He's probably miles from here by now, but thanks for your time."

Jewell attempted to smile and nodded, relieved that he turned and walked toward the woods, although she would have preferred he go down the driveway. It was frightening enough that he'd just shown up like that, but something about him gave her the chills even though he was a neatly dressed, very attractive man. If she hadn't known how unlikely it was, she'd swear he'd brought a hint of magical energy with him. But, of course, that was nothing more than her being paranoid, because everything in her life right now was related to her family and the more frightening aspects of their mystical abilities.

With nervous energy, she picked up the pieces of the cup and re-entered the house quickly. She dropped the pieces onto the kitchen island on the way to her room, wiping her wet fingers on her pants. It wasn't until she was standing in front of her mirror that she realized she'd gone there out of habit, not remembering she was supposed to avoid the room, until it was too late.

And it *was* too late.

A loud popping sound stunned her as it came from the reflection-glass that should have only shown her, not a ghostly her with a scene of violence coming from within its depths. Instinctively, she ran forward barely stopping before running into the mirror.

Within the bejeweled wooden frame, her other-self was obviously screaming at the young guard who'd wrapped her in that rug. He bobbed first one direction and then another with his arms held up to protect his face. Jewell watched in horrified fascination as Anippe ran around the room, lifting anything she could get her hands on, throwing object after object at him as he ducked or swayed to avoid being hit.

"Jewell! Back up!"

Jewell swung around at her mother's sharp command, her heart now lodged in her throat. "Mom!" She took a step away from the mirror, looked back, and saw Anippe staring straight at her, and then nothing was visible but the reflection of the back of her body and her pale face. She turned to her mother. "Did you see it? *Did you see them!*"

Rayne looked at her in surprise. "See what?"

"In the mirror. Anippe and that man. That guard. Amen-ra!"

Rayne moved forward quickly pulling Jewell into a tight hug. "I didn't see anything. I was just stunned when I saw you standing so close to it. I was afraid it would pull you back in."

Jewell exhaled, stepped back, and then grabbed her mother's hand to pull her out of the room. When they reached the small island where she'd set the broken teacup, she scooped up the pieces and threw them away before grabbing a bottled water from the refrigerator. She broke the seal, lifted it to her lips, and drank it all down. She turned to face her mother but couldn't say more when her body started shivering violently. Rayne pulled Jewell into another tight hug and held her. Minutes later Jewell felt herself relaxing. Rayne released her enough to be able to look into her daughter's eyes.

"Tell me everything."

Jewell nodded, a little breathless. "Okay. Um...I saw them. They were fighting. Or at least Anippe was. She was yelling. Even though I couldn't hear her, I could tell she was yelling. And she was running around the room like a mad woman, girl, whatever... She was throwing things at him. I don't think he was chasing her, but it may have been because he was trying to protect his gorgeous face." Jewell exhaled fiercely and shook her head, trying to clear it. "I think that's all."

Rayne nodded and pulled her to the couch. "Sit. Think. Are you sure that's all?"

Jewell thought for a few seconds then nodded. "I think so, yes. I'm pretty sure. *No!* She looked at me! When you yelled at me and I looked back, she was looking at me like she could see me through the mirror! And she smiled."

Rayne joined her on the couch. "Okay. First, have you ever seen them in the mirror before?"

Jewell shook her head. "Not them, me, her, him... Just Jacob, like I told you before."

Rayne bit her bottom lip, her eyes skittered as her eyelids blinked. "Okay. Start over. Only this time tell me what she was wearing."

Jewell opened her hands and shrugged her shoulders. "I don't know. Why does it matter?"

"Because it does. Think. Was it the same outfit, the wedding outfit, she wore when you were her?"

Jewell closed her eyes and replayed the scene, taking in the details. "Yes. She is still wearing the dress. Wait! I wasn't wearing that! I was wearing the servant's dress!" She looked at her mother, desperation gripping her. "What does that mean?"

Rayne took a deep breath and released it. "That means he got you back into the palace and he, or someone, redressed you, her." Rayne rolled her eyes. "Whatever! Damn. Again, let's just call her you.

"Okay, so, you are back at the palace, and you're angry at him. Tell me, thinking like Anippe, what *specifically* would you be angry about?"

Jewell leaned back and rested into the couch. "I would be angry he stopped me from saving Jacob."

Rayne's brow lifted. "And?"

Jewell shrugged. "I would be angry he stopped me from escaping a wedding to whomever the Nisu picked out."

Rayne nodded. "And?"

Jewell frowned. "I don't know of any other reason! Why are you interrogating me?"

Rayne's lips settled into a gentle smile. "I'm sorry. I don't mean to. It's just we need to look beyond the obvious. Something happened back then that messed with *Providence*. We have to find out what it was."

Jewell dug as deeply as she could into her memories about the scene in the mirror, but she could see nothing helpful. "I don't know what else to say. Anippe was mad and Amen-ra was covering himself to keep from getting hit by objects. That's all."

Rayne sighed. "Okay. Well, I have something I brought from home we need to look at together. First, Anippe wrote a diary. Or someone wrote one about her."

Jewell's heart kicked into turbo beats. "What! That's fantastic!"

Rayne shrugged. "Not all that fantastic, I'm afraid. The papyrus wasn't in good shape and has mostly deteriorated, but I have little pieces I believe belong together, from those I bagged up before moving to Mystic Waters all those years ago.

Jewell waited as her mother left the room to go out to her car and retrieve the box they called the *Royal Book of Kavanaugh*. Those specially boxed ancient documents, as well as all the diaries the Cavanaugh women wrote since, spanned more than three thousand years of their family's history. The oldest, written in the ancient Egyptian glyph script, were carefully preserved and interpreted by Rayne after several years of study. But some of the papyruses were in such bad shape to begin with, her mother could only bag each and every piece she'd found, and to Jewell's knowledge, they hadn't been taken out of the sealed box or touched since.

Rayne walked in carrying the awkwardly large, elaborately carved box. The carvings covering most of the lid were of a raised oblong circle encasing raised hieroglyphic symbols. Outside of the distorted circle were the sharp-tipped blooms of the Egyptian water lily. At the very center was an uncut jewel the family believed was the crowning jewel of Queen Nefertari's many royal jewels. As she was believed to have started the mystical family line, of the vast collection, that jewel was the one chosen by Rayne all those year ago to crown the box she'd designed and had commissioned to preserve the oldest of their family recordings.

Rayne settled on the couch and sat the box between them. Reverently she took out a tiny key and unlocked the fancy padlock, then opened the large top. One by one she lifted the Plexiglas-encased papyrus diaries and placed them aside, until at the very bottom she took out the one that held all the little bits and pieces of the destroyed scrolls.

Jewell watched as her mother pulled on a pair of gloves before taking a small knife to wedge between the two pieces of Plexiglas just enough to break the seal she'd created all those years ago, and the nearly destroyed ancient Egyptian material felt air for the first time in over two decades.

"Mom…."

Rayne looked at her and smiled. "I know. You can smell the history. I have ached to touch these again. But they were safer being in the dark. Being frozen in space."

"Thank you for doing this, Mom. I know it hurts them to be exposed."

Rayne looked at her is surprise. "This family's treasures are the women, and now men, who live or lived. There is nothing I wouldn't sacrifice to have you safe."

Jewell smile and reached over to cover her mother's

gloved hand. "I know. And I know everyone else feels the same, just like I would if it were another of us. But how do you know there is anything in there that will help?"

Rayne smiled. "Because I kept a journal of my own when I was translating the ones that are intact. I was reading over it at the house right before I came back. I noticed I had a little notation about what, at that time, I called the trash-worthy pieces. I couldn't make myself throw any of it away.

"But, anyway, I wrote down a list of words and names from what I could decipher, and though several of the names were only partially intact, there were some that were whole. One of those was Anippe and another: Jacob."

Jewell's breath caught. "Really?"

Rayne nodded. "I noted in my journal there were pieces that seemed to come from the same, and I'm certain *oldest*, papyrus sheets. Each parchment will vary a little from the others, especially if they are generations apart. I tried to group the pieces I found by age and what I'll call thread-count. Only a few actually fit together like puzzle pieces, so I never tried mounting them on anything. But maybe we should try now. Even if we have gaping holes, maybe something will make sense."

Not as excited, Jewell nodded. Of course it couldn't have been as easy as a puzzle with all the pieces. "Okay. We can try. I just hope there's something here to make pulling all this out worth the effort."

Morning turned into afternoon and afternoon into evening. The only reason Jewell noticed was because Dia popped in from her trip to her new home full of bubbling enthusiasm and wanted to know what was for dinner. Jewell and Rayne stood and stretched for the first time in hours, and Jewell knew her mother had to be as stiff as she was. Unfortunately, their hard fought puzzle-piecing hadn't yielded much more than what Rayne had recorded in her journal all those years before.

Discouraged and tired, she looked at her radiantly happy sister. "I haven't even thought of food…" She turned to her mother. "Mom, I think I have to go back. Whatever is happening there is happening without my knowledge."

Rayne shook her head. "We don't know enough. We haven't searched all the diaries."

Jewell almost snorted but stopped herself. "It would take years even with all of us searching. There are just too many of them."

"The aunts are headed back. Lune Brille and Soleli know more than my sisters and I. They will be here within the next twenty-four hours. Please hold on if you can!"

Jewell yawned and nodded reluctantly. "I'll try, Mom. But I'm tired, and I'm afraid to sleep, but I'm eventually going to have to. I really don't know if I can fight going back as weak as I feel right now. If it happens, I may just have to find whatever it is that went wrong from the other side."

"But what if you repeat what went wrong just because you don't know what it was, and the answer is right here and we just need to find it?"

Jewell sighed. "I don't know." She shook her head. "I don't know anything right now." She rubbed bleary eyes. "What if this isn't about her doing something wrong? What if it isn't about anything—but just is? How do you stop something like that?"

Rayne shrugged, her eyes so sad Jewell wished she could say something to eliminate her mother's fears. She didn't know what to say or what to do. Worse, she didn't know if there was anything she *could* do but ride it out and see what happened.

Dia approached them, and Jewell could tell she was trying to hide her excitement by how hard she was biting her lip. She grinned at her younger sister, hoping her own problems didn't make the rest of the family feel as if they weren't allowed to express joy.

"So, what did you think of Uncle Tom's cabin?"

Dia threw a quick glance at their mother. "It was perfect."

Jewell tried not to sigh. Just as she feared, Dia was suppressing what would have normally been bubbly enthusiasm. She walked across the room and threw her arms around her sibling. "That's fantastic! I'm so happy for you, Dia! Tell us about it."

Her naturally exuberant smile appeared, and Dia allowed Jewell to pull her on into the room. Together they headed for the small kitchen area where Rayne joined them. She looked at both her daughters and Jewell could tell she was trying to shift gears.

"That's great, baby. Daddy and Tom, well, all of us really, are relieved you'll be somewhere barely anyone outside of the family knows about. You can practice your craft to your heart's content."

Dia laughed. "Thanks, Mom. But I know you mean explode things." She turned to Jewell. "Did you tell Mom about me making gold?"

Surprise lit Rayne's eyes as she looked from one daughter to the other. Jewell shook her head. "No. I'm sorry, Dee. I forgot."

Dia made a face that normally would have made Jewell smile.

"Jewells, I'm an idiot. Don't apologize. It was a stupid thing to ask with everything you are going through." She turned to their mother. "I blew up something the other day and small golden nuggets were in the debris. I think they may actually be gold, but we're afraid to have them tested in case they end up being something unexplainable."

The strain that had sharpened Rayne's eyes all day softened and her lips lifted in a small smile. "That's great, baby. Maybe we can have the aunts look at them when they get here. They have ways of finding out all kinds of things." Her gaze swung back to Jewell. "I hope they come before anything else happens."

"Me too. But in the meantime, I have to eat a little something and then lie down. I'm not really hungry, but I think I better keep my strength up, and I'm beat. If I don't get some sleep soon I am going to fall on my face."

"Jewell, go sit on the couch. Dia, honey, help me throw something together for her." She looked back at Jewell. "And then you are going home with me."

She nodded. "Since I don't have the strength, or the bravado, to argue, okay. But I don't want Daddy scared by all this."

Rayne's eyes were haunted for a second before she visibly shook it off. "The only thing that will ever scare your dad is losing you." She teared up. "The months Gavin went missing nearly destroyed him. He really wouldn't survive losing a precious daughter."

That was her fear. Jewell, her siblings, and the two sets of identical cousins had all heard the stories of Gavin White's horrible kidnapping, and how their moms had saved him with the help of Uncle Tom. Since it had all happened the year before their births, and Gavin had immediately moved to the family home in Los Angeles still owned by Rayne and her sisters, they barely knew their oldest cousin. He hadn't returned to Mystic Waters in all Jewell's twenty-three years, and though her generation was never told the details of what Gavin had suffered, she knew it had to have been really horrible to keep him from ever returning to the home of his birth and to the large family, on both sides, that loved him.

"How is canned soup? Chicken noodle?"

Nodding, Jewell sunk back into the plush cushions of the couch. It felt so good to be lying back she forced herself to relax from her stiff neck to the tips of her bare toes. With a deep sigh she listened to the sounds of her mother and sister as they moved things around until finally the electric can opener hummed. They were speaking too quietly for her to decipher their conversation, but that was fine. She was tired of talking. She was tired of listening. She was tired of thinking.

"Jewells?"

"Jewell!"

"Jewell! Open your eyes!"

"How did that mirror get in here!"

Chapter Nine

"Anippe!"

Jewell's eyes flew open and she stared up at the face of Amen-ra in terror. For a moment she couldn't breathe, or move, or clear her mind enough to remember...*anything.*

"I didn't think you'd awaken. I would not have been so rough last night, but you gave me no choice."

As she had no idea what had transpired since she was last here beyond the fight she'd witnessed through the looking glass, Jewell could do nothing but stare up at the guard. She waited for Anippe's mind and memories to try to take over, but so far she was still Jewell in her thoughts. She exhaled a shaky sigh and took a mental inventory of the body she occupied. There was definitely soreness, *all over,* but mostly at the juncture of her thighs.

With a gasp, shaken to her depths, Jewell lifted her hand and smacked his cheek as hard as she could. "You brute! You raped her!"

Amen-ra barely reacted to the slap, but the words had him leaning back, as his charcoal lined eyes looked at her in wide-eyed confusion. "I raped no one! Of whom do you speak?"

Feeling a little self-conscious, Jewell couldn't maintain eye contact so she looked lower and then realized she was staring at his very broad, hairless, muscular bare chest. Slowly she allowed her gaze to slide downward only to see his bare rippling abdomen led to his very bare...*everything.*

His very well endowed, very cleanly shaven, bare everything, which sprung to life as she watched.

Jewell's gaze flew back up to his face and heat filled more than her cheeks. She cleared her throat. "You're naked!"

Amen-ra grinned wickedly. "Yes." His gaze turned

hungry. "So are you."

Without moving her head, Jewell lowered her gaze until the dusky tips of Anippe's breasts came into view. Frantically she jackknifed into a sitting position and reached for the linen sheets pooled below her feet. Her entire body infused with splotches of color that matched her hair as she grabbed and tugged at the corner of the cloth but Amen-ra seemed stubbornly content to remain kneeling on it rather than assister her. Jewell glared at him. "Move!"

Amen-ra frowned. "That is no way to talk to your husband and master."

"You are not—" Jewell groaned. She released the linen and quickly drew her knees up to wrap her arms around them before lowering her head to hide her face from his view. She had to remember she was Anippe as far as he was concerned, though she couldn't for the life of her figure out why Anippe wasn't attempting to overtake her thoughts at all this time.

How the hell had the princess ended up married to the guard!

Jewell knew she was supposed to remember she was herself and not Anippe, if she could, but how in the world could she proceed with no knowledge or even an idea of what had transpired between Anippe and Amen-ra the night before? She'd never once in her life expected to end up naked in a bed with a naked ancient Egyptian man and be married to him on top of it! She swallowed and peeked up from her kneecaps. "We need to talk."

Amen-ra's grinned wickedly, and if she wasn't so horrified by her predicament, she'd actually think he was too hot for words. "Please allow me to cover myself."

He slowly shook his head. "You should have no shame. Your body is beautiful. It is the gold lining in the clouds."

Jewell rolled her eyes. "It's a *silver* lining, you dolt! And I'm not ashamed of my...*this* body. But I would be more comfortable dressed. And what clouds are *you* talking about? I was the one forced to marry."

He seemed to give her words consideration for a moment then slowly slid back off the bedding. "You remember little, I see."

Jewell immediately reached for the sheet and pulled it up and around her as she rolled off the side of the bed, eyeing him warily. *You have no idea.*

Once standing, she looked him up and down, and thought maybe Anippe should be thanking her lucky stars. The man was freaking magnificent. As in m-a-g-n-i-f-i-c-e-n-t! There was no way to be a female and ignore such a work of masculine art. A smile played at her lips before she could stop it, which evidently was interpreted as an invitation by Amen-ra. He moved forward slowly as if he was prepared for her to bolt. Jewell had no idea how her absent other-self would have reacted, so Jewell stood her ground but raised her hand to stop him from coming any closer than arm's length. There was nothing to do but tell the truth.

"I am Jewell."

Amen-ra nodded, his eyes suddenly lit with humor. "Yes. The jewel of the Nile. *My* jewel of the Nile, now."

Jewell shook her head. "No. I am not *the* jewel of the Nile. I am Jewell Cavanaugh-White. And…I can't believe I'm going to say this…but, I'm from the future."

For the first time since Jewell awoke to realize she was once again back in Egypt, Amen-ra's countenance slipped and his eyes filled with confusion. "Why are you saying these things? I told you last night to stop such foolishness. I am no happier about any of this than you are. But I am a man of my word. I will try to make the best of it if you will."

Jewell took a deep breath then slowly blew it out. "I don't know what you are talking about. I wasn't here last night. Anippe was." At his growl she hurried on. "You have to listen to me! I know this is hard to believe, but I keep travelling back and forth between my time and your time. I think my soul once belonged to Anippe."

Amen-ra stared at her for only seconds before he burst out laughing. Jewell pressed her molars together to keep from saying more. But she had to somehow make him understand he had no rights, and certainly no *husbandly rights*, where she was concerned.

"Stop laughing. I'm serious."

Amen-ra shook his head, his eyes suddenly grave. "You will not repeat what you have just said to anyone. Your father will have you killed for sure, and me as well for promising him I would make you into an obedient wife, as you were never an obedient daughter."

Jewell kept her mouth shut. After all, what more could she say? The last thing she needed was to get killed. Even now she worried what kind of impact her mental disappearance was having on her family. She could picture them all standing around her, begging her to wake up. It killed her that they were living in fear of what was happening, and she felt a little guilty for not being more upset about it herself. After all, compared to every other male she'd ever encountered, none, not even the extremely good-looking ones, had actually made her feel so filled with this sense of femininity.

She clutched the sheet around her and grappled with the reality that she was completely powerless, both in her predicament and her reaction to him. Both were unprecedented. The first should have been an impossibility, and the second…she'd *never* been shallow when it came to a man's looks. She'd always based her relationships with the opposite sex on their personalities, pure and simple. And though Amen-ra seemed honorable enough, she didn't know him well enough to find herself this attracted to him. It was ridiculous!

She bit her bottom lip as she struggled with her devious feelings, even though in reality, she had no other option but to play the part of Anippe until she could get back home. Shaking inside, Jewell moved closer to Amen-ra, mortified by the act she was being forced to play out. If survival meant she had to be an obedient wife, then all she could do was be thankful he wasn't some big, hairy, toothless old man who wanted to beat her into compliance. "What am I to call you?"

His features relaxed. "My love."

His answer was such a surprise Jewell took a step back. "I don't love you." And neither did Anippe, unless something had changed drastically on their wedding night!

Amen-ra shrugged his massive shoulders. "You will. My father said it takes time, but eventually all his wives came to love him. Even the ones who were forced to marry him. I will pleasure you often. And you will learn to pleasure me. This too binds us."

Jewell didn't have an answer to that. It was all she could do to try not to notice that his especially well-endowed *everything* was on full alert again. She pulled her lips between her teeth and looked away, and was ashamed that she wanted to look back.

"You may look upon me with lust."

Jewell's gaze flew back to his face and this time she laughed, though it was a little garbled. "You are quite full of yourself."

Amen-ra reached down and grasped himself. He ran his large hand from the thick base up the length to the engorged head of his penis and then nodded. "Yes. I am quite full. It is good for you to see that I am man enough for you to enjoy."

Jewell had no idea how to respond to *that*. Though he was, hands down, the hottest looking male she'd ever met, she had to remember he was technically married to another woman, even if she was currently inside that woman's body. Somehow she had to buy them both some time.

She sighed. "I cannot enjoy you if I don't know you."

Amen-ra seemed to give her comment real consideration. "But you will know me more, each time we consummate our marriage."

"I don't mean in the Biblical sense!"

"I don't understand your words. What is this *biblical sense?*"

Since Jewell had no idea exactly where she was on the human species time-line, she shook her head. "It doesn't matter." She stepped back. "Look, I need some time to get to know you. Like what kind of person you are. What you like to do for fun. What you do with your time all day. What am I supposed to do with my time? Am I even a *princess* anymore or just some dumb guard's wife?"

As she ran out of things to say, she turned away from him and looked around the room. It was a relief she was still in a place that was somewhat familiar. Though, without *all* of Anippe's thoughts, it wasn't nearly as familiar as before, and that was worrisome. She needed to find whatever it was that went wrong in Anippe's time and correct it, and she had to get back home.

Jewell bit her lip as fear fisted her chest. She turned back to Amen-ra only to find him inches away again. She took a shaky breath, bewildered that being so close to his massive chest affected her womanly senses so strongly. "Will we be allowed to stay here, in Anippe's...*my* old room?"

She looked up, way up, into his angry eyes. Surprised, she stepped back quickly.

"I have no idea what this *dumb* is, but I know an insult when I hear one. You are an *ungrateful,* spoiled, unpleasant child, Anippe. You will stay in this room until you accept that, although still a princess by birth, you are now mine to do with as I please. It is by my request that you still live, though I look a fool for making it. It is by the grace of the Nisu, who favors my family greatly, that you are still housed in these rooms where you shall know all the comforts you have always known, although you will never know freedom until you accept your fate as a woman.

"You will speak with disrespect to me no more, or I will treat you like a wayward babe and spank your bottom until it stings in pain. And you will not, *ever,* speak to anyone else about being from another time.

"I am your master. You will obey me or there will be grave consequences."

He stared at her a moment then turned abruptly, grabbed a length of linen from a nearby pile of cushions, and left the room. Jewell stayed where she was as she listened to his movements until there were none. She swallowed against a tightness in her throat.

I've hurt his feelings.

"We are here to assist you bathe."

Startled, Jewell looked at the three young, identically dressed and wig-donned women, who'd entered her room so quietly she hadn't noticed them. "I can bathe myself."

There was silence as all three looked at her from charcoal lined eyes. Jewell sighed. She would have to go along with whatever was demanded of her if she was to be given any degree of freedom. And she would need it to be able to try to figure out what was going on. Resigned, she nodded. "Yes, of course."

A pleased smile lit their faces as one of the three moved forward. "I am Her-uben. Your husband picked us to serve you, as those who did are no longer in the palace. "Heneny will take your sheets to be laundered. If you please, come with us to your toilet. We will begin with your bowel cleansing first, as your husband commanded."

Jewell stared at the women in horror as she shook her head. Though she was not privy to Anippe's current thoughts and feelings, she had a very clear memory of the last *cleansing* they'd shared. "I do not wish to have one. I only wish to bathe."

The young women looked to each other then back to her. "Your husband demands it, so it must be."

Jewell shook her head. "I will not. I will bathe, but I will allow no one to touch me!"

Again the three women stared at her. Her-uben moved forward with sympathy in her eyes. "We will not hurt you. It is known throughout the palace what was done to you the last time. We will do no harm to you. Your husband only wishes for you to know comfort."

Jewell swallowed. "Then please, just let me bathe this time. I am not recovered from the last time."

Her-uben nodded and turned to the others. "You will speak of this to no one. We are very privileged to be servants of Princess Anippe, and are here for her pleasure, and for the pleasure of Prince Amen-ra."

Though the title before the guard's name startled Jewell, she remained silent as the other two servants nodded. The news that she would not be abused again relaxed her enough to smile at the woman. "Thank you."

Her-uben nodded and bowed before she stepped back and indicated for Jewell to precede her to the arched doorway Amen-ra took to leave the room.

Since she didn't have Anippe's memories of the palace anymore, panic flared. The last thing she wanted to do was have the people in the palace whispering she'd lost her mind and couldn't even remember the layout of the home in which she'd lived her life. But... "Please, lead the way. After everything that has happened, I am a little confused today."

Her-uben smiled. "Yes, after a night in the arms of Amen-ra, one does get a little light of the head." Her laugher was that of a happy memory. "He is the greatest of lovers."

Jewell stared at the woman. "You have slept with...my husband?"

Her-uben's brows lifted. "No, we did not sleep together. I leave after we are done."

Realizing that her American slang was lost on the servant, she nodded slowly. "But you had sex with him."

Though there was still confusion in her eyes, Her-uben smiled. "Yes. We mate often. But now he will be with you more, I'm sure. Please, follow me." She turned and started from the room, looking back when she realized Jewell hadn't moved. "Princess?"

Jewell shook herself and moved forward, following as Her-uben led the way to the large bathing room shared by all but the Nisu and immediate royal family. She was confused by the flare of jealousy she felt at learning the woman had slept with the man who was now Anippe's husband. She had no right to feel jealous and was pretty sure Anippe wouldn't either, since she was in love with Jacob.

Jewell had forgotten all about Jacob!

"What happened to Jacob?"

The women looked at each other and then Jewell. Her-uben shook her head. "We are not to speak of it."

Jewell nodded. So he had been put to death. She felt bad for him and Anippe but had no personal feelings of loss, only those of sympathy for what he must have suffered. Wondering again where her other-self was, Jewell turned back to what she was coming to think of as her head servant. "I need to know."

Her-uben shook her head. "This I cannot do. I am sorry. It is the orders of the Nisu that he never be spoken of again, under penalty of death. You must focus on pleasing your husband, Princess. It is the road to your happiness."

She smiled again, and it was obvious to Jewell she was in love with Amen-ra. Convincing herself it was only curiosity she felt stirring in her gut, she waited to speak again until they were in the pool, and Her-uben was shampooing her hair. As her head was being scrubbed hard, she kept her eyes closed. "How often do you sleep, I mean *mate* with Amen-ra?"

The servant's fingers halted in the process of the massage then resumed seconds later. "He is a man of much need. Nearly every day unless he is called away by duty, sometimes two or three times a day, if he has need of me. It is my pleasure to serve him."

Jewell pushed the liquid from her face before opening her eyes. "Will he not be faithful to his marriage?"

The servant's brows pulled together. "Of course. He is most honorable."

Jewell stepped away from the servant and allowed her knees to buckle so she could rinse whatever the servant had used as shampoo from her hair. She swam away a little to an area where the water was still clear and rubbed at her scalp to try to get as much of the substance out as possible before standing again. Mostly she took the time to process the information without the prying eyes of the servant. And to try to figure out why she even cared if the man was faithful or not to his wife.

Once she pushed the hair and water from her face, she opened her eyes and more servants were right beside her holding large jugs. She waited as one after the other poured clean water over her head before wrapping her hair in a long strip of linen until it perched like a turban on her head. She allowed herself to be led from the pool where she was wrapped in more linen before being taken back to her room.

She suffered through the women fussing over her as they oiled her body, brushed her hair, and helped her to dress in what she believed were Anippe's own clothes. She was glad the young princess would not suffer being thrown out of her home into the streets, and she was still going to be treated with deference and was allowed to keep those things that were hers. Jewell was growing more and more concerned that Anippe wasn't trying to break free and enter her mind at all. It was like she had completely vacated her body.

Shivers vibrated through Jewell as she stared at herself in the mirror that looked as if it was an exact match to the one her father, her *real* father—Garrison White—had built. What if Anippe was gone forever and she was stuck in this body, and time, for eternity?

"Are you chilled, Princess?"

Jewell looked at the servant, and for a moment her mind was blank. "What?"

Her-uben sent her a gentle smile. "You are shivering. Come, we will put you to bed and call for your husband."

Jewell nodded and then shook her head. "Bed, yes. Thank you. But please do not alarm Amen-ra. I am only in need of a little rest."

Her-uben smiled knowingly. "Ah, yes. He can wear a girl out."

It was hard to admit, since it made no sense at all, but Jewell was getting more and more annoyed the servant spoke so happily about making love with Amen-ra. She pushed the retort that sprang to mind aside and pretended not to care. "Actually, I think it has more to do with the harsh treatment my father commanded befall me. I am tired. Please leave me."

Her-uben's smile faltered. "As you wish, Princess."

She bowed and left the room with the other servants following like ducks in a row. Jewell breathed a sigh of relief, hoping everyone just left her alone. She really was mentally and physically exhausted. Her mind was overloaded with all that was transpiring. Her body really was hurting so much from all that had happened the day before, as well as from what Anippe apparently suffered at the hands of her new husband the night before.

If he'd been any kind of gentleman at all, he wouldn't have forced himself on the poor girl.

Jewell climbed onto the plush bedding and lay back, hoping she could sleep. But there was too much to think about, too much to figure out. As she thought of what her family must be going through, tears gathered and she emitted a cry.

"You are unwell?"

Jewell closed her eyes and groaned. She needed time alone, and apparently that wasn't going to happen. She opened them and looked over at him and her breath caught. Amen-ra was massive. Even dressed in the kilt held up with the golden rope he'd fashioned for himself, and the ponytail he'd pulled his hair back into, he was as intimidating covered as he'd been naked.

As he advanced across the room, Jewell rolled over, taking herself as far away from him as she could. He stopped and stared at her with a look between concern and irritation. "Why do you fight me at every turn? I will not harm you."

Jewell exhaled slowly. "I am sore! Do you not think your actions last night were harmful?"

Amen-ra frowned at her. "What did I do to you last night?"

"You raped me!"

Since he was as still as a statue with a stunned expression widening his eyes, Jewell had an urge to squirm. "Well, I know you don't think of it like that, but you did."

Indignant anger entered his eyes. "I did nothing but care for your injuries last night!"

Jewell frowned and searched his eyes for deceit. "What do you mean?"

Amen-ra shook his head as if he couldn't believe she was asking. A look of frustration lined the edges of his tightly clamped lips. He came closer to settle himself on the edge of the bed with his back to her. Jewell stayed where she was, afraid moving further from him would only be a sign of weakness, or worse, insult.

"Do you not remember?"

Realizing his tone was of hurt, Jewell debated over what lie she could tell him and then settled on the truth. "I do not."

Amen-ra turned his body so he could face her. "It is not surprising. The events of the day were difficult for you. But *I* did not harm you." He studied her face. "I *will not* harm you, Anippe. I have desired your notice since we were children. I am honored to call you wife."

He stood, keeping his back to her as Jewell processed what he was saying. She rose from the bed and walked around so that she could face him, but she kept a distance between them because she didn't want to give him the impression that his words meant everything was okay. It wasn't. She had no idea how Anippe would react, though she suspected the fifteen-year-old would throw his words in his face. She couldn't do that. It wouldn't serve her to antagonize him.

Jewell exhaled heavily. "I am sorry for making the accusation. When I awoke naked, with the pains in my...*body*, I thought that it meant you..."

"Took you against your will?"

Jewell nodded. "Yes."

"And even though you do not remember the events of last night, you believe me now?"

She nodded slowly, relieved to see that some of the hurt was leaving his eyes. "Yes. I do."

A small smile relaxed the rest of his face. "Good."

"But I am not ready to sleep with you," she added quickly, hoping to hold him off until she could get Anippe back and herself back home. As gorgeous as he was, she had no desire to sleep with another woman's husband.

He studied her then. "You do not wish me in your bed to sleep?"

Jewell nodded, thinking to tell him to go look up his *concubine*, Her-uben, but the words wouldn't pass her lips. Not only because she had no reason to treat the kind servant with scorn, but because it bothered her thinking of him with the other woman, though it boggled her mind that she cared. She swallowed. "I need time."

A fully relaxed smile lit his eyes and showed beautiful white teeth. He moved closer and Jewell forced herself to hold her ground. When he stopped a couple of feet away, she remembered to breathe.

"I have time. I gift it to you.

"I wish to gain your love, Anippe. It is not required. It is not even expected, and many would laugh that I even care. But I wish it to be. I have seen love matches. I wish to have one with you."

The sincerity of his words touched Jewell. His gentleness, given his massive size, made his words even more special. If he weren't married to the woman he believed she was, she would seriously have to consider giving into the physical attraction she felt for him...*no*, she couldn't think like that.

"Perhaps we can become friends," she threw in quickly to halt her wayward thoughts.

"That would be a good start. I desire you, but I will direct my physical needs from you until you wish to lie with me." He grinned with unexpected arrogance. "And you *will* wish to lie with me."

Since he'd thrown it out sounding like a teasing challenge, and Jewell had grown up in a family where teasing and challenges were welcome and enjoyed, she tried to smile. "We will see."

Amen-ra laughed and Jewell's heart stuttered a little. He was as gorgeous as her cousins Zeus, Apollo, and Heracles and would have made a ton of money showing off his face and muscles in the twenty-first century. But more importantly he seemed willing to give her time, which she strongly suspected went against how he'd been raised. Jewell could only hope Anippe was conscience on some level, so she'd know she could have ended up a lot worse off than being married to the very marriage-marketable man standing before Jewell. Women in her century would have fallen at his feet, and if Her-uben was any indication, women of this century were no different.

"If only I'd met you before..." Jewell clamped her mouth closed. She couldn't remind him she'd claimed to be from another century.

"Before you met the slave?"

Jewell nodded, though she hated to lie. But there just was no other choice.

The pleasure that had lit his eyes was replaced with irritation. "You will speak of him no more!"

Jewell nodded and looked away. The last thing she needed was for him to be angry with her. She needed to gain his trust. She needed to make him believe whatever she said and did was an indication she would comply with his wishes, especially since he was kind enough to give Anippe time to accept her fate. But mostly she had to remember this was not her place, or her time, and any attraction she felt for him could not manifest beyond thought.

Someday, sometime, Anippe would return to claim her mind and her body, and if the young girl had a brain in her head, her husband as well. At least Jewell hoped so.

"I will not."

Amen-ra's features relaxed immediately. "That is good."

Jewell attempted a smile, but depression was trying to take hold. She looked back to find him studying her. "Am I a prisoner to these rooms?"

Amen-ra nodded. "Until your father trusts you will be a good wife and forget your love of the one who will not be mentioned again. You will be permitted the run of the castle when you are with me or are being guarded by another of my choosing, as your father has elevated my rank, and I am to oversee the Nisu's safety along with my father. As my wife, you will be granted the privilege of great rank, though, for now, not that which you once held. But you will only be allowed outside of the palace when I accompany you. Then, once you are with babe, it is decided you may have more freedoms as your father believes you will have settled into accepting your place."

Jewell swallowed. She, or Anippe, would be watched every moment she was outside of her private rooms. There would be little opportunity to search for answers to the questions she had to find to ask. She nodded. She had no choice.

Amen-ra moved the remaining steps to stand before her and Jewell forced herself to remain immobile. He lifted her chin so she was forced to look into his eyes. "I will give you great pleasure if you allow me to. We can find a place of happiness if you will only take the path leading to it.

"You are yet a child, Anippe. I understand this, and I have convinced your father that is the only reason you dishonored him so deeply. But you must put away your childish ways now and become a woman.

"It would bear you well to start by humbling yourself before the Nisu, so that he may see you are still his daughter and not a traitor to his royal line."

Jewell inhaled and then slowly let the breath release. If nothing else, perhaps she could help mend the rift between father and daughter for Anippe. "Will he see me?"

Amen-ra shook his head. "Not yet. It is too soon and he is very angry right now. But I will speak to him after a time and let him know you are growing up, and your actions were nothing more than those of a spoiled child."

Jewell looked at him sharply but said nothing. He was wrong. Even as young as she was, Anippe's feelings for the

Jewish slave were sincere. That much Jewell could remember. "You underestimate the feelings of a young woman."

"And you underestimated the consequences of misguided youth. It is only the fact that you were yet a virgin that your life was spared. Had your examination proved different, I could have petitioned until I had no breath left, and it would have made no difference."

Jewell nodded. "I pretty much figured that out while I was being violated yesterday."

Amen-ra's eyes turned sympathetic. "Then do not cause such actions to come against you again. I will give my life to defend you against others, but I cannot fight the Nisu. I will dishonor myself for no one. Not even you."

Seeing both she and Anippe owed him a great debt, Jewell took the last step separating them and reached up to pull his face down to hers. "Thank you." She kissed one cheek, and then turned his head and kissed the other before releasing him to step back.

She could do nothing but respond to his pleased smile with one of her own. "I will do my best to honor you in the eyes of others, especially the Nisu. Thank you for saving my life."

Chapter Ten

Once Amen-ra left to resume his newly elevated duties, Jewell wandered the room she had only known before through Anippe's eyes. Since she hadn't really paid any attention to the details, as Anippe took her rooms and belongings for granted, Jewell examined the differences between the quality of the linens, the bejeweled urns and jars, the table of primitively produced makeup, and finally the other two small rooms off her main bedroom. One was something of a sitting room with a gilded, canopied lounge covered in richly colored sheer netting and plush pillows. And to the side were small platters of dried dates, figs, large grapes and raisins. Though she was becoming hungry, Jewell ignored them to continue her inspection.

The second small room was a private toilet. It was designed so that the one using it could sit on the six foot or so long bricked seat with its off-to-the-right hole and relieve bladder or bowels into the large-mouth jar stored below. The fact that there was no foul odor assured her it was cleaned often, a vast relief. In fact, all of the rooms carried a light pleasant scent, which Jewell could only surmise came from the large and small hand-basins throughout the rooms. The scented oily liquid filling each basin was topped by floating Egyptian Lily heads. The flowers were again used as decoration around the base of each basin.

Jewell noticed the tall vase holding the reeds at the far left of the toilet's opening, and the linens stacked there. Memories of the pre-marriage cleansing nearly took her to her knees. She didn't know how she was going to act compliant and refuse to cooperate with another cleansing at the same time, but she was determined to find a way.

"Are you feeling better, Princess?"

Jewell started and then exhaled as she turned to face the servant. "I am, a little." She turned back and pointed to the offensive objects. "Please remove those from my rooms. I will no longer require that service."

Her-uben looked from her to the reeds and back and though her eyes held surprise, she only bowed and moved forward to take the offending objects. "I will do as you ask, Princess. Please let me know if you change your mind. I came to tell you your meal is here."

Jewell nodded. "Thank you."

A pleased smile lit the servant's lips. "It is my pleasure to serve you, Princess. I am at your disposal for any pleasures you seek from me," she added, her tone seductive.

Jewell lifted her brows but only nodded in response. She knew well that same-sex encounters and even multiple partners enacting love-play was common in ancient Egyptian times. She had enough to deal with holding off Amen-ra. She didn't want to think about multiple partners at all.

"Thank you, Her-uben. I wish to be alone with my meal. Please leave it in the other room."

The servant bowed and backed away. Jewell walked over to look into a basin that had a somewhat translucent bar of soap sitting beside it. She put her hands in the cold liquid then lathered with the soap before submerging her hands again. A small hand towel of rough linen sitting to the side was obviously for drying her hands, and she was again thankful that, although primitive, the palace had rather modern conveniences. The only thing missing was a mirror over the sink.

Jewell's breath caught and she hurried from the room to the room where she'd been primped following her bath. She needed to get a better look at the mirror! If it was the portal through which her spirit transferred....

She stopped dead and stared at the empty wall where the mirror stood only moments before and her heart sunk. She ran to the room where, fortunately, Her-uben hadn't left. She was arranging the food on a table that was pulled closer to the lounge. "Where is the mirror?"

Her-uben turned and looked at her with raised brows. "I'm sorry, Princess. I don't know anything about a mirror."

A sense of panic engulfed Jewell and she turned in a circle, frantic. She turned back to Her-uben, her heart pounding. "There was a large, full-length mirror that I stood in front of while you and the others were doing my hair. It had jewels surrounding it. I need to know what happened to it."

Her-uben bowed. "I will see if anyone knows."

Jewell nodded, knowing the servant thought her panic strange, but she could barely breathe and could do nothing to hide the fear. Though it hadn't yet been proven, Jewell felt certain the nearly identical mirrors had something to do with her spirit's ability to transport through time.

The servant left and Jewell forced herself to the lounge. A large platter held what looked like several roasted small birds, a long loaf of bread glazed in what looked like honey, as well as two bowls of stew that held an array of vegetables peppered with spices. The aroma was quite pleasant and made her stomach growl, but she was afraid she'd choke if she tried to eat anything. She poked her fingers in the first of the two small finger bowls also on the tray, happy to see the ancient Egyptians were so serious about cleanliness.

"I had enough sent so that I might join you."

Jewell didn't jump this time, although she hadn't expected Amen-ra back so soon. She turned to him slowly. "My mirror is missing."

Amen-ra nodded. "Your father had it removed moments ago. He believes you must put away your vanity and submit yourself to humility. It is a good plan."

Jewell stared at him, dumbfounded it was truly out of her reach. She searched for a response that might help get it back. "I *need* it. Not for vanity. But so I may present myself before you—and him—properly attired. I cannot put on my wig or the make-up without it."

Amen-ra frowned. "Make-up?"

Jewell made an outline around her right eye and Amen-ra nodded. "Her-uben can do that for you. She is at your disposal for anything you wish. She has served me well this past year and will do the same for you."

Annoyance lifted her head. "*Yes*. I am well aware that she serves your needs."

Amen-ra's brows lifted and surprised pleasure lit his eyes. "You are jealous."

"I am not. I only think it improper."

"You wish me to only lie with you."

Jewell looked away, having no idea how Anippe would respond to his going to the servant for pleasures, even though the princess would probably not want him for herself. So all she could do was tell him how she would feel, were he married to her. "I cannot consider it a pleasure to lie with you if you are making love to another woman, too."

Amen-ra studied her. "So you wish for time and do not wish to lie with me, but you would deny me the pleasures of another woman."

Jewell licked her dry lips. "Yes."

Amen-ra walked over to the tray and washed his hands in the finger bowl. He dried them on another small towel before lifting one of the small birds to take a bite. Since he was watching her watch him the entire time, he chewed slowly, then used the linen to wipe his mouth before speaking.

"I will give you three days."

Jewell shook her head. "I may need more time."

Amen-ra shook his head. "I will give you three days."

Knowing he could change his mind and give her no time at all, Jewell could only hope she would be gone, and Anippe would be back to deal with him when the time expired. "Three days."

Amen-ra smiled. "Now, come sit with me and eat. I cannot have a fainting wife."

He clapped his hands and the two servants who originally arrived with Her-uben earlier appeared and waited as Jewell moved closer to him where she settled as far away from him on the cushions as she could. He grinned at her and moved closer, and Jewell forced herself to grin back and stay put as the servants carried the bowls over to kneel before them.

Amen-ra smelled wonderful and was too attractive for words, and though she wanted to deny the attraction she felt for him, Jewell finally had to admit it was there. Desperate to stay true to the girl whose body she occupied, she turned away from his entrapping eyes and realized the servant kneeling in front of him had moved as close as she could between his spread knees.

"You will maintain your distance, woman!"

All three looked at her in surprise, and although the servants had the grace to look away, and the one in front of him scampered back, Amen-ra's face lit up before he turned back to the servants. "You may go. My wife and I will feed ourselves."

Mortified, not sure if Anippe had suddenly awakened within her and had decided to come out, or if she herself had reacted so strongly in what was obviously nothing short of jealously, Jewell rose suddenly and crossed the room. She couldn't look at Amen-ra, so she spoke with her back to him. "I am sorry. I need to apologize to that woman."

She felt him at her back, his body pressed into hers and Jewell inhaled a shaky breath.

"There is no need, though I am happy to see you concerned for another's feelings. It is a good start to becoming the woman you were meant to be. My servants understand you are frightened and have gone through much pain and loss. They will do nothing to displease you."

He turned her slowly, and Jewell forced herself to look into his eyes. He studied her again in that way he had since her awakening, and Jewell wondered what it was he saw. "I will still apologize to her. I did not intend to be unkind."

His smile held satisfaction. "Only two days ago I watched you threaten servants and their families if you did not get your way. I am pleased to see this change. Your father will be also."

Jewell sighed. Was this her quest? To become the woman Anippe refused to be? If so, it was good Anippe had disappeared. Jewell just hoped the princess didn't decide to take over her mind at an inopportune time and blow everything up in her face.

It was imperative she gain the privilege of getting the mirror back, or she could be lost to her family forever. "Thank you." Hoping she wasn't going to regret it, Jewell held out her hand to him. Amen-ra responded with a heart-jolting smile as he took her hand and led her back to the couch.

The sounds of a harp playing a slow and hypnotic tune began as Jewell allowed Amen-ra to spoon-feed her the stew. While she was chewing, he would take a bit for himself and then place the spoon back in the bowl as they stared at each other. Jewell shivered, but not from cold, as everything inside of her was transfixed and attuned to both his gentle ministrations and the music coming from outside the room. She allowed herself to be lulled, realizing how stressed and strained she'd felt since awakening back in Egypt.

Before she knew it the bowl was empty and Amen-ra was handing her a bejeweled stemmed brass cup filled with wine. She took the cup and waited as he lifted his, and together they drank of the tangy liquid. She lowered the drink and returned it to him when he held out his hand. He settled the glasses then broke off a stem-filled bunch of grapes and offered her one. She shook her head, as her stomach was still too upset to eat more.

"Why are you being so nice to me?"

Amen-ra looked at her curiously. "Why would I not? I told you. I wish you to fall in love with me."

Jewell smiled, bemused that he found that such an easy concept. "Why? From what you have said, I was nothing but a spoiled child."

Amen-ra shrugged. "I am hopeful *was* is a good word.

But the truth, as I have said, I have desired you from afar for a long time. You are the fairest of face and figure in the land. You have been the fantasy of many, though often as not those fantasies likely had people's hands squeezing your throat as well." He chuckled.

"It was not until your father demand that I marry you and be held responsible for you, or put you to death and save everyone the trouble of dealing with you, that my youthful fantasy had a chance at becoming reality."

Jewell shook off the urge to tell him objectifying a woman was wrong, and Anippe was still just a child, since he'd have no concept of what to do with the information. She frowned and tried to remember to respond in ways he'd understand. "Why would you want to, though? I am no longer a prize. The Nisu hates me. He will not even acknowledge me."

Amen-ra waved that away with his large hand. "He is yet angry. But you are most special to him. Once he sees the changes you are already making, he will lose his anger."

Jewell had no idea if Amen-ra was right or not, but she sure hoped so for her other-self's sake. "I am told you are now a prince. Is that why you wanted Ani...me?"

Looking at her like she should know the answer to that, he shook his head. "I have always been of the royal line, which gives me the title of Prince though I am of much lower rank than you. I am the great-grandson of the Nisu's uncle Nakhti."

Jewell stared at him a moment as she did the math. "So does marrying me raise your rank?"

Amen-ra laughed. "No. Marrying me has raised yours, as you would have been dead by now, had I not."

He grinned and she realized he thought that a great joke. "That isn't funny."

His features settled. "I am honored by your father because he and my father are close, and my branch of the family has always protected the most royal of our family. It is an honor and a privilege we take very seriously. When your father assigned me to watch over you, it was the greatest day of my life. I have proved to be worthy in the eyes of the most High and Mighty Nisu."

Jewell tried not to roll her eyes. Amen-ra's sense of self-worth was something she could use, hopefully, since it seemed to be his top priority. All she had to do was to continue to feed it, and hopefully he would stay so full of himself he wouldn't notice what she was doing.

"So you turned her, I mean *me*, in to the Nisu."

Amen-ra looked at her like he was trying to figure her out. Jewell knew she was going to have to start thinking of herself as Anippe all the time or questions would be asked that couldn't be answered.

"You are confused still." He pressed his lips together then leaned close to her and lowered his voice conspiratorially. "We should not speak of this, but you must know why, so you stop asking questions that can get you in more trouble. The one who cannot be mentioned was a traitor to you and a danger to our people. The slave was trying to steal you from the palace so that he could ransom you."

Jewell frowned. "For what purpose?"

Amen-ra seemed to wrestle with the disclosure, but continued, "He wished to petition for his father's freedom or kill you if he didn't gain it."

Jewell shook her head. "Freedom from what? And how do you know this?"

Moving even closer, he looked her in the eyes. "It was discovered his father has long been poisoning the land to keep the papyrus from growing, so there would be no reason for his people to work in the fields. When he was caught, he was taken to a location to be questioned, but he killed the guard and escaped. He was quickly recaptured and killed. The Nisu did not want more than a few people knowing of the escape, or of his death, since it was suspected more people were involved. His son was not very smart in his spying to find his father, as it came to our attention quickly. Since he couldn't discover the place he believed his father was still being held, he decided to try a new tactic. You. Everyone knows the jewel of the Nile has always been the Nisu's weakness, so you were the slave's target. If he had you, he believed he would have the Nisu on his knees."

Jewell was torn between expressing her feelings about slavery, in general, and knowing the difference in time periods wouldn't allow her to express them without her also being suspect. She bit her bottom lip as she processed what Amen-ra said.

"You must let go of the feelings you had for the slave. He was only using you to get to your father."

Jewell didn't know what to say. Which led her back to... "How do you *know* all of this?"

Amen-ra leaned back. "I have said all that I can and more than I should have. You must let this go now and mention it no more. That is over. Your father is allowing me to give you a chance at a new life. Please take it."

Her father... The Nisu, not Garrison White. She sighed. "I am no longer a weakness for the Nisu."

Amen-ra shrugged. "It is a good thing. A Nisu should have no weaknesses. But now ours has a broken heart." He looked at her with aggravation. "He loved you above all others."

Jewell closed her eyes, wondering if her own father was suffering from one too. She cleared her throat, afraid thinking about him and her mother would break her own heart. But if there were something she could say to him, it would be how much it hurt her to hurt him. "Please tell him I am truly sorry."

Amen-ra smiled and leaned forward to place a gentle kiss on her cheek. "I will tell him."

Startled, Jewell smiled back. "Thank you."

It was hard not to get lost in his eyes. They were beautifully large and deeply brown, but the light of humor and care in them was what captured and held her immobile at the moment. "I don't understand why you chose me when there are others who would give you no trouble. You are...beautiful."

Amazingly color rose in his cheeks, and Jewell was even more captivated that her words embarrassed the man. Women would fall all over themselves just to gain his notice. She didn't need to see it in the ones who served him. Or in any others, because for the first time she knew if she were free to express her own desires, she too would do anything to capture his attention…in this life or the other.

It was a startling realization. And more than a little unnerving to realize she liked hunky men with superiority complexes. She studied him, befuddled. Was that why she could never commit to Kevin? Was that why he'd never made her heart beat wildly or her fingers itch to reach out and touch him suggestively, because Kevin was so compliant? So easy to deal with? Attractive, but without this kind of billboard-worthy gorgeousness?

Am I really that kind of a woman? Or is this simple chemistry?

Jewell swallowed, realizing this was the type of attraction her mother had once talked about regarding her father. When they'd first met, he was a worn-out young man who looked old before his time. He'd placed his own life on hold following the murders of his brother and sister-in-law to take care of their son Gavin. The teenager had been kidnapped soon after the murders and was missing for months before he was found, but the torture of worry and the physically draining toll hadn't stopped Garrison White from falling in love with her mother. And for her, the stakes had been as high. A three-thousand-year-old family curse had made it impossible for the Cavanaugh women to fall in love and not suffer great loss or death as a result, yet her mother couldn't resist him, no matter the danger, no matter the fear. Their love was one that made them throw caution to the wind, the situation and consequences be damned. It was a story she loved to hear her mother speak of time and again. But that was their reality.

And this was hers.

Amen-ra had been physically attracted to *Anippe* all those years growing up. Not her. His desire for the Princess was a result of a young man's lust, not love. He hadn't even liked her, thinking nothing better of her than a tool to appease male needs, as long as he didn't have to deal with her personality. How could she be attracted to this man, who in her own time she would look at with scorn? It made no sense at all!

But nothing made sense anymore. The only thing she had to hold onto was who she was. The real her, not the woman-child's body she wore.

"I know you don't believe me, and I promise not to say this to anyone else, but I'm *not* who you think I am. I'm not Anippe."

Disappointment took the light from his eyes. "Don't say such things."

Jewell knew she could be signing her death warrant, and it would not only cost her forever, but her family as well, but she couldn't lie about this. "Amen-ra, I am not saying this to anger you or scare you, but I need you to look at me and, more importantly, listen to me. This body and this face are very similar to my own, but this is not mine to share with you.

"It frightens me to tell you this, so please do not think I am doing it without fear, but I am Jewell Cavanaugh-White, and I believe I am a descendant of Anippe. I come from a long line of women who know and practice magic. I am not able to change things, or move things, or anything like that, but my gift is also my curse. I have been transported back in time, to this time, and I have somehow become the young girl who you married."

He shook his head. "I cannot believe this." His eyes turned angry. "You will not say these words!"

Jewell hung her head. There was no way to explain the unexplainable. "I *am* sorry. But one day Anippe may decide to reappear, and I will be returned to my time, to my family. At least I hope so. When and if that happens, *she* will be the girl you know. And she may not be willing to mend fences with her father nor live with you without a fight. She may still want to fight you and her father for killing the man she believed loved her. I am Jewell. I did not love Jacob. I am sorry for him, and I am sorry for her, but I am not her."

Amen-ra looked at her and frowned. "If what you say is true, then where is she?"

Jewell shook her head. "I don't know. My spirit entered her body before, and at first I still had my own memories before I had to let go and let her take over. Before that, when it happened, I thought everything happening was only a terrible dream. But this time I have only my memories, and those that she and I shared in those brief instances."

She pleaded for his understanding. "I'm not lying to you. I swear!"

Amen-ra turned and walked away but didn't leave the room as she'd expected. Jewell gave him time to process what she'd told him, hoping he would at least consider the possibilities. He turned to her and her heart sank. It was clear he couldn't fathom any of it.

"Three days."

He turned and left the room. Jewell knew she had no choice but to save herself. She closed her eyes and called to Anippe but, as she expected, nothing happened.

"I found the mirror."

Jewell swung around and smiled at Her-uben. "Where is it?"

Her-uben looked nervous, but she walked closer so she could talk quietly. "It is in the Nisu's rooms. I believe he has decided it is to be a gift for his new bride. The palace is full of chatter this morning about the woman he chose."

Jewell's hopes took a dive knowing the mirror was now truly out of her reach. She already knew the Nisu's servant would be there every minute guarding not only the Nisu's personal belongings, but now the mirror as well. And she knew firsthand trying to get to it in a disguise wouldn't do her any good. She could care less about the news of a new wedding for Anippe's father, but if she was going to play her part, she knew she should at least pretend interest. She sighed and thanked the servant for the information on the mirror. "So, I guess months of planning will go into the wedding. When is it?"

Her-uben gave her a tolerant smile Jewell found curious.

"It is said the Nisu is going to marry his cousin Princess Kiya in a matter of days. He and the Princess are to take an *all-night* ride down the Nile in celebration once the vows are concluded. Everyone is ordered to attend the celebration, which will last well into the night and for most up until morning. There will be much beer and wine...."

Her-uben looked away then back at her. "There will be almost *no one* in the palace once we are deeply into the celebration. Only a few guards will be left behind, but they too will be captivated by the partying at the rear of the palace." She smiled. "And will be happy to accept much liquid refreshment from one such as I."

Jewell stared at the lovely servant. Was she telling her this so Jewell could sneak back in and get to the mirror? Was it a test to see what she would do? She had no idea who lingered about, listening to conversations, and the servant was Amen-ra's lover. Maybe it was a way for her to get Anippe in trouble again and out of her way.

"I have the gift of sight," she said quietly. "I know you are out of place." She swallowed. "No one knows this about me because it would be dangerous, but I knew you were coming before you came."

Stunned, her heart thundering, Jewell continued to stare at Her-uben. Since her own family had such gifts she couldn't discount the servant's words, but neither could she confirm them. It was too risky to take a chance. "I need to know more."

Her-uben smiled. "I understand your caution. It is both a gift and a great curse to see and know things before they happen. Those things can change, depending on the decisions someone makes. I saw you before you came the first time." At Jewell's sharp look the servant nodded. "Yes. I know you were here before, and that you are the one who experienced all the pain. I also see that you will return to your family in that other place with the magic lights that come on by touching something on the wall."

Electricity! Jewell nearly fell to her knees. "*How?* How do I get back?"

Her-uben shook her head. "That I cannot see. That depends on you. On the path you choose to take."

Certain she was telling the truth, Jewell moved closer to her. "Do you know where Anippe went? She won't come back this time."

Again Her-uben shook her head. "That one is gone from my mind. I don't understand why, but it is as if her soul has vanished."

Chills swept through Jewell, leaving every hair on her body standing on end. "Is it possible she took my place?"

Her-uben didn't move nor speak for several seconds. "I do not know."

The thought of Anippe finding comfort in the arms of her family terrified Jewell. What if Anippe was there and her family thought everything was all right and they no longer searched for a way to pull her back? "I think I am going to be sick.

"If you saw me there, can you look to see if she is there?"

Her-uben shrugged. "Often the things I see are chosen for me and are not of my will. And those things are always things to come. I do not see Anippe returning to this place." There was sadness in her eyes for Jewell. "If she does not, it may alter what I see for you, and may be why I cannot see how you are to return. Her decisions affect your future too."

Jewell made her way to the lounge and sat, dizzy with the reality of her situation. She knew she was going to have to get to the mirror, no matter the risks.

"You should embrace your place here. The Prince is a good man and will make you happy if you allow it. If you cannot return to your world, then you can make a good one for yourself here. If you do and she returns, perhaps the Princess will benefit from your actions now. It is all about the choices you make."

Jewell didn't know how to respond. On one level she knew Her-uben was right, but that was her head. Her heart was screaming and making it impossible to think of accepting she would never go home. But she nodded, knowing there was no other answer to give. "I will try. But I will not give up until I know there is no way back."

The servant nodded and turned to bow as Amen-ra entered the room. He acknowledged her with a small smile then turned his attention to Jewell. "I have come to take you for a walk. You need exercise and fresh air to clear your head of nonsense."

Jewell glanced at the servant, but she was gathering the remains of their meal and then hurried from the room. "Thank you. That would be nice."

As she expected a smile in response, the lack of one gave legs to Her-uben's analysis of her future should she not comply with the dictates of those who held her life in their hands. With nothing more to say, she walked to Amen-ra and looked him in the eyes before preceding him to the doors that led to the large room where many mingled. Everyone stopped talking and turned to her. To Jewell's surprise, they bowed. She glanced back at Amen-ra and wondered if their actions were for her or for him. She followed his lead and nodded once to acknowledge them, then headed to an opening that, many stairs later, led outside.

She stopped there and waited for Amen-ra to join her. "Was that for me or for you?"

Amen-ra looked down at her, his brows lifted. "What?"

"The bowing. I don't know if I am still a princess in their eyes, or if they were honoring you."

He smiled slightly. "It is good that you question such. Your arrogance in the past would have made the assumption a given. But it was for us both. As my wife, you hold high rank."

Though that didn't exactly answer her question, Jewell let it go. "Where are we going?"

Seriousness entered Amen-ra's eyes as he looked at her.

"We are going to walk in the garden of Ra, then we are to visit the High Priestess to gain her blessing on our union. In three days you will lie with me, and we will begin a family."

Jewell wouldn't allow herself to react. Finally she nodded. If she was stuck in ancient Egypt forever, then there were worse people to spend it with than him. She just hoped she would be able to go through with it when the time came, if she was still here.

"You fear becoming a woman?"

Jewell shook her head. She didn't fear that at all. Mentally and emotionally she was years beyond the child whose body she wore. Even though Anippe was clearly marital age in this time, and was fully capable of engaging in a sexual relationship in Jewell's time, she was actually still a child as far as Jewell was concerned. But there was no way to express that to Amen-ra. Nor to explain that, as attractive as she found him and as much as she liked him despite his caveman attitudes, there were too many impediments for them to pursue a relationship. But she had to say something he might understand.

"I fear being in a marriage with a man I do not love."

Amen-ra reached out and stopped her forward progress and turned her to him. "It is out of our hands. If we do not consummate this marriage, it is not real in the eyes of the Nisu. As he knows I am more than willing to fulfill my duties, it falls on you to prove to him you have changed." A gleam entered his eyes.

"You look upon me with interest, at times even with desire in your eyes. Can you not let that be the basis of taking a step toward the love we both seek?"

Jewell sighed. "It isn't that simple."

Amen-ra grinned. "It is if you allow it to be."

Jewell resumed her walk without responding, taking the bricked path that led in the direction of the Nile. She knew Amen-ra was close behind even though he walked with silent steps. There was really no choice in the matter. She had given her word she would comply with both the Nisu and with Amen-ra. It was strange, knowing she had no choice. She was going to have to let go of the woman she was raised to be and be the woman fate had thrown her into, unless she was willing to fight everyone.

The garden ended at a set of stairs that led from the garden down to the grasslands and on to the great river. From the tall perch Jewell could see the twists and turns of the Nile for quite a distance. She continued to look at it as Amen-ra stopped at her side.

"You are beautiful."

Jewell glanced over at him and smiled. "Are you trying to woo me?"

Amen-ra grinned again. "I don't know about woo. I am only stating a fact."

"Thank you. You are something to look at yourself."

Though his brows drew together, his grin stayed in place. "If you find me attractive, you will enjoy our joining."

Jewell knew there was no point in trying to make him understand attraction wasn't enough for her. Or even like. Or, come to think of it, being saved by him. She had always dreamed of something more. A flash. A sizzle. An earthquake...*something* more than having no choice. "If I told you that I needed more, what would you say?"

Amen-ra shrugged. "I would ask what you needed."

"What if I didn't know the answer, only knew that something was missing?"

Clearly perplexed, Amen-ra sighed. "What do you need from *me*, Anippe?"

Jewell smiled sadly. What she needed was for him to not think of her as Anippe but to look at her with adoration because she was Jewell. It wasn't his fault, but that made no difference. "I need for you to believe me."

Amen-ra stood up straighter and looked out over the landscape. His silence was disheartening, though Jewell knew she shouldn't expect more from him than he could fathom. She reached over and placed her hand on his bulging bicep. When he looked down at her, she gave him a smile. "Would you let me prove it to you?"

Amen-ra's brows lifted. "How would you do that?"

"I could tell you about all the amazing things that are going to happen in the future."

He shrugged. "You might be a good storyteller."

Jewell shook her head. "I'm not. I'm not a good liar at all. But you have to give me a chance.

"You asked what I needed from you. This is it. This is the only thing I need. That you give me a chance to prove to you that I am Jewell, and not Anippe."

Chapter Eleven

Amen-ra's agreement to spend *getting to-know-you* time with Jewell didn't happen. Within minutes of their discussion, Anippe's father surprised everyone abiding within the palace with a grand announcement. At least everyone *else* seemed to think it grand. All it did for Jewell was increase her fears that she'd never find a moments peace, to look for a way back home. Security was to increase and the wedding celebration preparations were to begin immediately and last the next couple days. The only shining light, as far as she was concerned, was that Amen-ra was needed elsewhere. As the castle was thrown into action, she was handed over to the guard who'd delivered the message. Without so much as acknowledging her before he left, Amen-ra directed the guard to escort her back to her rooms immediately.

The number of voices and the sounds of many fast moving feet just outside of her rooms increased by the hour. The usual relaxed atmosphere of the royals and their caregivers was replaced with turbo-charged energy that seemed to vibrate in the air. While everyone was running to and fro, gossip about the Nisu and the beautiful young girl was shared and speculated upon by those who came and went throughout the keep, even by those carrying out the duties as Jewell's servants.

As launderers, cleaners, food bearers, and seamstresses came and went, she learned the bride to be was a distant relation just come of marriageable age, though Jewell had no idea if anyone actually knew how old the poor child was. What she did know was her new husband had been assigned to guard and protect the *Queen-to-be*. He'd have no time for his own princess, and he wouldn't until after the festivities, at which point she'd be expected to fulfill her duties as his wife.

When the wedding day arrived much too quickly, though her stomach was in knots, Jewell prepared herself mentally as best she could for the wedding celebration, while trying to keep thoughts of the upcoming night at bay. Were it not for her position as Amen-ra's wife, she knew she wouldn't even be allowed to attend the ceremony, a celebration of magnificent proportions according to all. She wished she could beg off attending, but she already knew she would be watched every minute until she was handed to her husband following the wedding. Her only hope was to somehow slip away from whoever was assigned to watch her, sneak into the Nisu's apartments, and find the mirror to see if she could somehow return to her own time.

Jewell's mind churned with possible escape scenarios and then discarded each one as too dangerous. Her-uben took care of all her physical preparations. She braided, pinned and made ringlets of Jewell's auburn hair with devices that strongly resembled modern cosmetology equipment, without the electricity. While the servant used a small wooden stick to paint the almond-shaped outline around Jewell's eyes, she explained each step. The kohl, made from black galena and shaped to resemble the falcon eye of the God Horus, was used as a form of protection. Her-uben then applied green eye paint below Jewell's eyes, to ward off evil spirits and help prevent eye disease. She painted purple shadow upon Jewell's eyelid saying she chose the color because it complemented Jewell's hair color and skin tone, and because it was Her-uben's personal favorite of all the available colors. The makeover ended after the servant applied a mixture of sesame and Moringa oils to Jewell's face and body, to preserve youthfulness and prevent wrinkles. *Not that Jewell had any*, Her-uben was quick to add.

After Jewell's body was draped and bejeweled, sandals were placed upon her feet and tied by the servant, though she'd tried repeatedly to convince Her-uben it wasn't necessary she be waited on hand and foot.

"It is my pleasure," was always the response, so Jewell eventually stopped protesting and allowed the servant to do as she willed, relieved Her-uben sent the other two servants away so that they were alone.

"I need to know something."

Her-uben stilled while in the process of tying Jewell's golden rope at her waist. "Yes, Princess?"

Jewell swallowed. "Am I always watched, even in these rooms?"

Her-uben nodded and lifted her index finger to cover her lip. She stepped back and walked to the apartment's main entrance, then returned. "Because I am in here with you, the guards are several feet from the door. But when you are alone, they stand right outside the opening." She exhaled. "Never assume you have privacy. There are those who listen for any opportunity to make trouble for another. And you made many enemies when you were actually Princess Anippe."

Jewell frowned. "How? Why?"

Her-uben lowered her voice even more. "She was mean. Very full of her own power. There was no kindness in her."

Jewell sighed. "She was a brat."

Her-uben smiled. "I like that word. Yes. She was a *brat*." Her-uben looked at Jewell and then smiled. "She would have never spoken to me unless it was to shame me in some way. She certainly never would have thanked me for anything, as you always do. It is most pleasant serving you."

Jewell kept her voice as low as the servant's so she was almost whispering. "I do not believe in one being forced to serve another. If it was your choice, and you were being paid to do so, or if you volunteered because it was a cause you believed in or out of love, then I would have no problem with it. I do not need you to wait on me, but I am very appreciative of your friendship."

"And I yours. It is a wonderful thing to know another who has mystical powers. I have long feared mine, and always kept them to myself. If it were known I could *see*, I would either be feared or put somewhere where my only purpose in life would be to feed the Nisu information, to help him remain ahead of his enemies. Either way every minute of my life would be that of a prisoner. I have heard stories of this before. Mystics are exalted but also must be controlled so they do not become more powerful than the Nisu."

Jewell nodded. "I understand. My own family is full of mystics, but we too must tread with caution. There are those who fear such things, even in my time."

Her-uben nodded, her eyes serious. "I think you must be very careful even with Amen-ra. He is a romantic and at heart a generous man to the women here, unlike most who treat us as vessels for their pleasures and care not for us beyond that. But he is still a man who believes his duty to the Nisu is the purpose of his existence. You will endanger yourself if you give him reason to fear you could be a threat to the Nisu."

Jewell nodded, realizing she may have already placed herself in danger by trying to convince him of who she really was. She would have to correct that mistake as soon as possible, which meant she would have to retract her story and vow to submit to him as her husband, unless she could disappear back into her own time before the evening ended.

"I have to get to the mirror tonight while everyone is celebrating. I just don't know how I will manage getting away from those guarding me. If Amen-ra must stay with the bride until she is wed, it has to be before then. Once he has me, I don't believe he will let me out of his sight."

Her-uben frowned as she nodded. "If you can, it would be best for you to slip away as the ceremony begins at the temple of Isis. All will remain outside praying, as the Nisu is to be alone in the sanctuary gifting Her and paying homage for Her favor. She is the goddess of motherhood and fertility, and producing more children enhances his position with Her. He will then supplicate himself and give offerings to the other gods so they will uphold *maat*, which will keep order in the universe. Order keeps him in the highest power until he joins them in the afterlife. After this is done, he will be led to the Nile where he will reveal his body to all those gathered so they may see his might and prowess, and so his young male slaves may wash his body in the waters of the *Mother Who Sustains All Life*. As he will be expected to impregnate his wife this night, he will allow them to stimulate him so he may release old seed into a virgin male slave, so only fresh seed will fill her womb. Afterwards the boy is taken to be killed in sacrifice to the gods."

Jewell listened intently, horrified to the point it made her stomach hurt, while trying to figure where this allowed time for her to slip away. "He will do all this in front of a crowd of people?"

Her-uben nodded, her eyes sad. "It has gone exactly this way with each of his unions. I expect this time will be no different. And, as you can imagine, it captures the attention of all. They will not be paying attention to you."

Jewell nodded. "I'm sure! But where are Amen-ra and the bride through all of this?"

"They are standing at the front of the gathering. This display of sex-play between the Nisu and his male slaves is meant to stimulate her womb into accepting his seed. The sacrifice of the chosen one is meant to show her all bend to the will of a Nisu and are put to death when they do not."

Jewell would think it more likely to scare the poor child to death, but she kept the thought to herself. "But why kill the slave?"

"Because the boy will be untutored in male love-play. The intercourse will be forced upon him, and pain and instinct will cause him to try to get away, possibly even fight the Nisu. The other slaves will allow this only until the Nisu commands them to hold him still until the deed is done. It is hard to watch, yet we are commanded to do so."

"This is horrible!"

Her-uben nodded. "Yes." She lowered her voice even more. "Princess Anippe got her cruelty honestly." She looked at Jewell, her eyes fearful, as if she regretted saying anything bad about the Nisu and his daughter. Then she shrugged. "Amen-ra will likely have to carry the child bride to her wedding and hold her up throughout the ceremony, as most are falling apart by this time. From stories older servants have told, your mother…*Anippe's* mother, was the only one of all of his wives that did not. She watched, and smiled, and enjoyed the spectacle. She was always his favorite wife. When she died, the Nisu was in mourning for a very long time. Anippe was only a baby at the time, and he turned his love for the mother onto the child. According to the elders, he is grieving still over the loss of both, now Anippe has disgraced herself."

Jewell nodded, torn between understanding the pain of loss and the horror of what was about to happen. "How can everyone allow this? It is wrong!"

Her-uben shrugged. "The Nisu is a god on earth, and we must obey our gods or evil will befall us. We are born to serve the Nisu. He is our vessel to the heavenly gods and the afterlife we seek."

Jewell blew out a breath, knowing she would have to find a way out of this as soon as possible. To protest what was about to happen would only land her in more trouble. When Her-uben stepped back and declared her ready, she wished for a mirror to see what she looked like in all the finery Her-uben had placed on her. Which brought her thoughts back to her quest. "I will try to make the guards stay at the back of the group while this is all going on, and since I have no desire to watch the rape of a slave, *ever*, I will try to slip away. If you can distract the guards, I will make my way to the Nisu's room to find the mirror. I only hope finding it makes a difference."

Her-uben stood very still for a few seconds, and then she frowned. "It is not the mirror you must find. It is the stone. I just saw you standing before it so I believe you will make it to the Nisu's room. There is someone standing behind you, and…I don't know what happens because the vision ended. But the stone at the top, it was throwing off light. I think it is what is making you move from your time to ours." She searched Jewell's face. "You need the stone."

Jewell nodded, ignoring the chill that swept through her. "You could not see who was standing behind me in the reflection?"

Her-uben shook her head. "No. Only that it was a guard with large arms. He was too tall. I couldn't see more than that."

Jewell nodded again. She would have to be very careful to make sure she wasn't followed into the Nisu's apartment. "I'll need something sharp to dig it out. No one has allowed me access to a knife, or any sharp object for that matter. Can you secure one?"

Without hesitation, Her-uben nodded. "I will. But you must be very careful not to get caught with it, or we will both be endangered."

Jewell's heart nearly burst with the love of friendship for the young woman standing before her. "You are placing yourself in great danger by helping me. I would not hold it against you if you feel the need to back away now."

Her-uben smiled. "I am meant to be here. To be your servant. I know you are blessed of the gods, and even if my actions take me into the next life, I will find favor. You are the daughter of kings. Even if not in your time, it is your heritage."

Jewell looked at her in surprise. "How did you know that?"

Her-uben asked permission, and then took Jewell's hand. She raised Jewell's arm so she could point to the small winged, dragon-shaped birthmark, nestled beneath, just above the armpit. Jewell gasped, surprised to find Anippe had the same mark she'd carried since birth. Though she hadn't thought about hers for years, Jewell looked at the fanciful stain on Anippe's skin, and wondered if that was their connection.

"That is the symbol of our royal ancestors. You are always under their protection, no matter what time you dwell in, and by assisting you, so am I, even if not in this lifetime."

Jewell hoped she was right. There was nothing she needed more at the moment than protection. "Thank you for all you are doing. But please don't endanger yourself any more than necessary. I could not bear to think my actions would cause you pain or worse."

"It is time."

Jewell and Her-uben turned to face the servant named Heneny. Jewell nodded and turned to smile at Her-uben and followed Heneny from the room. The guard who had escorted her from Amen-ra days before met her at the door. He was almost as tall as Anippe's husband and certainly had arms as muscular. Jewell knew she would have to make sure he was otherwise occupied when she attempted to escape him.

Rather than turning in the direction that lead to the gardens she and Amen-ra had walked through, they went straight until a wide hall led them to the throne room. Jewell swallowed, remembering the spectacle that led to the torturous wedding preparations. Only this time the large room held only a few people. All of them turned to her and bowed, and Jewell exhaled a breath she hadn't realized she'd been holding.

She nodded in acknowledgement to each as she approached them and responded with a small smile of her own when they did the same. Though there were a few who looked at her with distaste, she smiled at them as well.

"We are to head to the temple of Isis and await your father's return. It is good to see Amen-ra has tamed you," the guard said, grinning.

Jewell glanced at him, but said nothing. If everyone thought Anippe's husband had something to do with the difference in her behavior, it would work in her favor. She simply nodded and continued to move forward.

"I meant no insult."

Jewell glanced over at him again, this time really looking at him. She could see a resemblance between the guard accompanying her and the one Anippe had been forced to marry. "Are you related to Amen-ra?"

A hint of pleasure lit his eyes. "I am his younger brother, Akins."

Jewell nodded. No wonder they had such similar features and build, though Akins features didn't look quite as stern. "And you are being forced to guard me. Does Amen-ra have no faith in his prowess as a man? Does he think I will flee while he hovers over the poor woman who must marry my father?"

Suddenly the sternness appeared. "It is disrespectful of you to speak of such things. I think my brother will have to beat you regularly."

Jewell wanted to punch him in the nose. "Your brother will not beat me, *ever.*"

Akins shrugged. "You are right. Amen-ra only pleases the women. Perhaps he will allow me to do so in his stead."

You and what army?

Jewell kept her thought to herself, but the younger brother would find his hands full if he tried to lay a finger on her. "I am still a princess, *guard*. Do not test me."

With a mocking bow, he indicated for her to precede him. Jewell was glad he could no longer see her face. Everything she'd said was in an attempt to sound more like Anippe, but it made her insides quiver at men thinking they had any right to abuse women. She had to slip away from him before she ended up battered and abused…again.

When they reached the end of the palace, they proceeded down a long bricked walk that led to the temple. Though it was not as large as the palace, it was still quite impressive and had a huge courtyard where hundreds gathered to kneel and pray. Jewell stopped at the back of the crowd, hoping she wouldn't be forced to move forward. She turned to Anippe's brother-in-law. "I will stay here, if I may."

He looked at her curiously for a moment and then nodded before pulling a rolled matt from behind his back. He unfurled it and placed it before her. "As you wish."

Jewell sighed, relieved. But her relief was short-lived.

He stood behind her and waited. All those kneeling in front of her lowered their faces to their mats then rose, only to lower themselves again as they prayed. She mimicked their motions, wishing the matt were a little more comfortable. It didn't take long before her knees were numb, and she felt awkward knowing Amen-ra's brother was there to watch her behind every time she face-planted. Thankfully, before she begged to be able to stop, a cheer went up and the Nisu appeared at the entrance to the temple. She allowed Akins to help her to her feet then stood back as a procession followed the Nisu from the temple to the path leading to the Nile. His personal servant was there, as well as the young slaves who would play a part in the upcoming ritual, though from her distance she couldn't see that any of the young slave-boys were resisting what was to come.

A long line of what Jewell suspected were the priests of the temple followed next. Each carried a jar out in front of them, and though Jewell would have been interested in what those were for any other time, for now she could only hope the rituals to come would keep everyone's eyes glued to the ceremony, including her watchdog.

She glanced over to Akins to find him following the progression and couldn't help but smile to herself. When he also smiled, she nearly groaned, thinking he was still watching her with his peripheral vision, until he waved and she turned back to see Amen-ra looking over at them. She nodded to acknowledge him, which seemed to satisfy him, as he turned back to the woman at his side. Once everyone in front of them followed the procession, Jewell looked up at Akins.

With her heart pounding, Jewell waited until the large crowd was once again tucked between her and the man who was supposed to be her father. She bit her lip as she followed the last of them, hoping to escape at the onset of the spectacle that was about to commence. She knew she would need time, and she desperately hoped Her-uben had found an object that would allow her to remove the precious stone from the mirror's frame.

So much depended on so many things falling into place, yet she had no control over any of them. Akins had to be so distracted he wouldn't notice her departure, the guards at the palace had to be likewise occupied, the mirror had to be easy to find once she entered the Nisu's apartment, and the stone had to be the object that could get her back home.

If any one of those things failed to work out, she was likely signing her death warrant attempting the escape.

Refusing to overthink any of it, Jewell settled at the back of the large crowd, relieved Akins wasn't trying to get them closer. She covertly scanned the crowd and gauged her distance from the stairs leading to the palace gardens. She peeked occasionally to see what Akins was paying attention to while she pretended to watch as the priests lined up on either side of the Nisu along the Nile. As the Nisu threw off is robe to reveal his aging body, a cheer went up and continued as he held up his arms, turned around slowly, and was then led into the water with the assistance of his young slaves.

A gagged and bound naked young man was led forward and made to stand upon the stage that had been built just for the wedding celebration. The chatter of the spectators increased, as did periodic cheering and clapping. The sacrificial lamb looked terrified, as he should be. Sickened, Jewell had to stop looking. She glanced over to find Akins straining to see what was going on down at the river and took a small step back.

She waited a heartbeat and took another step, and another, each time holding her breath. She feared he would turn to her and demand she return to his side. With a quick glance behind her, Jewell continued her slow progress until she was at the tall grasses someone had planted as decoration sometime in the past. Her stomach hurting in earnest now, she turned and crawled up the stairs quickly, fearing someone would shout her name. When she made it to the top, she stayed low, not wanting those below to see her lone figure standing out.

Sweat formed and ran down her brow. She continued her progress through the maze of plants decorating the garden she and Amen-ra had walked through only a few days before, nearly vomiting when a loud scream tore through the air. She jumped, realizing the poor slave's gag must have been removed. Sapphire shivered in horror, but refused to look back... She didn't need to. There was no doubt that he was now in the clutches of the Nisu, and she could do nothing but try to save herself. The screams continued but were soon covered by what sounded like victorious shouts.

Not knowing if the shouting was for the Nisu and his disgusting ritual, or if someone had discovered she was missing, Jewell made a dash for the steps leading into the palace. She had to stop short when she saw two guards chatting with Her-uben as she flirted and poured them liquid from a long-necked jar. Her-uben flashed a look her way and then smiled coyly at one as she stepped closer to the other to rub her body against him. Both men were completely engrossed in the beautiful servant, and Jewell sent her a silent *Thank you.*

Her heart felt like a jackhammer had taken up residence in it, but Jewell knew she had no time to hesitate. Even if Akins hadn't noticed her disappearance yet, it was only a matter of time. At least there weren't feet already pounding her way, so she made her way as quietly and quickly as she could to the hall that led to her rooms and then to the stairs leading to the Nisu's apartment.

And there, at the bottom of the stairs, was a curved knife. It was beautifully made with a jewel-encrusted handle and was larger than she would have expected, but she had no time to give it more thought as she scooped it up and ran up the stairs.

She paused at the entrance to the Nisu's apartment and tried to listen for any sounds coming from inside. Her heartbeats were pounding in her ears and it made hearing impossible. Jewell wet her dry lips and took a step inside. Unlike the time before when she'd been trying to escape as

Anippe, the room was completely decorated in flowers and filled with large trunks, which she could only surmise belonged to the new bride. Knowing servants could arrive at any moment to begin the process of moving the princess into her new home, she left the sitting room and made her way to first one bedroom, then a smaller one where the mirror leaned against the far wall.

Jewell ran across the room and stopped before it. Seeing her reflection as Anippe startled her for only a moment and then she quickly looked the frame over. Shaking with emotion, knowing this *was* the mirror her father had made, she ran her fingers over the raised hieroglyphics and felt the wood vibrate.

Excitement gripped her as she looked up to the stone Her-uben believed held the magic to get her home. She ran her fingers over the stone, and it lit and threw colors across her hand and Jewell could feel it pulling her forward.

"Anippe!"

Jewell screamed as Amen-ra ran across the room and grabbed her. He locked his arms around her waist and lifted her as he knocked the knife from her hand. She elbowed him in the stomach and he dropped her instantly. She landed on her feet and jumped forward to touch the stone again. The room started spinning around them and increased until the speed of it made her dizzy and nauseated. Amen-ra's eyes were huge as he stared at her in horror. He blinked and jumped forward to wrap his arms around her again. Lightning flashed and thunder boomed within the walls of the wind tunnel closing in on them. Jewell glanced up to find Amen-ra looking down at her. His eyes held fear but also stark determination. She had no idea if he meant to protect her or kill her, but whatever was happening was happening to them both.

Since she hadn't gone through this type of transition before, at least not that she remembered, Jewell's heart nearly stopped when the floor dropped out from underneath her and she felt herself falling. Amen-ra's arms tightened around her almost to the point of suffocation, but Jewell couldn't protest as the wind had already stolen her breath. As oxygen depleted she felt herself traveling downward on the spiraling road to oblivion. Too weak to fight it, she gave in and blacked out.

Chapter Twelve

Jewell's vision was too blurred to make out all the faces hovering over her, but she could clearly hear the distress of several female voices. She tried to sit up, but something heavy was holding her down. Whatever was pinning her to the cushions was also tickling her nose. She blew out a breath, and the softness lifted and then fell back over her nose again.

"What is that?" She'd tried to shout it, but her words came out as a breathless whisper.

"Oh my! She's awake. Help me get him off of her!"

Jewell was able to take a deep breath once the weight was pulled from her chest and what she'd thought blurry vision suddenly cleared as long hair slid over, and away from her face. She stared up at the familiar faces of her mother, aunts, sisters, as a thump sounded beside her. Before she could speak her mother dove onto the couch and pulled her into a hug, again cutting off her oxygen. As happy as she was to realize she'd made it back, she was afraid she was about to pass out again.

"I thought we'd lost you for good!"

Rayne's tears splashed on her face as she pulled back and smiled down at her daughter. "But who is he? How did you bring him with you? Are you all right? Does anything hurt?"

"Rayne, child, I think you're cutting off her oxygen."

The droll sound of a much older woman's voice caused Jewell to turn her head enough to see her great-aunts had arrived. She was still struggling to breathe and couldn't acknowledge them. She turned back to Rayne who was climbing off her. Finally, she took several cleansing breaths before questions were bouncing around the room. She struggled to sit up and was relieved when Sapphire stepped forward and assisted her.

"Thanks."

Sapphire's eyes were wet with unshed tears. "I thought we'd lost you too!" She pointed down to the floor where the backside of Amen-ra's large immobile body was on display. His loincloth skirt was flipped up so that his butt cheeks were visible to the room of seemingly frozen women. Jewell stared at him before looking up at her family.

"How did he get here, too? He held on to me. That's all I know."

Immediately the room came to life. Dia bent over Amen-ra and poked at him repeatedly, lifting and dropping his arm. Haven moved over to Jewell and placed her hands on different parts of Jewell's body for a few seconds at a time. As her aunt had learned over the years not only to control the healing aspects of her touch, she'd also learned to use her senses for diagnostic purposes. Within minutes she took a step back and smiled, pronouncing Jewell healthy right down to the bone marrow. Rayne ran to the kitchen to wet a washcloth, ran back and wiped at Jewell's brow, and then returned to the kitchen area again to pitch it into the sink before snagging a bottle of water from the refrigerator. Seconds later she thrust it in Jewell's face.

Jewell took the drink and swallowed the refreshing liquid gratefully as she occasionally glanced down to make sure no one was stepping on Amen-ra. Her two great-aunts stood back with smiles that said they found the whole thing amusing. Smiling at them in response, she followed their gaze only to realize Dia was poking at Amen-ra's behind. "Dia! Stop that."

Her younger sister glanced up and smiled. "It's like a rock!"

Jewell rolled her eyes and decided she needed to check on him, though she had no idea what she would do with him once he woke up. Her gaze flew to Haven. "He isn't dead, is he?"

Haven shrugged as all the women moved to stand

around him. Jewell nudged him with her foot, only to have his big hand grasp it, and squeeze.

"Ouch!"

Amen-ra released her foot and rolled himself over, then on up to his feet, startling everyone into scurrying back. His crouching stance made it clear he was ready to do battle, but the confusion in his eyes bespoke his befuddlement to find himself in a small modern living room filled with nearly identical-looking women…discounting the three distinct generations of red-heads, Sapphire's black hair, and Dia's very blond wacky hairdo of the day.

Haven stepped forward and held up her hands so that the palms faced each other. Lightning crackled between them. "Believe me, buddy, you don't want a piece of this."

Amen-ra slowly stood up straight and took his time looking around the room until his gaze landed back on Jewell. She couldn't help but grin as her eyebrows shot up. "I told you so."

He frowned at her as if trying to decide if she was the woman he'd followed through the whirlwind. Finally he spoke, though the words made no sense.

Rayne step toward him slowly but directed her words back to the room at large. "I don't know this language. It must be older than Aramaic." She bowed as those in the palace had bowed to him and his deep and relieved breath was obvious to Jewell. He spoke to her mother, and though his words were indistinguishable, it was obvious he was asking about his confusing situation.

Rayne shook her head at him and held her hands, palms up. "I don't understand you."

He frowned and glanced over to Jewell, speaking again. This time there was an edge of anger to his voice. Jewell walked toward him, stopping at her mother's side. "I don't know the language either. Somehow I easily communicated with him when I was in Anippe's time, even though on this last trip to Never-land she never took over my mind."

Amen-ra's frown deepened, and he took a large step forward. Before he could reach out and touch Jewell,

Destiny stepped between them. She stared at him hard and the floor trembled beneath their feet. Jewell hurriedly placed her hand on her aunt's arm, knowing a full-blown earthquake was a real possibility if Destiny felt her family was in any way threatened. "It's okay, Aunt Dee. He's confused, not dangerous." *At least I hope not.*

Jewell smiled at him as she stepped around her aunt. She hoped her soothing voice would override the problem that he couldn't understand them any more than they could understand him. "Amen-ra. I am Jewell."

He stared at her suspiciously then glanced at the others. His gaze returned to her. He nodded and pointed around the room. Though he spoke again, this time it was like he was explaining something to her. Jewell could only hope it meant he understood, that what she'd told him before, about being from a different time, was true.

Jewell took a step closer and though her mother protested, Jewell held her hand out to him. Amen-ra instantly grabbed her and pulled her against him. Though his hug was crushing, she was more concerned about her relatives forming a circle around him. She thought about telling them to leave him alone for a minute. She considered stomping on his foot to get him to let her go. But the only option she could think of that would throw them all off enough to pay attention to her was to reach up, grasp his jaw, and pull his head down for a kiss.

Immediately his arms relaxed, but his hands tangled in her hair as he plundered her mouth, setting her lips on fire. For a fleeting second Jewell thought she should remind him they had an audience, but even she forgot about them as he deepened the kiss, separating her lips, absorbing her breath, her strength, and her soul. When he lifted his head, he stared down at her, his eyes searching, his breath as shaky as her own. When someone cleared her throat, he glanced up, warily scanning the women encircling them.

Held in a slightly dipped back position, Jewell glanced to her left to see her mother's mouth hanging open and her brows lifted in amusement, while Haven stood at her side with lightning crackling all around her. Jewell turned her head to the right to find Dia looking at him like she was about to test out her magic on him if he moved a muscle, and Sapphire, who stood with a gun pointed straight at his head, glared at him with her sparkling sapphire eyes. She had no idea where Aunt Destiny had gone, but she hoped Amen-ra was steady on his feet is she was behind him.

Great-Aunt Soleli stepped forward and gently lowered the gun until Jewell could no longer see it from her swayed-back position. Somewhere in the back of her mind, a thought—that Dia was more dangerous—registered, but Jewell was still floating on the cloud his kiss had placed her upon, and she couldn't form the words to warn anyone.

Sapphire wanted him to do it again and maybe again, but a sudden hard pounding on the front door had him jerking her against him. He swung her around and clamped her against his back, protectively, as he turned toward the sound. Figuring it was another family member, Jewell peeked around Amen-ra as Destiny opened the door. Kevin stepped up to the opening and then stopped dead, irritation lining the corners of his mouth.

Jewell tried to move around Amen-ra, but she barely got further than a few inches as he was either shielding her or trying to prevent her from escaping his hold. She patted his arm and smiled when he looked down at her. After a few seconds hesitation, he eased his hold enough so that she could move to his side, facing the intruder. Jewell groaned. This was the last thing she needed! "What are you doing here?"

Kevin looked from Jewell to Amen-ra, to the others, and back to Jewell again. "I thought something had happened to you! I thought the fact that you weren't answering my calls or texts meant you had gotten hurt or had died, or *some* stupid thing. But I see you are just fine. Throwing a damned party! A damned costume party! What the hell, Jewell! Is he a stripper?"

With each of Kevin's angry words, Amen-ra's body tightened, as did his grip. Jewell patted his arm again and tried to take a step forward, but he wasn't allowing her to budge.

"Serves you right for showing up uninvited, Butt-face."

Jewell nearly groaned and wanted to tell Dia to *shush*, but she had bigger fish to fry...as in one trembling-with-energy Egyptian. She reached up and placed her palm on Amen-ra's jaw and caressed it, until his attention was once again on her and his body was no longer straining toward Kevin. "It is fine."

Though it was clear he couldn't understand the words, his lips lifted slightly. His garbled language came back at her gently, and Jewell couldn't help but smile.

"If you're done playing with the stripper, I'd like a word."

Amen-ra's head whipped back around to face Kevin, and Jewell knew things were about to get ugly. The last thing she needed was for the ancient male to snap the modern male in half. Wishing there was another way to handle things, but knowing too much in the category of unexplainable was a real possibility, she turned to her great-aunt. "Momma told me a story when I was small. You have the power to make someone forget something, and they never remember it. I need someone to forget me."

The aunts smiled at each other before Soleli stepped toward Kevin. Though he looked at her like she was about to stick a knife in his heart, he stood his ground. "What the hell is this woman going to do? Wipe my mind clean?" He laughed nervously when there was silence in the room.

Soleli lifted her hands and immediately Kevin's body stiffened and strained as it tilted her way. Although Jewell couldn't see the magical pull, it was obvious as Kevin rose up to the tips of his toes and slid across the floor until he was inches from her aunt. Soleli inhaled deeply and softly spoke the incantation, ending it with, "Go thee well, remember no more, go thee well."

Amen-ra held firmly to Jewell from the moment Kevin reacted to her great-aunt's powers. When Kevin returned to his normal stance and simply turned to leave without a word to anyone, the Egyptian turned Jewell so she was facing away from him as he lifted her off the floor and turned a full circle. Words of angry fear flew from his lips, and Jewell knew he was panicking. He'd not only landed in another time, he was obviously aware he'd landed in a den of mystics. She wanted to reassure him, but he was spinning with her as if trying to make sure none of the women encircling him would be at his back.

Aunt Soleli stepped toward them and he stopped spinning, though Jewell's mind did not. She shook her head hoping to clear away the dizziness, but it only helped a little and she felt like a half-stuffed floppy toy in Amen-ra's arms. She forced her head up and back, so that she could use his massive chest as a pillow.

"Don't hurt him, please."

Soleli simply smiled at her gently before bowing to Amen-ra. When she began speaking to him, in what was obviously his own language, Jewell felt his hold ease, and as they conversed, his heartbeat started to slow. She didn't want to interrupt the bonding of her great-aunt and the man who still had her dangling in his arms, but she was becoming exhausted with the entire circus and a little nauseated as well.

"Aunt Soleli, will you please ask Amen-ra to release me. I'm feeling a little sick."

With a concerned nod she looked back into Amen-ra's eyes, and again spoke his language. Though he seemed to hesitate, he eventually lowered Jewell so she was again standing on the floor, but he didn't ease his hold on her. He looked down at her, and then to Soleli, and spoke to her great-aunt again. When Soleli smiled and glanced at Rayne, Jewell couldn't help but question their conversation.

"What is he saying?"

Soleli took a deep breath before turning to the women filling the room with the threat of magic. "First, we need to let him know we will not harm him. Haven, dear, please put away your lightning. Destiny, darling, you're wearing out Mother Nature. Stop making her vibrate. Dia, honey, I know you mean well, but we don't want the young man to explode, or any of the rest of us for that matter. Please, no more pointing." She turned back to Jewell as the others complied, amusement glittering in her eyes. "Jewell, child, he says you are his wife, and he wants to know where he can take you to bed."

"Now we're talking!"

Jewell shook her head, not in the mood for Dia's sense of humor at the moment. "Dia, don't."

Dia looked Amen-ra up and down. "If you don't want him, I'm up for a new challenge."

Sapphire glared at their youngest sister. "She's married to him, you dolt!"

Jewell shook her head. "Not really. He married Anippe."

Dia smiled. "So there. He's free. She's long dead and probably mummified."

Soleli chuckled. "Well, as far as he's concerned, Jewell is Anippe. And he has no intention of letting her out of his sight."

"So what's this thing about wiping someone's memory? Can't you do it to him, too?"

Soleli shook her head at Sapphire. "No. He has been allowed to come here for a reason. If I wipe his mind, and we attempt to send him back, it could drastically change the balance of more than just his life." She concentrated on Jewell. "You and he are connected, for whatever reason, and until that reason is revealed, we must proceed as though wiping his memory were never an option."

Jewell nodded. "Okay. So, can you make him understand that I am me, and not Anippe?"

Soleli shook her head. "I have tried, but he refuses to accept it. I think he is on sensory overload at the moment, which is understandable, but given time, he may come to accept it."

"*May?* And what if he doesn't?" Rayne asked, moving closer to her daughter, keeping a wary eye on Amen-ra.

Soleli shrugged. "Then Jewell will need to teach him to

be a man of this time." She smiled. "And she will be the one to decide if she is willing to consummate their marriage." Soleli laughed. "It seems to be of great concern to him."

Jewell's heart thudded. She'd forgotten the promise she'd made. Had she not managed to transport them back to the present, she would have already been forced to sleep with him. Jewell cleared her throat. "Please tell him that this changes everything and that I am not his wife, but we will try to figure out a way to get him back to her."

Soleli nodded and translated. Jewell felt his arms loosen, but he still wasn't releasing her. She turned in his arms and looked up at him. As if fearful to have his attention diverted, it was several seconds before he glanced down. Jewell smiled at him sadly. "Please translate for me. Amen-ra, you are safe here. No one will harm you. But I am Jewell Cavanaugh-White, not Anippe, like I told you before, when we were in your time." She paused and was rewarded with a slight nod.

"I will do my best to help you return to your time, if it is possible, but I do not want to go back. Anippe...the *real* Anippe, should be there, waiting for you."

He stared at Jewell a moment longer and then turned his attention to Soleli, to speak to her. When he was done, Jewell's great-aunt translated for him. "He says he doesn't want her. She was a pain in the rear. He wants you to go back with him."

Jewell didn't know what to say. Dia, however, was pointing again, and had several words to share that had Amen-ra backing up with Jewell in tow, as if he'd recognized the danger of that pointing finger.

"Diamond! Stop that." Rayne took a breath and shook her head at her youngest. "You are going to get someone hurt," she stated more calmly and then turned her attention to the Egyptian. "Aunt Sole, please tell him there is no way we will willingly allow Jewell to go back with him. If he wants her, and *if* she wants him, then we will concern ourselves with a way to keep them both here. But that is our only offer."

"What in the world would make you think Jewell would want him?" Sapphire asked.

Rayne turned to her oldest daughter. "Have you not noticed?"

Sapphire's brows pulled together as she slid a glance at the couple. She turned back to her mother and shrugged, and Jewell couldn't help but wonder what her mother was talking about either...unless the attraction she'd always felt for Amen-ra was apparent. She bit her bottom lip and slid a glance up to his face.

"Aunt Soleli, please tell him to release me. I am not going to flee nor will I allow anyone to harm him."

Amen-ra looked down at her when she spoke, and as the words were translated, his arms relaxed even more so Jewell was able to take one step away from him. She turned back to those gathered and made a face. "I don't know how this is going to play out, but I'm going to try to do for Amen-ra what he did for me when we were in his world. I'm going to give him time."

Everyone looked at her curiously and Jewell felt her cheeks heat. "He could have forced himself on me, believing I was Anippe, his new wife. But he didn't. I asked for time to adjust to the situation, though it wasn't the one he thought it was, but that aside, he gave me time."

"So he and this Anippe, a.k.a. *you*, have not consummated the marriage?" Sapphire asked.

Jewell knew her face was probably as red as her hair. "No."

"But you want to, right?"

Jewell slid Dia a glance, wondering if Sapphire had been right all along about how annoying their youngest sibling could be. "Dia, that isn't any of your business."

Dia just grinned so big she showed nearly all her beautiful teeth.

Jewell closed her eyes and shook her head. "Dia is moving out."

"Moved, actually. You've been out for three days."

Jewell nodded but was distracted by the fact that an equivalent amount of time had passed in both worlds. Wondering if it was significant, she asked her mother, who promptly turned the question on their resident time-traveler. Aunt Soleli nodded. "It is very significant. Everything is. We need to know every detail of every moment that passed while you were there."

Jewell nodded and then turned to Sapphire. "I hate to ask you to do this, but can you stay with Mom and Dad for a few days? I think it might be best if I introduce Amen-ra to his new world without anyone around ready to kill him."

Sapphire smiled, a pleasant surprise. "Sure, Sis. As long as you're sure he won't hurt you. I think you could have a lot of fun introducing him to life as we know it." She glared at him and her sapphire eyes shimmered. "But if I even suspect for one second that harm is coming to you, Sis, I will chuck my badge and put a bullet in his skull. Make sure he knows that, Aunt Soleli."

The older woman chuckled. "Honey, he'd have no idea what a bullet is, but I think he's got the gist of your words by your glare and the heat of your tone."

"Good enough."

Jewell rolled her eyes heavenward. "Thanks, Sis." She looked around the room at the women she loved, and smiled. "Well, you guys get out of here. If he is as tired as I am, we won't have any issues tonight."

"Do you think the danger has passed, then? Of you going back again against your will?"

Jewell had forgotten about that. "It is the stone and incantation on the mirror's frame, I believe, that has made all of this possible. I am not entering my room again until we find out how to use it to our advantage to get Amen-ra back to his time, or destroy it for all time if he decides he wants to stay. Either way, once we are done with it, we have to know how to safely place it, or its parts, where no one can ever stumble across them again."

Soleli nodded. "That is very wise, my dear. I think you are coming into your own as a mystic."

Jewell wasn't sure where the great-aunt was going with those words, but she was tired of talking and tired of standing, and she knew Amen-ra wouldn't relax until everyone was gone. Simply smiling at Soleli, Jewell turned to each member gathered. "I have been through much and will fill everyone in soon, but for now, I am tired. Amen-ra is surely tired, and I think I'd just like to lie down and sleep for a while."

"What about him?" Dia asked.

Jewell grinned. "I'm putting him in your room on blankets if I have to, and I'm taking Sapphire's bed."

"What if he refuses to stay in my room?" Dia asked, her grin more than a little telling.

Jewell shrugged. "I'll cross that bridge when I get to it. But please. Everyone go. I'll handle this."

Surprised pleasure lit Rayne's eyes. "Yes, you will. Bye, baby. Call me if you need me." She headed to the door and each aunt and great-aunt said her farewells in turn. Soleli also said parting words to Amen-ra that made him shake his head, but he was grinning. Dia winked at her and said her goodbyes. By the time everyone else was gone, Sapphire had packed a bag and moved forward to give Jewell a hug.

"Be safe. And call me if you need me. I'm staying at the station, rather than going to Mom and Dad's, but I'll be here with an army if you need one."

Jewell smiled and nodded, though she was suddenly nervous once Sapphire walked out the door. She turned to Amen-ra, to find him grinning at her, obviously pleased to have survived the ordeal long enough to have her alone.

Chapter Thirteen

This is awkward.

It would have been hard enough to explain separate sleeping quarters to an archaic man who believed he was her husband, but the language barrier made it downright impossible. After repeatedly leading him to Dia's room and pointing at the stack of blankets she'd placed there, then getting him to lie down on them, before having him follow her back out of the room when she refused to join him, was wearing her nerves to a frazzle. After the fourth attempt she thought he finally got it so she headed to Sapphire's room, but before she knew it she and Amen-ra were facing each other with Sapphire's king-size bed the only barrier between them.

Hoping to distract him from his obvious intent, Jewell motioned for him to follow her into the bathroom where she indicated the toilet. He looked at it curiously for a moment then back at her. She blew out a breath and then lifted the seat. Knowing of no other way to make her point, she stood in front of it, turned to make sure he was watching, then pretended like she was holding a penis and aiming it at the water in the bowl.

Relief filled his eyes and he immediately untied the golden rope holding the loincloth in place. When it landed at his feet, he moved forward and nearly pushed a stunned Jewell into the shower stall before relieving himself with a loud sigh. He started talking, his indistinguishable words flying from his lips as his hard spray hit the bulls-eye, and Jewell could only guess he was expressing gratitude.

With heat-filled cheeks she turned away and tried to ignore the fact that for the first time in her life she was sharing a bathroom with a man, and one who had no modesty at all. When he was done, Jewell hesitated to turn back, but being the neat freak she was, she knew she had no choice but to help him finish the bathroom ritual.

When he reached for her with the hand he'd used to take care of his business, she shook her head and swatted his hand away. "Oh no, you don't." She quickly showed him how to flush, which made him smile at her in surprise, and then took him by the wrist and turned on the water at the sink. She made him hold out his hands so she could squirt liquid soap into them and smiled that he got the idea and washed his hands himself.

"This is going to be like raising a child."

Amen-ra responded in some way, though she was certain he had no more of an idea of what she'd said, than she had of what he'd said. Pushing that thought away as a given, she glanced at him before she had to look away again. Since he was already undressed, she pointed to the shower stall, which he immediately stepped into. With no hesitation at all he turned the knob just like she'd shown him at the sink. When steaming water hit his naked flesh, he jumped out of the shower with a high-pitched scream.

Trying not to laugh, Jewell reached in and turned on the cold as well and waited until the temperature was more than slightly warm and took his hand and held it under the spray. Looking at the showerhead warily, he stepped back in and flashed her a smile followed by another stream of words she couldn't understand. Since he seemed to think he was just supposed to stand under the shower, Jewell reached in and ignored how wet she was getting to grab the shampoo bottle. She squirted a glob in is hand before she indicated he was to put it on his head and scrub at his scalp.

Even though she had to show him the remaining steps to washing and rinsing from head to toe, Jewell couldn't help but enjoy the process as much as he seemed to be. When he was completely rinsed, she had him step out before turning off the water herself. The last thing she wanted was for him to get scalded again.

Amen-ra knew how to dry himself, which was a relief, but it was only then Jewell remembered she had nothing for him to wear. She and her sisters all owned sweatpants, which would have been the only appropriate unisex option, but Amen-ra's thighs were nearly as big as, or possibly even bigger than, their waists.

Not that he seemed to care. Once he was done he dropped the towel to the floor and looked at her like he was awaiting the next adventure. Jewell pressed her lips together and pointed at the towel. "You don't get maid service here, big boy. Pick it up."

He looked at her curiously. Jewell pointed at the towel again, this time jabbing her pointing finger to indicate her displeasure. With a raised brow he bent over and lifted the towel. Satisfied, Jewell pointed to the bar attached to the wall. Though he sent her a frown of displeasure, he hung the towel up and then turned back to her.

"Good boy. Now go away and let me shower." She pointed to the door.

Amen-ra bowed and swept his arm out in a way that indicated he expected her to precede him so she shook her head and flapped her hands to shoo him out of the room. He shook his head and indicated she was to go first again, and Jewell groaned in frustration and led him from the small room. She pointed at the bed and he eagerly jumped on it. Jewell cringed, hoping Sapphire's bedframe hadn't cracked.

She turned abruptly and re-entered the bathroom, quickly locking the door behind her. As expected, he was immediately trying to open it, but she ignored him and stripped off her clothing as quickly as she could.

The warm spray was amazing, but not something she could enjoy as Amen-ra was now banging and shouting at her. Afraid he'd break the door down, she washed her hair and body in record time and then grabbed one of Sapphire's towels from the clean stack to dry her hair and then another to wrap around her body, after deciding she couldn't use Sapphire's robe without asking her permission first. It was bad enough she'd invaded her sister's space when they were all so careful not to do that.

The door splintered and Amen-ra pulled at it, throwing the pieces behind him. Jewell watched in horror as he stepped through the oval opening, looking around as if anyone else could have come in through the walls to abduct her. She pressed her lips together and shook her head. "My father is going to kick your ass and Sapphire will shoot you for sure now."

Clearly unmoved, as he couldn't have understood the threat anyway, Jewell gave up trying to make him feel bad. "Shoo. Back out of here. I need a minute alone."

Amen-ra must have understood *shoo* because he shook his head no and crossed his arms over his massive chest. She pointed at the toilet and then at herself. "I need a minute alone!"

This time his eyes brightened with understanding, but otherwise, he remained as still as a statue.

"Get the hell out!"

That got his attention, and he turned and climbed back out the hole he'd made. When he turned around and peeked back in, she pointed. "Go!" He glared at her, but turned and walked away.

Knowing she was left with no choice but to have him follow her if she tried to make it to a bathroom that still had its door intact, Jewell groaned as she dropped the toilet seat down and lifted her towel enough to sit down and take care of business. Once she was done she looked the door over, unlocked it and swung it open.

Amen-ra was gone. Torn between relief that he hadn't stuck around and fear that he was into something, she held the towel close and ran from the room. He was in the kitchen area. All the cabinet doors hung open, the water was running full blast in the sink, and his bent over strong back, naked butt, and long thick legs were all that were visible as his head was behind the refrigerator door.

Feeling like she had a two-year-old on her hands for sure, she headed to the sink and turned off the faucets, first. When he swung around, it was very clear she was not dealing with a two-year-old. Deciding she was going to have to stop being embarrassed every time she laid eyes on his manhood, Jewell slowly closed each cabinet door and eyed him warily, wishing she'd taken a moment to forage through Sapphire's drawers for clothing, while he'd been scavenging the kitchen for food.

He smiled at her and held up a container. Jewell nodded and held out her hand, having no idea what he'd found. When she stepped closer, she saw the refrigerator was full of plastic containers and realized her family had probably stocked up while they held vigil over her body for the past few days. She smiled at him and lifted the rubber lid to find a seven layer salad, but he'd already turned back to lift out another.

Jewell pointed to the counter and then sat her container on it, and he did the same. This time he didn't wait for her to open it, but did so himself, then looked over at her with a smile that she could only interpret as saying, *I killed that there bear.*

Imagining the country twang that made up the thought caused Jewell to laugh. Amen-ra looked at her curiously, as if trying to decide if she was laughing at him. Whatever he decided was lost on her as he moved quickly and pulled her into his arms. His lips were soft and tasted of springtime; his arms were like steel but held her in warmth. His rock hard body was an anchor in her storm-tossed life, and all the arguments she should have come up with vaporized and were no more. She gave in and kissed him back with an urgency that left her breathless and shaking with need like she'd never known existed.

Amen-ra lifted her and headed straight to the bedroom. Jewell knew she should protest, but there was nothing she wanted more at the moment than to get lost in the wonder of him, the taste of him. Thoughts melted as he gently placed her on her feet next to the bed and grasped her jaw so that he could look deeply into her eyes. Though his voice was deep, he spoke with honey-coated words and even though she couldn't understand them, she felt like he was asking her permission. Mesmerized, Jewell nodded, and he smiled right before she felt the towel slipping from her body to land at her feet.

He lifted her again, anchoring her back with one bulging arm, and scooping her legs up so he held her just above her knees with the other. He took her mouth in a laboriously slow kiss that melted time as well as her strength. He moved with a slowness that seemed deliberate. His masterful lips glided from her lips to her cheeks, to the outer edges of her eyes, to her temples and forehead, until he had worshiped every nuance of her face. He pulled back to smile at her before climbing onto the bed to gently place her in its center.

The cool sheets at her back contrasted sharply with the fire building in her body, and Jewell never wanted anything in her life as much as she wanted him. She reached up and ran her fingers over his jaw, her thumbs over the sides of his strong nose, then brushed each over his full lips.

He smiled at her and Jewell couldn't help but smile back. His words began, sounding like a chant, or an incantation. She listened intently as everything inside of her strained to have his lips back on hers, his body pressed harder against hers, his manhood filling her.

She wished she understood. Wished he could understand her words as well, as she wanted so badly to tell him how he made her, for the first time in her life feel like a woman, how he made her want with a passion she never knew existed, how he made her dream things she had never before known to dream.

When he finished speaking, he lowered his head and took her mouth again to tease and tantalize, to tickle and torture, and somehow she knew whatever he'd said had just been sealed with a kiss and a promise.

His gentleness as he paid homage to her body stole her breath time and again, and she responded by giving back in equal measure. Touches were followed by tastes, kisses made her high and weakly dizzy at the same time. The warmth of him as he slid over her body in his quest to know all her secrets made her writhe with want until *finally*, he slid into her, filled her, and what had been slow and easy became wild and frantic.

Jewell strained against the building pressure of crashing, cresting, and receding waves ricocheting within her body, and the heat of molten lava where he joined with her. He began speaking again as his strained body moved with the precision of a satin coated piston, creating a friction that had her gasping for breath, and digging her fingernails into the flesh at his back. A moist sheen coated his face and body, and he moaned through clenched teeth as he continued his sweet assault. Her own body glistened with the labor of their union as she continued to hold off against the inevitable that would truly make her his...until with a scream of defeat, she could hold out no more.

Amen-ra's shout followed as hot liquid spilled into her and filled her. His body strained against hers, motionlessly but for desperate breaths, and that which was still throbbing and thrashing inside of her as if it had a life of its own. She rode out the climax and slid down the aftermath with him, and then found her lips locked once more in a celebration of satisfaction, and Jewell was very much afraid, *love*.

Time lost meaning as he continued to kiss her, to speak soft words to her, to snuggle with her before he again explored her body, taking her to paradise and back once more. As they lay there in the afterglow of a second coupling, Amen-ra's stomach grumbled, and they smiled at each other. Jewell forced herself to sit up, unconcerned now about her nudity, or his.

"I guess we need to eat," she said, making the motion by putting her hand to her mouth. He nodded, though she could tell he was in no hurry to leave their bed. "Then get your lazy butt up. You're in my world now, and modern women don't wait on men hand and foot!"

He grinned at her and she would have sworn he knew what she was saying, but he still didn't move. Shaking her head, Jewell rose and headed to the bathroom. Although the door had a large splintered hole in the center of it, she shut it anyway, hoping he would get the message that she needed privacy. Since he didn't appear just outside of it, she quickly cleaned herself up and pulled on the robe Sapphire had hanging on a decorative hook. Sapphire's concerns once she came home to see her door destroyed made using the robe seem like nothing.

Jewell returned to the kitchen to find Amen-ra lifting the container of lasagna to his nose. She grinned at him and held out her hand. He hesitantly handed it over then took a step closer, his eyes once more filled with hunger. She had no idea if it was for her or the food. As if reading her mind, he grinned at her then pointed from the container to his mouth.

Since she wasn't sure if he thought she was going to feed him, or if he was simply asking permission to eat her food, she had no idea. But she was going to make sure he knew the days of women feeding him were over if he ended up staying in her time. She took a couple of plates from the cupboard, purposely showing him she closed the cabinet door after she had. After placing a small helping of spinach lasagna on her plate and a much larger portion on his, she smiled at him. "You're going to love this. My aunt Destiny makes it." When he reached for the plate with the larger helping, she swatted his hand away, making him frown at her again. She laughed and opened the microwave door and sat both saucers inside.

Jewell knew he was watching closely as the lit inside of the cooker revealed that the glass turntable was spinning the plates around. He glanced back at her, his eyes wide, and then turned back to watch the show. When the device dinged, he jumped back and watched warily as she took a potholder from the drawer and pulled one plate after the other out.

He held his hand over the steam and jerked back and then looked back at her in wonder. Jewell smiled at him. "Microwave cooking."

He attempted to repeat what she'd said, but the words were still barely distinguishable. She smiled at him anyway.

"Very good."

After placing the seven-layer salad on each plate, she carried both to the bar and indicated for him to take a seat. When he simply looked at her, she grabbed a couple of forks from the utensil drawer and then held the robe in place and sat on the stool herself. Without hesitation he took another. Jewell didn't hesitate to fork a small amount of salad and put it in her mouth. It was all she could do not to moan in appreciation. It wasn't too long ago she'd disparaged ever eating her family's fare again.

Amen-ra copied her bite for bite, and although he seemed hesitant at first, he eventually dug right in. When his plate was empty, he looked at the fork and then at her.

Jewell grinned. "More?"

He shrugged.

Jewell pointed to the containers and then to his plate. Amen-ra shook his head. Jewell nodded, wondering if she should make another attempt at getting him to sleep in Dia's room. She was beat. But whom was she kidding? The last thing she wanted was to sleep alone. Not only was she crazy about him, she didn't want to take a chance she'd be sent back and Amen-ra wouldn't be there with her. Chewing on the frightening thought, Jewell carried her plate to the sink and rinsed it out and then watched as he did the same. Smiling that he was so trainable, she headed back to the room. Amen-ra ran across the room and jumped on the bed, his eager smile self-explanatory.

Too exhausted to mince words, Jewell shook her head. "It isn't happening. We're going to sleep."

Amen-ra's brows shot up, and she was certain he knew exactly what she'd said, even if he didn't understand the words. Deciding her life was fast becoming an ongoing version of charades, she put her palms together and placed them by her tilted hear and closed her eyes. When she opened them, his face was inches from hers.

He reached out and gently framed her face with his hands, his eyes intent. He spoke sincerely, and again Jewell wished with all her might that they understood each other.

"...and I will cherish you, always."

Jewell's heart thudded as Amen-ra's eyes widened. He took a step back as excitement filled Jewell's chest. She advanced on him, grasping the huge muscles of his arms. "Say that again!"

Amen-ra shook his head. "No."

Panic flared in his eyes. "How can this be?"

He flinched with each word he spoke and then let out a shaky sigh. "I understand you!"

Unable to contain her smile, Jewell jumped into his arms and kissed him wildly. "And I understand you!" Her laughter eventually caused him to smile, but his eyes looked haunted.

"How is this possible?"

Jewell shook her head. "I don't know. I was just wishing we could understand each other, and suddenly we can!"

Amen-ra looked at her warily. "You are a sorcerer, too?"

Jewell shrugged. "It looks like it." She grinned. "This is great! Wait until I tell my family!"

Though it was obvious he wasn't as excited, Amen-ra nodded. "They will be pleased about this?"

Almost giddy at learning she had a power she could control and thus hopefully determine her own future, Jewell nodded. "It is fantastic! We have to tell them. Come on. Get dressed."

Amen-ra frowned. "My cloth is soiled."

His tone and predicament finally had the power to temper her excitement. "That's right! We need clothes for you! But don't look so upset. This is a good thing!"

Amen-ra turned from her and walked across the room to pull the top sheet off Sapphire's bed. In two quick motions he ripped it so that he had a length of cloth that closely matched what he'd been wearing. Jewell cringed, knowing the sheets were expensive, and that Sapphire was going to kill her for allowing him to destroy her room. But what concerned her more was the look in his eyes. He wasn't at all happy to learn that she had mystical powers that could master his ability to know and understand another language.

Jewell's heart sank. This wasn't supposed to happen. Not now. Not after she'd found someone who'd transformed her dull, lackluster life into excitement and passion. She moved closer to him, but didn't corner him. "It's going to be okay. I know this is all too confusing for words, but I'm still me."

Amen-ra shook his head. "No. You are not. You are special, and I have lost my heart to the kindness in you. But I am out of place. This is not my time. Such things are dangerous. I must go back."

Jewell stared at him, torn between heartbreak and anger. "I am not dangerous! My family is not dangerous!"

Amen-ra closed the distance between them and pulled her into his arms. "I have love in my heart for you, just you, *not Anippe*, as you are the woman I would have loved her to be. But I do not understand these things that happen in this house, but even those things do not matter. I am in a land of women who need nothing they cannot attain themselves. I am a man. A provider. A protector…and I am powerless against magic. I cannot protect that which is stronger than me. I do not belong here."

Jewell couldn't believe she was losing him to his pride and then remembered Her-uben's words. "I will always need your protection. My family will too. We must always be careful. And you are not just in a land filled with women. I have a father who is as normal as you are and an uncle too. They do not know or use magic, but they accept it because they love us."

Amen-ra shook his head, his eyes filled with sadness. "It is not enough. I am not a man to sit idly by while others take care of me. I have nothing to offer you."

Her heart sick, Jewell knew she couldn't convince him otherwise. He was a proud man, and to try to make him into something else just to make her life complete wasn't fair. She nodded, determined not to let the tears filling her eyes fall. She took his hand and led him from Sapphire's room to her own. She opened the door and walked them across the room, wondering if she could even wish him back to his time, wondering what she would do with her own life once she had.

The truth hit her in the face and she knew no matter when or where, she was meant to be with him, that the reason her life had never held meaning or purpose was because only he made it complete. Peace settled over her and a shaky sigh escaped.

Jewell didn't look at the mirror but stopped them both in front of it. She turned to him, wanting to beg him to reconsider, but his dejected stance and pain-filled eyes relayed the torture he was already experiencing at the thought of their separation. "If it is possible, I will send you back. I can't immediately follow, but I will try to come back to you as soon as I let my family know. I can't just leave them without a word. It would hurt them too much."

Amen-ra pulled her to him and held her tightly. "I will wait for you. I will always wait for you. No matter how long it takes."

They stood there for long minutes before he pulled her into a deep kiss. The length of it and the wet tears that mingled upon their faces bespoke the fear it could be the last time they touched. Finally Jewell pulled away, unable to prolong the pain. She turned to face the mirror, and her breath caught in her throat.

Anippe's mirror was gone, and the one her father made was once again back in place. She moved forward and touched it, running her fingers over the carving that spelled her name. She touched the crowning stone, and then the rest of the frame, but there was no magic in the mirror. Jewell turned back to him, her heart pounding. "It isn't the same mirror. It isn't a portal to the past."

Amen-ra walked over to it and touched it as she had. He frowned down at her. "What is this trickery?"

The accusation caused Jewell's cheeks to fill with heat. "I am not tricking you! How could you say such a thing after all we have said to each other?"

Furious, she fled the room and headed straight for the front door. She would send his ass back one way or another. She had her pride too! If she had to, she'd have Aunt Soleli or Destiny send him back, and then she'd....

Jewell found herself halfway to her car before she remembered she hadn't grabbed her keys, but that was the least of her worries as a very large, horribly mangy wolf was no more than ten feet away. Even in the darkness she could tell its yellow teeth seemed as large as its emaciated body was bony, and all she could do was remain frozen to the spot.

Her heart thumping in triplicate, she took in the redness of its eyes, the ready-to-pounce stance and the foamy substance dripping from its mouth as it growled. She heard Amen-ra step onto the porch and wanted to scream to him to go back in, but she couldn't make herself speak.

"Jewell! Do not move!"

Jewell swallowed, knowing this must be the rabid dog the man had spoken of, but this was no dog. This was a wild animal, and a deadly sick one at that. She stared at it and tried to remember what she'd done to enable Amen-ra to speak English. But before she could begin wishing, Amen-ra jumped from the porch and ran to her and scooped her up. The wolf reached them seconds later, and Amen-ra kicked it so hard it flew backward and landed on its side. Amen-ra didn't waste time and hit the grass running so fast he was able to get them back up on the porch and into the house before the animal fully recovered. He slammed the door with his foot as the wolf hit the door hard. Only Amen-ra's throwing his weight against the wood kept the animal from pushing the door back open. Jewell came to her senses enough to turn and throw the deadbolt. Almost immediately there was silence, and she and Amen-ra gasped for breath as they kept their backs anchored against the door.

Several seconds passed before Amen-ra lifted her and carried her back into Sapphire's bedroom. He turned and fumbled with the lock before having it secured. He turned to Jewell and pulled her into his arms. "What was that monster?"

Still shaking so hard she could hardly talk, Jewell tried to tell him about wolves, and that this one was sick, but her adrenaline was making coherency impossible. He pulled her to him and held her tight. "It is over. You are safe. I won't let anything happen to you. I'm here, and you are safe."

A peace settled over her, and she could once again breathe normally. She leaned back and smiled up at him. "I told you I needed you. That animal would have killed me and could have killed you. You saved me. Again. Only this time it's me. Not Anippe."

Amen-ra smiled. "I will never try to leave you again. I was wrong before. This is my home. This is where I belong.

"*You* are where I belong."

Jewell snuggled into his warmth. He was where she belonged too. As a thought occurred to her, she leaned back and looked up into his eyes. "I think I was wrong, too. I kept thinking the reason I was going back in time was because Anippe had done something wrong, and I needed to make it right. But that wasn't it at all. It wasn't her life that needed fixing. It was mine. I had no purpose, no passion. And with you, I have both and more."

She stood on tiptoes and pulled his head down for a long kiss. When she released him, he scooped her up and placed her upon the bed. She giggled when he pulled the robe from her body and the torn sheet from his loins.

"I will give you good purpose, woman. Pleasure me often, and give me children to bear my name."

Jewell laughed and shook her head at his old-fashioned expectations. He was still an archaic male, and he'd need a little tweaking now and again, but she knew she wouldn't have him any other way.

THE END

For a sneak peek into the next book in The Cavanaugh Series, read on!

SAPPHIRE BLUES

Can a werewolf be defeated when a mystic denies her magic?

Police officer Sapphire Cavanaugh-White turned her back on magic soon after her *ascension* eight years earlier and hasn't looked back. But now, with all the local humans and wildlife living in fear of a murderous maniac, Sapphire may have no choice but to hunt down the animal who may also be a man.

To protect their nearly extinct species, Nicolae Lupei must find and destroy one of his own, while keeping their existence a secret. But, when he runs across the policewoman his brother may have infected, he finds his loyalties torn. Save her, or those he calls family?

SAPPHIRE BLUES

Chapter One

Sirens blared, lights flashed and blinded, fiery emergency flares marked off areas where hundreds of bits and pieces and a few larger chunks of human remains lay in drops or pools of blood. The air held the scent of death, of decay, of fear and vomit. Even Mystic Waters' seasoned police officers weren't accustomed to seeing this kind of carnage. Having only been on the force for a few months, Sapphire Cavanaugh-White tried to distance herself emotionally from the horror as she held a sanitizer-covered hand over her nose to mask the death smells with the scent of rubbing alcohol. There was no way to soften what she was seeing while she studied the largest piece of the deceased's carcass.

Chunks of flesh clung to what remained of the hip, but it was clear only two-thirds of intact spine was still attached to the sacrum at its base. The coccyx was missing as well as any sign of genitalia or digestive organs. Whatever kind of animal tore this person apart had been indiscriminate as to what it was eating. The lack of a crotch area as well as the fact that there was only a four-inch stub of one remaining leg could have made it difficult to identify the sex of the victim. Were it not for the completely intact tattoo of a big-breasted woman on the remaining butt cheek, it could have gone either way.

"I've found what I think is part of the liver and a kidney, and Jackson found both eyes—blue—but everything else looks like skin and muscle so far. What do you think?"

Sapphire rose slowly, only realizing she'd been stooping for too long when her legs protested the movement. She shrugged, taking in the distaste on Brad Cunningham's face. The veteran officer was her partner and was basically training her on Mystic Waters police procedure. She thought it ironic he was asking her. "I don't know. Maybe a pack of wild boars?"

Brad nodded. "Possible, but where is the rest of it?"

It was Sapphire's turn to shrug. "It's a *him*. I'm thinking maybe the rest was carried off for later, or maybe Mr. Casey scared them off when he came around the curve, but he said he didn't see anything but what we're looking at now. He thought at first it was an animal hit and broken up by a car." Sapphire sighed. "He's pretty upset now he knows it's human."

Brad nodded again as he lifted his hand to hold it over his nose. "Yeah, I think we all are. I've never smelled anything like this. It makes me want to puke."

Sapphire nodded, still keeping her hand close to her face as well. "I know. There's something strange about it. But I can't put my finger on it." She glanced back down at the chunk of meat that was once part of a man. "I wonder who he is, and what he was doing out here on a mountain road in the middle of the night."

Brad shrugged. "Guess we'll never know. Isn't much to identify him by."

Sapphire pointed to the butt cheek. "It's a tattoo. If he's a local we'll see if anyone comes forward claiming a missing person. That's a pretty clear identifying mark."

"You're right. I didn't notice it before. It's hard to look at this too closely. How do you stand it?"

Sapphire almost smiled but knew it wasn't appropriate. "I wanted to be a nurse when I was growing up and spent a lot of time watching law enforcement shows that leaned heavily toward forensics. By the time I got to college, I was captivated with the idea of studying forensic science, which led me to law enforcement. So I got a degree in criminal justice, with a specialty in forensic science, and hope one day to work in a law enforcement lab or for a coroner. Maybe even for the FBI."

Brad looked at her for a long moment then shook his head. "That would be a terrible waste. You're too attractive to be hidden away in a lab somewhere studying things that used to be human beings."

Since Brad's tone didn't carry any *flirt* in it, Sapphire let the comment pass. She wasn't one of those people who jumped on the sexual harassment bandwagon without due cause. So she took it as the compliment she was sure he'd meant it to be, but it was still an issue she wished never arose. "Thanks, but one of the perks of being hidden away is your work is what matters to people, not your looks."

"I didn't mean it that way."

She did smile now. "And I didn't take it that way. But you've heard some of the guys at the station. It gets a little old after a while. All I want is to be good at what I do."

Brad nodded. "I get it. But men are men, and you are gorgeous. You can't expect us to ignore something that is impossible to ignore. That isn't even fair." He looked down then and his brows pulled together.

Sapphire sighed heavily. "I appreciate my genes. But they don't define me." She didn't know what else to say. To continue to try to make her point would continue to force him to make his, and neither one of them were comfortable now.

"Look, don't worry about it. I appreciate it that you are always respectful, and have never treated me like a piece of meat rather than a colleague. Let's get back to work."

Brad nodded. "I never will, you know. Treat you like

that, I mean. I like you. You're smart. You are willing to work as hard as it takes and you never complain. If we didn't work together, I might have eventually found the courage to ask you out. But this way is better because girls who look like you don't look at guys who look like me."

Sapphire was too stunned to speak at first. "Brad—"

He shook his head and looked back up at her with a grin. "Don't say it. You're nice. I don't want you to have to lie to spare my feelings. Just friends works for me."

Sapphire smiled and held out her hand. "Friends it is then. Not just friends, but good friends." She glanced over to see the coroner was finally arriving. He pulled his black ambulance as close to the wandering police officers as possible. She hoped the new coroner was already in place and had replaced the one who was to retire.

Doc Parsons had held the position long before she was born, and though she knew there had once been a mass murderer in Mystic Waters, and because that *too* had been before her birth, she didn't really know any details and doubted it had resulted in anything like she was seeing now. She was certain Doc Parsons would have a heart attack if he had to deal with this.

To Sapphire's relief, the man who stepped from the ambulance was the new guy. From the little contact she'd had with him so far, she figured he fit the bill as a coroner. Middle-aged, thick glasses, thinning buzzed hair but not yet bald, he looked born to wear a lab coat. He walked right to her, his lips pressed together.

"Hope you didn't touch anything."

Feeling more than slightly offended, Sapphire shook her head. "No." She didn't add that she wasn't stupid. There was little point. She grinned at the coroner, doubting he knew the falsehood of the pleasant gesture. "We've identified several body parts, have concluded it is a male by the tattoo on the remains, and will be here to help start packing it all up, whenever you're ready."

The coroner nodded though he wasn't looking at Sapphire. His attention was glued to the remains she'd been studying. "It doesn't look like this is a homicide. And if it is, there are too many people here making a mess of the scene for it to matter. Clean it up and bring the parts to me. We'll see if we have enough to make an identification."

Sapphire nodded. "Yes, sir." Again, she didn't add her thoughts that had he been on the scene when he'd been called, he could have orchestrated the process. She watched as the coroner headed in the direction of the different flares. He barely bent over as he glanced at each body part the officers had marked, before heading back to his vehicle. Sapphire waved her partner over. "Looks like we get to bag it all up."

Brad nodded, his eyes filled with distaste. "I was afraid of that. Doc Parsons would have looked harder."

Sapphire nodded. "Maybe. I don't think anyone is too anxious to look too hard," she said, looking at the group of officers standing together across the road. She had to get to the squad car to get supplies from the trunk but approached the more senior officers first.

"Doc says we are to bag it all up."

They turned to look at her, and irritation set in, as several pairs of male eyes looked her up and down with appreciation. She ignored them and turned to head to her car. Brad was already there pulling out a body bag and the black toolbox they used in such cases. The sound of a wolf's howl startled them both, and Brad looked at her warily. "Is that what I think it is?"

Sapphire shrugged. She hadn't seen any wolves in the area in all the years she'd lived in Mystic Waters. Though she knew there had been reports of them from time to time when she was growing up on Mystic Mountain, she'd never once gotten a chance to lay eyes on one. "I don't know."

"Would a wolf have done all this?"

Sapphire frowned as she pulled on a new pair of latex gloves. "I don't think so. This is too aggressive. I can't imagine wolves tearing a man apart like this. If they felt their pack was threatened, one would hold him off while the others got away. And we would see signs of them. There are no tracks. With all this blood we'd have seen bloody paw prints. We'd also see scat and hair. There's nothing here to indicate a wolf."

"Well, it's giving me the creeps."

Sapphire nodded as she followed him back to the biggest chunk. The wolf was continuing to howl, its call singular. She handed Brad a pair of gloves and knelt down to open the toolbox. "I think it's just one wolf. From my understanding, if a pack was close by, the alpha male would begin the communication and others would respond with howls as well."

"That's a relief. All we need is a pack of wolves moving onto the mountain. We'll get calls day and night."

As Sapphire began lifting and bagging the smaller pieces of flesh with the long tweezers, she agreed. "I think once word gets out something tore a man into a thousand pieces, we will get those calls anyway. I just wish we could identify him before word gets out. I'd hate for someone to have to speculate if a son, father, or husband is gone longer than someone expects."

Brad pointed at the largest chunk of flesh and bone. "If you'll hold the bag open for me, I'll put it in."

Although she normally wouldn't have blinked at handling a dead body, Sapphire didn't argue. She was thankful, in this case, to hand that particular job over to his willing hands. Unfortunately, just holding the bag didn't stop the smell from nearly knocking her over, as Brad had to hold it just below her face as he placed it in the plastic. She gagged, and chills washed over her body. Though she wanted to close the bag as soon as the body was in it, she knew there were other big chunks the coroner would want in the body bag as well.

She and Brad made the rounds gathering the larger pieces while the other officers used varying sized plastic baggies to gather the smaller pieces. By the time she was able to zip the bag closed, it only weighed about forty pounds. As well as they could tell, whatever killed the man ate him as well.

Fire trucks arrived on the scene, ready to spray off the road once the police left. Sapphire immediately looked to see if Apollo was among those on duty and smiled when she caught a glimpse of him jumping out of the extended cab. He was so cute in full fireman regalia, though she knew other women, those not related to him, would think him hot, not cute. He spotted her and smiled.

"Hey, cuz. We got the call about this. Can't believe something like this would happen on Mystic Mountain. Dad will be sick. You know how he reacts whenever anything violates Mother Mountain."

Sapphire nodded. "I imagine it will affect our mothers and Aunt Haven too. They are all so attuned to everything around here."

Apollo nodded as well, his gaze going to the officers loading the various remains into the black ambulance. He looked back at Sapphire and shook his head. "How do you stand it? The smell is enough to make me sick."

"It isn't easy, but it's my job. And I can't let the guys see me flinch. They've already made noises that my looks got me the job."

Annoyance flashed across Apollo's classic features making Sapphire smile. His Native American genes were slightly tempered by her aunt Destiny's, but he and his identical brothers Zeus and Heracles were their father made-over.

"Does it never occur to them that you being at the top of your class has something to do with it?"

Sapphire shrugged and pulled the latex gloves from her hands, making sure they ended up inside out. The last thing she wanted was to get the deceased's bodily fluids on her. "I'm glad you're here. Something is really strange about this. Not only about the way the remains were mutilated and left behind, but also the smell. There's something off about it."

Apollo glanced back to the officers and other firemen before speaking quietly. "I can smell it. I did as soon as I stepped out of the truck." He looked back again to make sure they were still far enough from the men moving in their direction. "Is there any way you can get a sample of the blood? We could have the parents look at it."

Sapphire nodded. "I'll try. Thankfully Aunt Soleli and Aunt Lune Brille decided to stick around to make sure Jewell and Amen-ra aren't in danger of being sent back to ancient Egypt. There's a good possibility they might know something, too. Or at least be able to help us find out if it's anything a *normal* police investigation couldn't make sense of."

Apollo smiled at her. "Since when do you involve yourself in the possibility of magic?"

"Never. And I hope that isn't what this is. But I feel really creepy about more than the obvious. And that makes me think it does have something to do with the mystical."

"Hey, Whitehawk! You gonna spend all evening talking to the pretty girl or you gonna help us clean this mess up?"

The flare of anger in Apollo's eyes was enough to keep Sapphire from pulling her gun on the other fireman. She placed her hand on Apollo's arm to calm him and then turned her attention to the idiot. "Apollo is my cousin. And you are out of line. You can call me Officer White, or you can just call me officer, or even ma'am, but pretty girl is not acceptable."

The fireman bowed mockingly. "Sorry about that, *ma'am*." Then he smiled at her. "But since the chief here is your cousin, maybe you'd like to get a drink later?"

Sapphire fumed, unable to believe how completely inappropriate the jerk was. This time it was Apollo who was the one calming her. "Don't bother. He won't last long in this job with an attitude like that. It doesn't bother me. But I'll bust his mouth for talking to you like that if you want me too."

She grinned at him. He'd always known how to make her feel better. It had been that way since they were kids. Apollo was a good guy who used his human skills to help others, and in that they were alike. Of all her cousins, and for that matter the rest of the family, she felt closest to Apollo because neither of them felt the need to call to their mystical side to get things done.

"Thanks, but no. I can fight my own battles, and he isn't worth the time for either of us. I'll head on into the woods and see if I can find evidence of the body being carried into the trees. Whatever did this somehow knew to keep their feet out of the mess, but too much is missing for there not to be more somewhere. Hopefully I can get us a blood sample, without anyone knowing what I'm doing. You head on, and get everyone done and out of here as quickly as possible. I feel like someone or something is watching." She bit her bottom lip as creepy-crawlers skittered up her spine.

Sapphire sent Brad a signal that she was heading into the woods. He nodded and continued packing away their supplies. It didn't take long to find where the animal dropped what must have been a large chunk of flesh onto the ground. From there, following the blood-trail was much too easy as the beast, or whatever it was that had destroyed the human, hadn't worried about hiding anything. With the high beam of her flashlight pointed only a few feet in front of her, it was clear a pretty good-sized body part had been dragged. The flattened bloody grass was fairly wide, not just a line, and there were additional bits and pieces of flesh or muscle that left a trail behind.

The smell got worse the farther she walked, which made her concerned the animal was definitely something out of the ordinary. Sweet yet vinegary, the scent was like nothing she'd smelled before.

As thinner young trees gave way to millennia-old established forest, Sapphire unsnapped her holster and pulled her gun into her free hand. She stepped over broken branches, decomposing leaves, and the wild bushes that grew whenever the canopy overhead gave way for daylight's solar rays to allow for it.

She wished for daylight now.

A pop to her right caused her to freeze before she thought to swing the light in the direction of the noise. Sapphire searched the area but saw nothing save more trees and shadows. A chill covered her body, sending goose bumps to dance over her skin, though she assured herself it was only that the wind was picking up. With a shaky breath, she turned the beam back in front of her until she had it lighting the blood-trail again.

"Hey!"

Thinking she was about to pee on herself if she didn't get over being spooked, Sapphire swung her body around until she had Brad in the flashlight's beam. He was frowning at her, which, she realized, never happened. "You nearly gave me a heart attack!"

He shook his head, his brows pulled together. "Sorry, but we need to get out of here. Dispatch just sent out word that a storm is moving this way rapidly. We're under a tornado warning."

Sapphire nodded, almost relieved she wouldn't have to

go any further into the woods. She started to walk his way hoping he would turn around and lead them back. She'd been so focused on the bloody trail she hadn't stopped yet to get her sample. When he continued to wait, she sighed. "Go ahead. I'll just be another minute."

A hard blast of wind whipped through the trees, nearly knocking her to the side. She caught herself and spread her stance in an effort to keep her feet. "Okay, run! I'm right behind you!"

Brad took off at a sprint and she followed, fighting to stay upright. The sound of what she could only imagine was hail sounded loudly overhead. The canopy didn't hold it off for long, and ice rocks pounded her head and shoulders painfully. Desperate to get out of the downpour, Sapphire sidled up against a large tree and called for Brad, but she had no idea if he responded. She could hear nothing over the deafening onslaught.

Blinding white light replaced the darkness, turning harmless trees into threatening beasts with flailing arms. The immediate crash of thunder followed so quickly Sapphire knew the storm was right above her. She debated her options as she pressed herself against the tree's trunk. If she stayed where she was, there was always the danger of the violent lightning striking either the tree or bolting through the canopy and setting a fire, even zapping her. Brad had obviously opted to get out of the forest fast, and she knew she should have too, but the violence of the wind and the harsh sting from the hail kept her glued in place.

A flash of movement caught Sapphire's attention seconds after her hair came undone and smacked her already watering eyes. Whatever was there was gone too quickly for her to be able to identify if it was an animal or a large branch flying by. Belatedly, the growing fiery heat across her wrists alerted her to the possibility of injury. She pushed her hair away from her face and studied the slash, realizing *something* had scraped her, as it passed by. She didn't have time to dwell on the pain as the hailstorm intensified, pelting her with the stinging ping pong-sized ice-balls, making her cry-out as she was slammed by it again and again. Knowing she would have bruises all over, she slid down the tree's trunk and curled into as small a target as she could.

Sapphire expelled a long breath and tried to gauge the extent of her injury only to gasp in terror when something covered her head and body, pinning her arms down in a tight grip. She struggled against the blinding material, not knowing if it was a blanket or tarp someone was using to hold her down. Fury filled her, and she screamed, desperately trying to push whomever it was away, and then sanity returned and she stopped. "Dammit, Brad! Get off me!"

There was no response in either movement or sound, and Sapphire growled. "I said get off me!"

The pressure around her eased and Sapphire fought against the covering until it finally landed at her side. There was no one around. The wind and the hail had stopped. She sat, frozen with confusion, before remembering to look at the arm that was still burning and now starting to itch. Blood seeped slowly from the three-inch-long gash. Sapphire clamped her hand on the wound to stop the flow as she struggled to her feet.

It was eerily quiet after the noise from the wind and the hail; *nothing* stirred. It seemed as if she'd stepped from one planet to another. She took a shaky breath, then more, until she was almost breathing normally. Swallowing, she looked around for her flashlight, but it was so dark it took her several minutes to find it. Once it was in-hand, she shined the beam at the ground and saw her gun was beside what turned out to be nothing more than a wool blanket lying on the ice. She frowned, wondering where its owner was, concerned he or she hadn't even stayed around for introductions, or to let her know that they were all right too.

Surely, if it *had* been Brad, he would have stayed put long enough for her to apologize for cursing at him. With that in mind, Sapphire shined the light around her, looking for any signs of…*anything*. She shivered, not just from the cold wetness against her head and skin, but from the reality that whoever, or *whatever* had come to her rescue, may have also been the person or *thing* that now had her forearm swelling.

Ignoring her purpose for entering the woods in the first place, Sapphire made a quick trip back the way she'd come. The melting ice balls and forest debris made her progress slower than she'd hoped. It was a relief to finally see the flashing blue and red lights through the trees, and it was only then she realized she had been on the edge of panicking.

At last she stepped from the woodlands and into the clearing of the roadway. The activity at the site of the massacre now was that of crews loading up to leave and of those already pulling out to head back to their stations or their homes. Relieved her shift would soon be over for the night, Sapphire took a deep cleansing breath. Which only reminded her that something smelled very wrong….

"Sapphire, over here!"

She rubbed her nose and turned at the sound of her cousin's voice. Apollo squatted next to Brad, who was sitting on the asphalt beside their cruiser, with a cloth held to his head. She hurried over and squatted down too, sending a glance to her cousin.

"Is he hurt badly?"

Apollo shook his head and rose from his crouched position and she followed suit, still looking at her partner.

"I don't think so. I think a branch hit him while he was

running back."

Brad glanced up, his blood-covered face either regretful or embarrassed. "I'm sorry I left you. I didn't realize you weren't right behind me."

Sapphire shooed away his comment with a wipe of her hands. "No problem. Are you okay?"

Brad frowned, and nodded, But Sapphire wasn't sure she believed him. He looked like he'd been in a prizefight, and he'd lost.

Apollo grabbed the arm she swung and lifted it to inspect it before looking at her with a frown. "What happened?"

Though he was gentle, the pain of his grip caused Sapphire to pull her arm away. "Something flew by me and scraped it." She frowned. "*I think.*" She glanced down at Brad. Knowing he already felt bad enough about abandoning her, she kept her next thought to herself. Apparently Apollo caught her vibe, though, as his eyes grew concerned.

"Brad, I need to talk to my cousin. Are you okay enough for us to step away for a minute?"

Sapphire's slid her partner a glance, frowning when he hunched down into himself. He seemed much more injured than his small head wound indicated. When Brad nodded, again, Apollo put his arm around her shoulder and pulled her away from everyone's earshot.

"What really happened out there?" he asked, lifting her arm again, this time taking her flashlight to shine it on the wound.

Sapphire winced at his touch. "I'm not sure. The storm came up so fast. Everything was flying all around me. Then suddenly something hit me, or something..." Sapphire bit her bottom lip, afraid the sudden onset of nausea was going to cause her stomach to revolt and embarrass her.

With his lips pressed together and his brows furrowed,

Apollo slowly turned her arm to inspect it before releasing her and looking into her eyes. "I don't think that's a scrape. You need to go see Aunt Haven."

SAPPHIRE BLUES... Available now!

Mystic Waters Books

The Cavanaugh Series

The Cavanaugh Series Books Now Available!
(The Cavanaugh Sisters Trilogy)
#1 Mystic Thunder
#2 Touch of Lightning
#3 Tempest's Embrace
(The Cavanaugh Series continues!)
#4 Jewel of the Nile
#5 Sapphire Blues
#6 Diamond in the Rough
#7 Luna's Landing
#8 Celestial Liaison
#9 Zeus: *Unbound!*
#10 Apollo: *Unleashed!*

The Cavanaugh Series Books to come!
Heracles: Undone
Soleli's Secret
Gavin's Ghosts

The Blood Moon Series

Blood Moon Rising

www.jcwardon.com

FOR MORE INFORMATION:

Visit my website: **www.jcwardon.com**

Facebook pages: **www.facebook.com/jc.wardon** and
https://www.facebook.com/JCWardonNovelist

Tweet me: @jc_wardon

Thanks for sharing my world. I'd love to hear from you!

JC Wardon

ACKNOWLEDGEMENTS

I would like to send out a special Thank You to all who have embraced the Cavanaugh women. May your lives be as enchanted!

Thank you all so much!

JCW

www.jcwardon.com

ABOUT JC WARDON

JC Wardon loves writing fantasy and spends her days weaving stories for those who love it as well. Though she has great appreciation for romances, a juicy and complicated plot is what she holds most dear. Danger, mystery, and magic are the life's blood for her Mystic Waters Books. She hopes you are captivated and stimulated, and that your hearts become engaged.

If you enjoyed JC Wardon's *Jewel of the Nile*,
please consider telling others and writing a review.

JC Wardon

Mystic Waters Books

www.jcwardon/com